D0877494

ENVY

THE SEVEN SINS SERIES

DYLAN PAGE

COPYRIGHT

Copyright 2022 Dylan Page

FIRST EDITION

All rights reserved.

If you are not reading this book via a licensed copy sold by Amazon, you have a pirated version.

This book should not be copied, duplicated, or stored on any retrieval systems except for brief excerpts quoted in book reviews.

Thank you for supporting indie authors by buying books or reading subscriptions through legitimate channels.

Edited by Angie Ojeda Hazen of Lunar Rose Editing

PA & Author Services by Wildfire

Cover Design by Merel Pierce Designs

Formatting Services by Bibiane Lybaek of Obsidian Author Services

TRIGGER
WARNING

Warning: This book is meant for mature readers, 18+.

Envy is an 80K+ word dark romance that contains some scenes and situations that may be upsetting for some readers. Includes several triggers and sensitive material such as: fatal illness, violence, and other possible triggering elements.

Please do not read if you are uncomfortable with any of the above. Thank you.

This book is a work of fiction. Names, characters, places, and incidents are the product of the author's imagination or are used fictitiously. Any resemblances to actual events, locales, or persons living or dead, are coincidental.

The Seven Sins Series

ACKNOWLEDGEMENTS

To the other authors of the Sinful Seven!
Tara, Billie, Brooklyn, Marissa, Drethi, and Talli... it was a pleasure working with
you all and thank you for the experience. As my first collaboration, this was truly an
honour.

To my Misfits and Weirdos,
NV Roez, MF Adele, Tia Fanning, Vivian Murdoch, Allie Stern, Alyssa Lynn,
Billie Blue, Dani Carr, Tara Hodel, Brooklyn Cross, Marissa Honeycutt.
Thank you so much for being such an amazing support system. You ladies always put
a smile on my face and I love what truly amazing, strong, smart, beautiful, and
funny people you are. I feel truly lucky to have found such a tribe.

To Kys, Ronka, and Afree
....
Sorry, not sorry.

ENVY

Heaven and Hell weren't the enemies everyone thought we were.

The mortal plane was more like a chessboard with humans being the pieces and us the players.

The divine was more bound by their rules.

If there was one thing the seven deadly sins could sense, it was the dark desires of the human soul.

The heavens wept when Cain raised his blade and brother struck down brother, for the fourth sin emerged in a rage of Envy that could tear down the strongest bond.

PROLOGUE

Leviathan

I take what belongs to me. I take what belongs to others. I take what is satisfying to me. I will take what satisfies others. I will take it all. And mine it will be. – Leviathan

The day I fell...

For once, Heaven wasn't a paradise; it was a battlefield. That ethereal light that had always shone over utopia was now clouded over by the smoke from Lucifer's new dragon, turning what was usually a bright rolling sky of white cloud into a murky amber. Scattered across the grassy, flower-covered plains, His angels were slowly pushing us back. The moment Lucifer returned with his army, I took up my sword, my decision already determined. I'd made my way down to the masses, caught Lucifer's crystal blue gaze, and nodded, affirming my choice, where I stood, before fighting my way through the throng of angels, cutting them down one by one.

I'd been relentless. Ruthless, my skills with my weapon were unparalleled to the others. As a loner, I'd delved into swordplay and mastered it, hoping that I would be considered the best at something for once. That I possessed a talent or skill no one else possessed. But as always, I had come up short. Michael, beloved Michael, and his symbolic blade were seen as the fiercest warrior, His best man. Gritting my teeth, I released all my bottled frustrations, feelings of imperfection, and inadequacies, to channel all of them into the Battle of Heaven.

Though I'd been victorious thus far, I'd watched as His army proceeded to sweep its way through Lucifer's beasts, and several angels had already been thrown beyond the shattered remains of the golden gates. Lucifer was thrown from Heaven first, clinging to the edge as he dangled, reaching for something or someone to grab onto. Maddix was gone. Lust was gone. And now, Michael was leading the charge in my direction. Despite that, I found myself now cornered, and I wasn't about to surrender yet. Call me desperate or stubborn, but I was not going to give up until the edge of Michael's sword was slicing through the back of my neck.

One of His angels shot at me, his wings carrying him through the air, the fool moving ahead of the others to take me one on one. His long, heavenly blade was raised high, ready to strike me down. Only these holy blades had the power to actually kill us, and I wasn't ready to die yet. Baring my teeth, I rose to the challenge, swinging my own silver sword high to block the attack. What this idiot wasn't prepared for was the second blade I had hidden that was strapped to my back. When our swords clashed with an echoing metallic peal that rang out over the hills of His paradise, I swung to the side, wielding my secret weapon, and struck. My blade sliced into my challenger's side, and as I glared up, a cruel smirk spread over my face as I drank in the surprise of his expression. Twisting the blade into his body, dragging it across his middle, I made sure to cause as much damage as possible to end his life.

His light, the pure embodiment we emit as angels, dimmed, his wings twitching as they lowered on his back, and I wrenched my weapon free, the blood spattering over my exposed legs. In fact, my entire body was covered in blood, traces of smoke, and dirt from the fighting, but I didn't care. My opponent fell limply to the ground, dead. I was trembling all over at the death surrounding me, my mind racing as I took in the sight of lifeless angels; some I'd known, some who were nameless, along with the remains of demons. As I stared at those I'd once known, I could feel my breathing quicken, my lungs soon gasping as I fought for air, my body trembling in rage and anguish, the two feelings clashing so violently in my mind that I felt like I might collapse. So much blood, so much death, so much chaos...

And then I remembered.

He forced me here, where I don't belong. Plucked me out of the darkness of the Abyss and tried to shape me into something I'm not. Every day since, I was stuck here, trapped, surrounded by those who only reminded me of how I was not good enough, pure enough, worthy enough... I would never be enough, would never have what they were all blessed with upon their creation.

Another angel flew at me, his spear raised, shield held high, but I was ready, despite my exhaustion. He came down, moving much too quickly. He'd never be able to slow down in time. I spun to the side, flying up before he could slow and change his trajectory, and swung both blades to his throat. The spray of blood flew across my face, right into my mouth. I spat it to the ground just as his head fell at my feet and I turned to face my next adversary.

Two angels advanced upon me next, but they were nothing. I don't even recall their names. Their faces only blended in with so many others I'd begrudged. I just wanted to get to Michael, who was making his way in my direction, his blue eyes locked on me, his expression determined and set.

He'd been the one to throw Lucifer out, to banish him from this place. My fury rose in my stomach like bile, driving me onward, and I easily cut through these two fools, kicking their bodies loose from the sharp edge of my weapons. *I* wanted to take him down. *I* wanted retribution for my fallen comrades. Our fight, this war, was all because He had lied. Because He had chosen *them* over us... tainted, imperfect, flawed humans were loved more than His angels.

And why? For what?

I tried so hard to exemplify the image of perfection that the others had, and yet, I always felt like I was lacking. Nothing I did was enough. Then He went and created those humans, those imperfect miscreants who chose to go against his word and his law, and yet, He chose to love them over us. Over me.

He made me what I am.

He forced me here.

And then, he abandoned me when it was clear I was not worthy.

I rolled to the ground, ducking beneath the shimmering metal of another foe's blade, and sliced my dagger back, quickly severing the tendons of his ankles. He screamed, his legs useless, but his wings still held him aloft. Soaring up behind him, I swiftly sheathed my weapons before I gripped the muscle of the golden feathered appendages and wrenched as hard as I could, flexing my strength as I twisted and pulled. The crack of the bones breaking was so loud I was certain that everyone in a hundred-foot vicinity could hear it before he howled in agony. Seizing the hilt to one of my blades, I brought it up and easily slashed his throat, tearing through the muscle and tendons before dropping him to the grassy plain to lie with his fallen comrades. Finally, I turned to Michael, the corners of my lips lifting as we finally squared off.

Here I was, covered in blood, my leather belt once a rich, mahogany brown, but was now shining red from the blood of angels. My white knee-length robes have turned into various shades of grey mixed with deep red stains, and my gold cuirass was dented and marred. Meanwhile, Michael was the epitome of perfection as he stood there, his beautiful sword grasped tightly in his hands, robes hardly wrinkled, looking like he'd just stepped onto the battlefield, when really, he's been fighting as long as I have. The fact that he doesn't even look winded or at all anxious to be facing off with me was infuriating as well as offensive. He was a warrior, but so was I. I've proven myself time and time again, and yet here he was, looking at me like none of my achievements mattered.

I glowered at him, my rage fuelling me, giving me second wind as I prepared myself to fight to the death against someone who I'd once considered a brother.

"Surrender," He called to me, his voice hitching a little, as if this pained him. But I knew it was an act. He didn't care. None of them did! He'd always had it easy, always been one of His shining boys. He never had a day in his life where he questioned his very existence as I have. For him to look down upon me, displaying no genuine sympathy for how I have struggled, fills me with blinding rage. My breathing quickened, and a tightness in my chest ached. It made me feel weak, and I loathed that feeling.

"You ask me to surrender as if I am the one at fault..."

"You *are*, Leviathan."

"He promised us eternal love!"

"He has."

"And yet he chose *them*!"

Michael's wings twitched as though agitated, like he was irritated by my sentiment, and his next words only enraged me further. "He *is* love."

I spat on the ground; a bit of my own blood mixed with what was left over from the previously fallen challenger. Up until now, I'd been confident, dauntless. But as I focused on Michael up the high ground of the grassy slope, I felt a terrible, twisting, sinking uncertainty in my stomach.

I am going to lose.

I blinked my green eyes several times to clear my vision and rolled my arms back, preparing myself for our inevitable clash. I refused to let him see how vulnerable

I felt. "His love is tainted. It is false. Fraudulent. He has never loved me as he has loved you or any of the others. And now, he rewards those who are inferior, those... those mortals that are so impure, unclean, so lacking in everything, more love than he has ever shown me!"

"You are blind, Leviathan!" Michael moved closer, but with each step he made forward, I took one back, careful about keeping the distance between us the same. I wasn't going to engage until I found an opportunity that gave me the upper hand. Michael had proven his prowess in battle, and I had always admired him from afar, but I've never put myself in a situation where I had to fight him.

Until now...

"No, Michael, for the first time, I can speak freely about how I feel. I can tell you all how it *really* is! And He is too prideful to admit he is wrong! So he threw Lucifer out!"

"It was Lucifer's pride-"

"Lucifer was right!" I cried, my voice catching in my throat, causing it to crack and exposing my failings. "Lucifer *is* right. And yet we are punished for it!"

"Enough!" Michael's face reddened, his blue eyes sparkled as if he was holding back tears. Deceptive, a ruse. "Enough, Leviathan. You have turned your back on Him. On us all! You cannot stay here!"

"So come at me, brother. Fight! Let us end this!"

"I don't want to kill you..."

"Why not? I am just The Flawed Angel, defective, the one he twisted and forced into a world where I did not belong. I have had to live every day since, forever reminded of the fact that I am not like the rest of you. That you were all created with the intent to carry that virtue and righteousness without question, while I come from the darkness of the Abyss, and am thus polluted."

"He still loved you, Leviathan. *I* loved you-"

"No!" I screamed, feeling as though my vocal cords would tear. "You all have something I can never emulate! I have been set up for failure... poor Leviathan, the corrupted angel. The one who will never be good enough, never have enough... I'm worth nothing to him. To all of you." My chest was heaving, and I furiously fought back the tears in my eyes. Although the moment I see the look of pity on Michael's face, my overwhelming emotion of despair is fleetingly replaced with fury. "Don't you dare!" I yelled, the grip on the hilt of my blades tightening, "Do *not* look at me like that. Not ever again!"

"Leviathan-" he started to say, but I was done. The calm way he addressed me, the way he shook his head, as if what I was saying was a lie, sent me into a blinding rage. Forgetting my initial plan of engagement, I flew at him, releasing an ear-splitting roar that ripped apart my vocal cords. I'd hoped to end it quickly, bringing both my blades inward to slice into his sides, but Michael was too fast. He flew back, just out of reach as our weapons crashed deafeningly together and brought his large, celestial sword down, forcing both my hands to the ground.

You fucking fool, Leviathan! I scolded myself.

I wrenched my arms up, using my strength to try to knock him off-balance. His sword slid over the top of mine, the sound ringing out like a piercing shriek over Heaven's now burning and bloody fields. I lunged again, hoping to knock him back, confident that with my superior strength and size, I could get him to lose his balance and fall, and then I'd have him. Overhead, the smoked cloaked clouds of Heaven were dark, storming without thunder or rain. *He* was displeased. He was angry. Good. He could watch as I took the head of his *new* favourite angel.

I rushed Michael as I spun with each step I took, first bringing down one blade upon him, only to whip around, immediately following with the other. He stumbled back but did not entirely lose his footing as I'd hoped and managed to block each strike with his sword. Snarling, I dived at him, swinging inwards again right to his throat. He wouldn't be able to block both being so high. But Michael jerked himself back once again just as I brought the sharp edges together with a resounding clang. Before proceeding with my next strategic ploy, a sharp, cold slice of metal was pressed into the back of my neck, and I knew... I knew

I'd misjudged his step. Somehow, he'd gained the upper hand and had me in his clutches.

It was over.

I sagged where I stood, inwardly berating myself for losing control and instigating the first move. *Way to go, Leviathan, you stupid, useless, broken angel... you have now fallen. You lost.*

I fell to my knees, my whole body sagging in defeat, knowing that I wouldn't have enough time to follow through on another move before Michael would apply just a bit more pressure and remove my head from my body. But he didn't budge.

"What are you waiting for?" I spat, furious at his hesitation. I wouldn't have. "Do it."

"You are not so far gone that you cannot be redeemed, Leviathan..." Michael whispered, his voice tight. "But you have sinned. You have gone against *Him*."

"So end me!" I cried, dropping my weapons as I clenched my fists. "End this, for I will not stop! I cannot! I can't come back from this!" My voice cracked on the last words. "I cannot live here, not with *Him*. Not with any of you. Not after all of this... not after all this death and betrayal. I do not belong here, Michael. I never have!"

He still did nothing, and it only fuelled my rage and resentment. In a flash, my hands swung up, reaching behind me, seizing the blade of his sword, squeezing it until I felt it pierce through my skin, freeing my "holy" blood so that it dripped to the ground. "Do it!" I hissed between my teeth, my jaw clamped so tight I thought the bones would crack. "If you have the courage He credits you with, you will end me. End my suffering!" I tugged a little harder on the blade, my palms and now the back of my neck bleeding with a steadier stream, though my eyes were locked on the plains of Heaven; the place that I did not deserve, trying to ignore the ache in my chest. "Put me out of my misery, Michael." I could feel him pull back on his sword, the metal sliding out from where it had cut into my neck, and I snarled.

"Coward! I did not hesitate when I tried to end you... and yet you pull away from disposing of me? You are weak!"

"It is not a weakness to wish for one's redemption."

I laughed bitterly, still clinging to the blade, "Redemption? I certainly hope you are not referring to my soul? I never had one. Have you not been listening?"

"You are capable of good. Ask for His forgiveness. You must not let Lucifer twist His love into something spiteful and untrue-"

"Enough!" I screamed, unable to bear more of this. "Do it! Now!"

Michael's sword ripped sideways through my palms, slicing through the skin, leaving a trail of blood following its wake as I hissed in pain. Before I could register what was happening, we were standing before the shattered remains of the golden gates where the dragon had come storming through. Michael stood at my back, my arms held tight in his clasped hands, and his whisper came out more like a prayer than a goodbye, "If your brother or sister sins against you, rebuke them; and if they repent, forgive them. Even if they sin against you seven times in a day and seven times come back to you saying, 'I repent,' you must forgive them."

"But I do not," I said firmly between my gritted teeth as the shattered remains of the gates clanged uselessly before us, swinging idly on their damaged hinges.

"Not today, brother,"

And I was gone.

I fell, and as I did, I could feel all that he made of me burn away from my body. I writhed in agony, my body growing, twisting, morphing into some twisted semblance of what I had once been... a demon, plucked from the dark abyss which was now Lucifer's Kingdom, combined with what I had become. I was shrouded by smoke and ash, all that was once holy and pure falling away, turning me into yet another unnatural entity, a shadow of the demon I once was. I was in Purgatory, the in-between for life and death. From here, I had two options to go... Earth, the human world. The very thought of being amongst the creatures that stole any sort of love He had once had for me made me sick. No...

I would return home.

The Abyss.

CHAPTER ONE

Leviathan

"Bloody *FUCK*!" I roared towards the cavernous sky.

All I could do was stand there and watch as my latest project was demolished. The dragon, Glazhale, came first, smashing over the largest turret of the white marble and gold trim castle. Then those ridiculous, brainless automatons that had followed it here began applying their own methods of destruction. Some had gathered loose, obsidian rock from the mountainous backdrop I'd set up in front of and threw those repeatedly at the structure until it began to crack and eventually fell apart. Some of these mindless varmints were throwing their own withered, little bodies against the stone, doing more damage to themselves than my newest work-in-progress.

Lucifer's angels... rather, Lucifer's *failed* angels. They were anything but holy, beautiful, or of the image we had all once been.

They had followed his dragon here, *needing* to be led, or they'd get lost along the way, most likely throwing themselves into the fires of the river Phlegethon because it was bright and pretty. These things were so pathetically mindless and weak that I wondered why he kept them around at all. They were barely three feet high, their skin similar to the crinkled, filmy layer that sits on the surface of lava. Red-eyed with razor-like claws, they buzzed around like annoying tiny gnats, continuously emitting a noise that reminded me of a human child who screamed when they didn't get their way. Every time I heard the sound, it made me cringe.

Speaking of the little pests...

I could feel one right now, striking me at the back of my thigh again and again with a soft little, *thump-thump-thump.* I nonchalantly peered down over my shoulder at it and couldn't help but raise a brow and sneer in disgust. The stupid little creature was headbutting my leg... the thing thought I was a part of the palace.

Bloody hell!

I lowered my head, sighing as I pinched the bridge of my nose as it continued to ram its head into the backs of my legs. It didn't hurt; it was just mildly irritating.

I sighed in defeat as the dragon finished off my project with a final blast of fire, weakening the supports so that it all came crashing down in one dusty mess, crushing several of the *Failed Angels* in the process. Good riddance to them, I supposed. Besides, he'd just replace any that were missing. The dragon, however...

I glared up at it as it let out a high-pitched, off-key shriek that had my own loyalists running for cover and muffling their ears, before it turned and flew off, back to the Kingdom of Pride where Lucifer resided... right at the center of Hell. It took all my self-control to refrain from summoning Beast, my familiar, and sit back to watch as he grew to rival Glazhale before challenging him to fight to the death. It would be immensely satisfying to see Beast take that dragon down, but there was no way that Lucifer would allow him to go unscathed should he conquer. So instead, I just watched as the remaining little beasties that haven't killed themselves tearing apart my destroyed design follow, all save for the one still headbutting the backs of my legs.

I turned, casually flicking my wrist in the little pest's direction, not bothering to watch as the harsh, green light bursts from the inside of its mouth. I knew what would happen. It will still, paralyzed by the pain, as the harsh inner flame I've cast eats it from the inside out. In seconds, it will be ash and nothing more. The best thing for it, really. What a miserable existence it had otherwise.

"Clean this mess up!" I snarled at my demons, who had since re-emerged from the smaller caves in the mountainside, to survey the smoking scene left behind.

"And rebuild, my Lord?" one asked tentatively.

"And have Lucifer send his vermin over to tear it down again? No. It's a waste of time. Retrieve what can be saved and store for another project." I turned away, heading down the black, sandy plain towards my old palace. Beyond this section where I'd built my fortress, it overlooked the expanse of misty plateau that was my realm. The original home I'd erected since I was kicked out of "Paradise" was the very part of Hell I'd once dwelled before it became Lucifer's kingdom. The castle I'd built set over the very cave system I'd dragged my broken, bloody body to the moment I returned. Lucifer had awarded it to me for my loyalty. It had been enough for some time, but then the Prince of Darkness constructed *his* new palace.

It was just so much larger than mine, and refined, a mirror image of Heaven's. I had figured Lucifer's head was stuck so far up his own ass that he wouldn't notice that I was in the midst of constructing a duplicate one to his own, only flashier and more grandeur. Was it so wrong of me to want more than I'd been settled with since the beginning of Hell's birth? Well, I guess today proved that apparently, it was.

I stopped in the courtyard before my fortress, sneering as it loomed high up against the black, obsidian mountains that bordered the highest plain of Hell, protecting the seven kingdoms from the fiery River Phlegethon. The only light here came from its flames, and as I stared up at my fortress, I could feel my hands tremble with rage. Why was I denied everything I've ever wanted? Why was I never satisfied?

Because for your whole existence, you have been denied it all. Because you are unworthy. You have never been good enough to deserve all that you desire. Because of all your fallen siblings, you are the only one who has known no pleasure...

I scoffed at the sight of my palace, finding the mere presence of it unbearable. This was all I was permitted to have. I'd thought that when I was thrown from Heaven that Lucifer would be different. I may respect him, but he's still a spoiled prick who prefers to keep the rest of us under his heel. Though here I am considered a prince, the Gatekeeper, which is more than I had when I was one of *His* angels, I am still deprived—still barred.

The Kingdom of Greed was the closest to my domain, but I couldn't bring myself to look there without feeling a tortuous sort of resentment toward my closest brother, Riker, who was once Maddix. To block the sight of his obsidian, gold kingdom, I constructed a wall of mirrors, hiding my realm behind the impressive beauty and wealth of his own. So whenever he was in Hell and looked my way, he would only see the richness he had attained and not the vast, foggy moor I had claimed to.

Thinking of the remains of my newest project was like a sickness stewing in my stomach, and I was tempted to call upon Beast and send him to destroy Lucifer's own palace. After all, had he not stolen the very image of His kingdom as his own? Was it so wrong that I should want it, too? Apparently, yes.

Well, if I couldn't have it, then neither could he.

My form shifted back and forth between its tainted angelic being to my demon body. As my mind continuously tortured me with these thoughts, a deep, echoing, unworldly, monstrous growl emitted from the pit of my stomach as I fought for control, and my subordinates scattered far from me as they cleaned up the wreckage.

I couldn't bear to be here. I needed to get away. Though I had taken my position as Hell's Gatekeeper seriously, sentencing and punishing those who have sinned, those who attempted to escape Hell hoping to find their way up the River Styx to the gates of Heaven, I wasn't in the mood now. And I certainly didn't want to sit around watching my followers clean up the remains of the new palace. *No doubt*, that smug pompous prick was laughing his ass off, probably having watched the destruction unfold at the hands of his pathetic little minions and dragon.

I raised a hand, the air before it swirling in black smoke as I opened a gateway and stepped into the ether. Momentarily caught in the middle of nowhere... not Hell, nor Heaven or Earth... and stepped out into the in-between. Purgatory. The Neutral Zone.

This place was as unimpressive and bland as you could imagine—grey, grey everywhere. A long, cavernous tunnel, split into two sides by the River Styx, which glows silver from the souls of humans who have died and are traveling to the afterlife. I strolled along the bank, not even bothering to look at the souls of the dead mortals. I could care less about them—these faulty beings—these weak, sinful creatures who He loves so dearly. If I could, I'd stomp them as they passed, but they were ethereal... I would sink through and disappear into the river that was neither gaseous nor liquid. More like a drifting fog, each soul being judged for their life, to be sorted when they reached the end where the river forked left and right. To the Gates of Heaven or the Mouth of Hell, the Abyss.

Occasionally, a lost soul would be found wandering on one side of the river or the other. The ones who clawed free, fighting the inevitable end of death, because of some unfinished business. *Those* souls were ripe for taking. The more we had in Hell, the less for Him in Heaven, and more humans we could punish for eternity... the biggest *fuck you*, to Him. I sent slave creatures to Purgatory every so often to collect any wandering, lost souls they found on the riverbank so that they could be dragged into Hell. Any opportunity to take from him, to deny those he'd see as worthy but were just... lost, and to deny them entry to Heaven so that they may never bask in his love, was the closest I ever felt to contentment. But today, the shores were empty.

The only light in this bland area of judgment comes from Styx and from Charon's new place... a cafe he built hundreds of years ago when his role became more obsolete, when the mortal's belief of paying for admission to the afterlife started to die out. But he was still here. Thus, The Last Stop was constructed, a structure built on a stone bridge that hung over the river, joining the side of Heaven and Hell to a single, neutral zone. It's done well, and attracts enough beings from both sides.

The dark, charcoal-coloured sand gave way beneath my booted feet as I walked towards The Last Stop. It looked like a mausoleum, made out of stone, but with thick, almost see-through glass that overlooks the souls traveling to where their eternal end. I climbed up the old grey steps covered with a black, practically dead-looking moss, and pushed open the thick, dark, oaken door, stepping inside. It's quiet today, and my presence is noted immediately. At a nearby stone table, I saw several of Dai's demon's drowning their sorrows in their brews. No doubt they'd had their asses kicked in one of her fighting rings. The crazy she-devil loved her brawls.

Psychotic jade... I thought to myself as the Princess of Wrath came to mind. I was glad her kingdom was far from mine, almost as far as that dallying, undeserving Sal, The Prince of Sloth. I didn't want either of them anywhere near me. Her demons, however, gave me a respectful nod, acknowledging my standing, but my mood is so soured at this moment, I just ignored them. I approached the counter, the gothic standing candelabras and hanging steel chandelier's candles flickering as I breezed past and took a seat. The light from the river glowed through the thick, foggy-looking glass windows that line the walls, helping illuminate the space, and I spotted Charon making his way over to me, bowing respectfully once he did.

He was a good one, Charon. He wore his dark robes, his face always hidden by a hood pulled up over his head, a towel slung over one shoulder, but you could see his long, withered, deathly white hands as he cleared tables and served drinks. His voice was gravelly, hoarse, like he'd gotten live flies caught in his throat. For extra money, he would open his robes to show off his favoured Lederhosen that he wore beneath them, something I knew Lucifer particularly enjoyed seeing when, on the rare occasion, he left his kingdom. But I didn't give him a hard time. I'd never seen his face, nor was I aware of how old he was exactly... all I knew was that I had respect for him. He'd been around since the beginning, and though he was no longer in favour with the mortals (yet another reason for me to despise them), he had found a way to keep himself busy for eternity.

"Leviathan," his strange, buzzing voice rumbled from beneath his cloak, "Your usual?"

"Yes." I leaned over the counter, resting my forehead against the palm of my hand, feeling suddenly exhausted. "It has been a long day..."

"Aren't they all?"

I snorted at his words, huffing a dispirited laugh at his statement. There was no day or night here. It just... *is*. I was grateful when Charon carefully poured me a smoking, white draught, a spicy sort of alcoholic beverage that I occasionally favoured. Not like the disgusting brew that the demon lackeys always ordered. I preferred the more refined dishes; after all, they were the best. And that was what I wanted.

"What's been going on underside?" he asked me as he wiped down the shiny, polished, dark green fluorite countertop.

"A whole bunch of rubbish," I muttered bitterly, thinking about recent events. Not only my would-be new castle getting knocked down, but rumours of Riker, Him and some human... and Asmodeus...

"There has been much talk, as of late," Charon's low, buzzing voice rasped. He heard everything that went on. Even though he was privy to such information, he wasn't one to spread gossip like some desperate minion, which was something else I liked about him and made him tolerable to be around. He simply offered an opening for us to vent and let us divulge what we saw fit and would leave it at that.

"Things have felt different somehow," I admitted, sipping my drink. It burned down my throat, but in a pleasant way, like a tingling sensation and a taste that reminded me of fruit-induced meats I enjoyed.

"How do you mean?" I could hear the confusion in his otherwise flat voice.

"I feel like... something is happening. Something is coming..." I downed my drink in two swallows and thumped the glass down, ignoring the burn in my throat. It was hard to explain, but I could sense a constant prickling of my skin, like that bestial side that still existed somewhere inside of me, sensed a disturbance.

"Like... another war?" Charon's voice wavered ever so slightly with fear. The last time there was a war, Lucifer became the king of Hell, and thus, the seven sins were born.

The corner of my mouth tilted as I shook my head at him. "No, Charon. Not a war."

His shoulders visibly relaxed just the slightest. He went to pour more into my almost empty drink, but I covered it with my hand, not wanting to return home intoxicated and belligerent for my followers to see. I was about to explain further when the pale, brushed gold inscribed door on the opposite side of the establishment opened, signalling the arrival of an angel from the Heavens. Unable to hide my curiosity, I peered over and frowned at the sight of Michael.

Bloody fucking hell...

"Leviathan," he nodded, taking a seat right at my side, invading my space. There were dozens of empty chairs and stools in this place, yet he chose the spot beside me. He was trying to make me feel uncomfortable, no doubt, and it was working. I cringed a little as the feel of his silken wings brushed against my left arm, and I shifted my weight, leaning slightly out of his way. Michael nodded to Charon. "Some of the sacred draught, please, Charon," he said politely, his blue eyes sparkling against the silver light of the souls that shone through the glass. He was such a pretty boy. I curled my lip at him and shook my longer, caramel-coloured hair out of my face, now wishing to finish my drink quickly and leave.

As Charon slid a golden goblet of that fancy, heavenly wine I'd once indulged in towards him, Michael nodded his thanks and partially turned his torso in my direction, resulting in me shrinking away in response. The last being I wanted to talk to right now was this uppity ass. I slid my stool back, preparing to flee, when he spoke up, "You heard about Riker?"

"Rumours..." I muttered, making sure I sounded as bored with his choice of conversation topic as I was of his face, "Something about palling around with humans?"

Michael nodded, lifting one of his light brows as he studied me. "And Asmodeus?"

I sighed heavily, hating him so much. "His latest folly failed."

"Indeed." He took a sip of his drink, but I could still feel his eyes on me. I could sense that he was hinting at something, perhaps, shoving it in my face. Why, I didn't know. I just wanted him far away from me. Charon, the intelligent being he was, obviously sensed my increasing displeasure and drifted away from us. In the corner where Dai's demons were still drinking, I sensed them watching the scene before them. No doubt they'd report back to their mistress. I didn't want her to think me weak in any way. I didn't want anyone to see me as weak. I stood so fast that the stool fell to the floor with a loud clatter.

"It is not a bad thing, Leviathan," Michael said quickly, realizing I was seconds away from tearing out of there.

"Relationships with humans are disgusting and an abomination!" I hissed at him.

"Those are Lucifer's words. Not yours."

"They are what I believe!" I snapped, turning my green gaze his way. He could piss off right now! According to him, apparently, my own thoughts were not my own. The audacity of him to think I could be so manipulated!

"Leviathan, why are you so unhappy?" Michael's voice gentled, and if anything, it made me angrier.

"What are you talking about?"

"Just that. Why are you so... unhappy? Why does nothing please you? What are you so self-conscious about?"

I burst out laughing at his words, tilting my head back as I did, both livid and amused at the same time. "Self-conscious? Enough with your gossiping, Michael."

Michael stood up, uncoiling his 6'4" frame and swimmer's body, tall enough, but not nearly as broad or as tall as me. Not after what happened to me when I fell. I grinned, enjoying the sight of him flinching at my slightly pointed fanged teeth. I ran my tongue over them, pausing at the sharp tips before my smile broadened, the effect having the result I was hoping for when I noticed how he took a small step back.

"I have a kingdom of my own. I have responsibilities and freedoms I was never permitted when I lived amongst the angels. I *belong* in the Abyss. I thrive in it. So, explain yourself."

"You are never satisfied, Levi..."

"Don't call me that," I hissed, sharply cutting him off, hating it when he used that shortened version of my name. "You have no permission to address me as thus. What are *you*? Just another soldier. Another lackey. While *I* am a dark prince, someone important. And you are *still* cleaning up after them... those humans. Those insects that he favours. You are nothing but an errand boy, Michael. Nothing but a servant, a slave."

Instead of angering him as I'd hoped, his face fell in disappointment. No matter. I was done. I hated how he looked down upon me, how he thought himself better.

He wasn't, I reassured myself. He might have been on the winning side in the battle of Heaven, but in the end, I ended up in a position of power that demanded respect while he still had to follow *His* bidding. I sneered as I turned away to leave, moving towards the oaken door which led to Hell's side of the Styx.

"As you are his..." His voice was so soft, I almost didn't hear him, but I had. And his words hit me like a blade had just sliced through my gut. Charon's place was eerily silent, and I knew all were waiting for me to detonate, to start a fight on neutral ground. But I wouldn't. I would save face and not even bother turning to even look at him. I didn't need gossip about how the *tainted monster* lost control and caused a scene.

"*He* is the only one who speaks the truth." I snarled, "I am the Prince of Envy, Grand Admiral, Ruler of the Chaotic Oceans, The Great Devourer, Dragon of the Abyss, and Gatekeeper to Hell. He has given me more than your God ever has! And I shall remain loyal to him!" I shoved open the door and stomped out, wishing Michael hadn't appeared. I didn't want to go home, nor did I want to stay another second near him. I know some demons, even the other Princes and Princess of Sin have ventured into the human realm, but I never did. Why would I want to walk amongst them? There was nothing on Earth for me. With that final option out, I remained where I was on the stone bridge, overlooking the river of souls.

They slowly drifted my way, disappearing beneath me, the dark moss hanging just inches above the surface before the dead human spirits reappeared on the other side. Idly, they made their way down the tunnel before arriving at that inevitable fork where it was officially determined where their souls would spend eternity... left to the golden gates of Heaven. Right, and they'd fall through the hellmouth which my familiar, Beast, stood guard over, watching and preying upon those who fought to free themselves from Satan's grasp.

They never made it out.

I leaned against the stone balustrade, lazily taking in the humans that were once living, but now no more. I curled my lip at the sight of their dead faces, a sick sort of pleasure pooling in my stomach, as I thought about when they came to us to face judgement. I loved punishing them. I could vent all my anger and frustrations on them, and I did it gladly. To the ones who got away, who disappeared through the golden gates, they were *His* problem now. I'd never have to hear them whine or lament or feel like they had the right to make demands. I hated them. *All* of them.

I released a long, strained breath, only now realizing I'd been holding it in. Why did I feel such a tight squeeze in my chest? Why did I feel anxious? Why was I shaking? But mostly, Michael's words seemed to affect me... why wasn't I happy? I was never happy. Not even when I had been rewarded my kingdom or Lucifer trusted me enough to be Hell's Gatekeeper. I was back in the Abyss where I'd been born. I should feel like I was finally home. And yet each day, I woke up with the same feeling... dissatisfaction. Misery. Resentment and discontent. I tried to mimic the others or secretly take from them, hoping to feel an ounce of their euphoria. I had my followers bring me the silks from Asmodeus's kingdom, knowing that Lust had the most exquisite furnishings and comforts, and decorated my palace with them. As Ruler of the Chaotic Oceans, I themed my kingdom after anything and everything I could find in the world I controlled. So... why was I feeling this way? Why did it feel like I was suffocating, like there was a weight upon my chest that felt as though something was missing?

Because no matter how much I wanted, coveted, and took, I was never satisfied with anything. It felt like I always just... existed. It was all meaningless... all of it...

My eyes drift over the endless faces of souls, feeling nothing but the stewing, bitter animosity, hatred, and the impulse to destroy what I could not have.

By the envy of the devil, death entered the world...

I felt such a suffocating sense of misery, and my eyes began to glaze over, unseeing as I held my head in my hands, loathing this sense of helplessness that made me feel genuinely ill, until for some reason... a face amongst the souls caught my attention.

At first, I didn't realize I was staring at it until it disappeared from view beneath the bridge. I found myself leaning over the rail in an attempt to keep the soul in my sight, but her slim, frail body, shrouded in the white cloak of death, vanished in the dark shadow of the stone. I didn't have a single thought in my head. It was like my body was acting on its own as it spun around and rushed to the other side of the bridge, searching for the beholder of that face.

She emerged again, another soul partially obscuring my view as it drifted over her, and I impatiently tapped my toe, waiting for it to move. When it did, I found myself breathing a sigh of relief as I studied her face once more.

Her eyes were closed, her mouth slightly open, looking like the others around her... like they were sleeping.

Something about this particular soul captivated me. She looked like... a doll. A delicate china doll that I'd seen human children play with on the rare occasions that I have travelled to Earth. I knew neither her hair nor skin colour, as she was like a glowing ghost, but her cheeks were rounded, though a little sunken as if she had recently lost a significant amount of weight. Her nose was small and slightly upturned, while her little pouty lips were full, the top shaped with a little cupid's bow. She was tiny, almost like a human child, but I could tell by the shape of her body that she was a woman, a young woman. But she was dead. They were all dead.

For the first time, I found myself wondering what happened to a human; why did she die? She appeared to be young, and besides the obvious signs of a bit of weight loss, there was no indication as to why or how she passed.

I watched as she floated farther away from me, and for a moment, I almost lost sight of her completely. That was, until I realized that my feet were carrying me down the stone steps, half walking, half running alongside the Styx, keeping her in my field of view. Why? I had no clue. All I knew was that for some strange, unknown reason, I *wanted* to keep staring at her. She was nearing the point of judgement, where she would either be granted entry into the Gates of Heaven or thrown into the Mouth of Hell, and I felt a small bubble of excitement in my chest at the thought of her coming to me. However, as I watched, she moved away, turning left, towards the golden gates, and that feeling instantly vanished. Of course, she would be good enough to go to His kingdom.

My hands shook with rage and indignation at the thought of her being amongst Michael and the other Angels for eternity. As much as it angered me, I should have expected it, what with her innocent and pleasing features that screamed holier-than-thou.

I really could have nothing I desired...

I kicked at the dull, grey sand, sending a spray against the rock wall of the cavern, and my fist went flying. Blinded by my fit, when I came to, I found I'd actually punched a sizable hole into the stone, my fists stinging slightly from the impact. My breathing was coming in heavy, quick pants, like I'd just engaged in battle for days, and yet, all I'd done was see a dead human soul drift away from me. Why was I so... *affected*?

There was a pang in my chest, knowing she was leaving me forever. Once again, I was not good enough, worthy enough, to have anything I wanted. But...

Did I want her?

I peered wistfully over my shoulder to where her soul was slowly approaching His kingdom. She was a human, I reminded myself. A dead human. So, what was she worth? Nothing. Less than nothing. I despised humans. I felt that strange, twisted sort of reassurance when I remembered how they screamed and writhed on the ground, oftentimes shitting themselves in the process as they endured the effects of my power as I punished them. Look at His favourite mortals now... covered in their own excrement, sobbing and snivelling on the floor of my fortress, begging for forgiveness when they didn't deserve it. And yet, he chose them over me.

But this one...

She was closer now. And soon, she would be gone from me forever. I found myself toeing the edge of the Styx, trying to keep her in my sights for as long as possible.

What if I steal her soul? I wondered. What if I somehow managed to reach it from the edge and pull her free? Then I'd take her down to my kingdom. The very fact I'd steal and torture a little soul meant for the Heaven's being the best *fuck you* to Him I could do. Yes, I'd summon one of my minions and have them risk the dangers of entering the Styx to collect her soul for me. I'd celebrate and gloat before the gates from my side, having gone a step further to spite Him. *This* would bring me pleasure.

But just as the decision was made, suddenly, her soul became alight. Odd... What was happening? Her ghostly white features and floating veil, which covered her, were becoming brighter, even more than those around her. Her soul was frozen in place, moving no further down the river. I paced on my side, wishing I could enter the Styx without the worry of being sucked into oblivion, wishing I could storm across The Last Stop and into Heaven's territory to be closer to her... but I couldn't. I was barred from Heaven and their side. I snarled as I moved as close to the edge as I dared, straining to see what was happening. I'd never really paid much attention to the souls in the river, but not once had I witnessed such an anomaly. That's what I was telling myself now as to why I was so fascinated, so curious as to what was happening to this particular soul.

I was about to summon one of my demons to venture to the other side and quickly grab her when the soul flickered, the light disappearing and coming back in quick succession before she vanished completely.

Wait... what? Where was she? She hadn't entered Heaven's Gates; of that I was certain. But I couldn't see her anywhere else, either. I rushed up one side of the river and then down the other, searching, but she was just... gone.

Where was she? Where did she go?

Why did I even care?

Why was I feeling so irrationally angry because of this? Why did I feel like diving into the River Styx to find her and drag her down into Hell with me? But it would do no good. Somehow, I could sense that she wasn't here anymore. Not Purgatory, nor Heaven, and certainly not Hell. The longer I stood in frustrated silence, the more sure I became about what happened. She was not here because she was no longer dead.

Which meant, she was back on earth.

CHAPTER TWO

Evangeline

Overhead, the sound of Mrs. Freeman's footsteps steadily paced back and forth, echoing over the floorboards, and I sympathized with her. I knew why she was so anxious... storms always had that effect on the old woman, and tonight, New York was being completely pissed on, a torrential downpour that battered the city. I was hiding out in my basement studio. The one window, covered in bars, peeked up onto the sidewalk where rain pounded the pavement and lightning flashed across the sky, casting the city in white, blinding light for only seconds before we were again cast into darkness.

But I didn't mind. I loved storms and found the unpredictable and chaotic weather exciting. And so, I snuggled up under my blankets in bed, listening to the rain, exhausted after a day of studying and then working on my small business, which was making small kits out of Altoid tins or ones I'd purchased in bulk at the dollar store to sell. First aid, sewing, and emergency kits were the top sellers and no-brainers and the easiest ones to put together. But I also branched out into more unusual products that were gaining traction, like pocket rosary shrines for the Catholic students who attended my school, or pocket games that most groups seemed to enjoy, travel paint containers, and my best-seller, the travel altar that the underground Wiccan group at my school loved so much.

I spent hours prettying them up and finding the right supplies. My little kits were trendy on campus and brought in enough money that I could feed myself and not dip even more into my debts and loans. I hoped that taking a few business courses would help me start my own company someday, though to be honest, I seemed to be doing alright on my own. I just needed to branch out more. The kits were fun, but it wasn't a passion. I was naturally artistic, but I wasn't sure where that could take me.

One day, I would own my own business, and I wouldn't have to worry about my next meal or what the hell I was going to do if I ever got sick again...

My hands wrung the blanket wrapped around me as memories brought back that familiar sting in my arms, which were hidden beneath my thick sweater... arms that were scarred from endless needles, and I shuddered. No matter how many times I'd been poked and prodded, I never got used to it.

It's all over, Evie... you're better now. That was two years ago; in the past. Look at where you are now. You're surviving. You're thriving. You're ALIVE! So tell that other shit to fuck right off.

I tried not to let myself get too caught up over things I couldn't control or worries that wouldn't be solved lying in bed in my shabby, little one-room basement studio in the dead of night during a storm. Life was too short to stress out over the small stuff.

I yawned and rolled over just as another flash of lightning briefly lit up the space. Sure, this place was basically a hole in the ground, the basement to a suite that a kind older woman rented out to college students. Yes, the area was somewhat sketchy, the space was cramped, and there was always a cold draft coming in from the doorway, which I had shut with several additional deadbolts and chain locks after I'd moved in and my neighbour got robbed, but the price was right. I wasn't going to be picky. At the end of the day, I was going to a great school, I had a place to call home, and I was fucking living!

I mean, it was literally one room with a couch that was a fold-out bed, lined up against the far wall from the window. I had two counters, a sink that I used for dishes and to wash my hands and face in, a cupboard with just a few plastic plates, bowls and cups and a pot or two, and a hot plate set up on one counter, leaving only one space free to cook on. I ate simply, healthy, but also so I didn't need much room. The only other furniture I could squeeze into this space was a plastic patio table I'd painted flowers and vines onto to make it a little more pleasing to the eye and two fold-out chairs. However, I kept one always folded up and set aside as I hardly ever had visitors, save for my landlady who would bring me baked goods on occasion. My clothes were all rolled up and stuffed into a duffle bag which I kept beneath my fold-out bed, and my toilet and shower were set up in what should have been my closet.

That was it.

But this was New York. I wasn't going to be picky. Not when I was going to school and had my health, something I reminded myself of every day. It could be worse... so much worse.

I shivered as a draft swept through the small space. Laying in the dark, listening to the storm, I flipped my wavy, chocolate coloured hair away from my face. It was down to my shoulders now, and it was comforting to have it so close to its old length before I lost it all. I was feeling more like myself again. I'd gained my weight back, though I was still very slender, thanks to my father's side of the family.

Lightning flashed once more, and even through my closed lids, I could see the blinding light. I remember back to a time when I feared going to sleep. For so long, I worried I would never wake up again, and once, that almost happened.

I felt that familiar pang in my chest as the memories of that dark time in my life came flooding back to me. The endless hospital visits, the way my parents looked at me with grief, like I was already dead. My mother's family was from Trinidad and Tobago, and though my father was as Irish as they come, I used to look more like her, with golden skin and silky dark hair. But the leukemia treatments had robbed me of so much, then. I had been incredibly frail, my complexion wan and paling, and my hair gone. I didn't look like myself anymore. Eventually, it became too much for my parents to watch me slowly wither away, so they stopped visiting altogether.

The day I died, nurses had surrounded me in my room, some cracking jokes to cheer me up, and I would weakly try to smile, wanting to laugh so badly, but didn't have the air or energy. One nurse I loved, Marsha, held my hand the entire time. Though she had a smile fixed upon her face, her tears fell upon my grey-tinged skin. Her comfort was the last thing I remembered before I closed my eyes one last time and then...

Nothing but blackness.

For the first time in years, I found myself thinking about the sensation I'd felt after I closed my eyes. I couldn't see anything, and it felt like I was floating, drifting. Where I was heading, I didn't know. I couldn't see. It was like I was just... *waiting* for something. But as time stretched out, I could recall another sensation. An uneasy feeling, like I was terrified of something and wanted nothing more than to get away. It was like... like I was being *hunted*. I was being watched, and whatever it was, the presence of evil had my frail little soul trembling.

Was I going to Hell? What had I done to end up there?

I thought I'd been a good person. I hardly ever thought bad of anyone, except for a few girls at school who teased me when I lost my hair. I never stole from the local corner store like most kids did as the first act of rebellion, and I was too much of a chicken-shit to lie to my parents about anything. I was just a teenager who spent several years battling a disease while doing my best to enjoy what time I had left. Did I really deserve to be damned for eternity?

The nightmare was building, and though at some point it lessened, like a distance was growing between myself and that dark presence, it didn't go away completely. I tried to concentrate on the growing sense of warmth, like a beacon that was beckoning me, promising safety, and I could feel it begin to pull me in. I was leaving the hunter behind, but I knew he was still close, still watching. I didn't feel safe. I felt... pursued. Whatever was stalking me, radiated pain, anger, voracity, and... intense yearning. It scared the shit out of me.

Next thing I knew, I was awake in my hospital bed. Nurses and doctors had circled around me, some bent over my body, in the process of removing syringes, tubes, and other life-sustaining devices. They stared at me in absolute shock when they realized I was awake, apparently not expecting me to open my eyes again.

"Surprise..." I whispered, the smallest of smiles curling up on my cracked lips.

It's funny, thinking about it now. Before, when I would go to bed, my mind whirled about my near-death experience, it was more that I was consumed with the thoughts of never waking again, of going to sleep and that being it. I'd pushed the memory of that creeping, haunting feeling out of my brain for good. But now, out of seemingly nowhere, it was back in full force, and I had no idea why. It made me curl up into a tight little ball beneath my comforter as I hugged one of my pillows tight to my chest. The memory of it was chilling, but that's all it was... a memory from long ago.

But then, I *felt* it.

For the first time in my life, I felt every single hair on my body rise, and a shiver raced through my very bones as a sinking feeling in my gut suddenly alerted my senses that I was *not* alone. It felt like it was *here* now, watching me. As if I'd somehow summoned it by simply thinking about it again. How was that possible? Was I just feeling this way because it was the first time I remembered it since it happened? Maybe that was it. That was all. Just my body reliving that horrifying sensation of evil stalking me through the darkness.

Although no matter how I tried to reassure myself, I was frozen where I lay on my side, the covers pulled up to my chin, and I wanted nothing more than to cower beneath them like a little kid afraid of the boogeyman. Keeping my eyes closed, listening to the sound of rain battering against my barred window, I repeated a mantra over and over in my head, *It's not real, it's not real, it's not real...*

Feeling my strength return, I counted silently to three, then slowly opened my eyes, studying the small space around me, but the shadows swallowed everything. A small voice in my head was screaming a warning as the sensation of something nearby only became stronger. I'd locked my door, and my window was *always* locked, the bars adding further protection. I knew no one else was here. There was nowhere to hide.

And yet...

I shivered and retreated beneath my blankets, squeezing my eyes shut, praying that this ominous, unsettling feeling would disappear. I slowly inhaled a long, shaking breath through my teeth and counted to ten, holding it in before releasing it in a low hiss. In the distance, I could hear the rumble of thunder. Poor New York was just getting absolutely shit on by mother nature right now.

I waited for this unsettling sensation to vanish so that I could get some rest, but it didn't. The pull got stronger as time went on, like whatever that darkness was, was closing in on me, calling me out. Summoning whatever ounce of bravery I had left in me, I peered out from beneath the blankets. Despite my eyes being wide open, I could see nothing but shadows and no hint of movement. I was losing my mind, I told myself. I needed sleep. That was all. I was about to lie back down when another flash of light illuminated the space, and to my horror, in the corner adjacent to the window, a huge, and I mean HUGE, shadowy figure was lurking there. It literally took up the entire space from floor to ceiling, and it wasn't... solid. Though it seemed wispy, black, and semi-transparent, I could still see that it was bulky, like a giant, and what looked like *horns* arching up to the ceiling, while two wide wing-shaped hazes stretched to the side, blocking my kitchenette from view.

I screamed, leaping up from my bed, and threw myself at my desk, feeling around for my bat, something I kept as a weapon of sorts for this very moment. Somehow someone, *something,* had broken into my place, and I was going to fight.

I spun around to face them, bat raised in the air, but to my shock, I was alone. I reached over to the old Victorian lamp at my bedside and yanked the chain down. The room was cast in its warm glow. Outside, the rain pattered against the glass of the window, the room was the same as it was when I'd been working on my projects. But there was nothing.

So what was that shadow? Was my mind playing tricks on me?

Shaking my head to clear it, I hurried over to the closet that was my washroom and quickly checked it, but it was empty, too. I moved swiftly around the space, checking the locks on the door and the window again, looking under the fold-out bed, yet I was alone. I tried to reassure myself that it had just been in my head. I was tired, overworked from studying all day, and then busy crafting for most of the night. I needed sleep. That was all.

I crawled back into bed but brought the bat with me, feeling safer as I clutched it tight to my chest, pausing before turning off the light. The feeling was gone. Like it had never happened in the first place. I was alone.

I fell asleep convincing myself that my mind was simply playing tricks on me. It was all in my head. A lousy memory had come to life as I'd reflected on my near-death experience. That was all.

That was all...

CHAPTER
THREE

Leviathan

I listened patiently as I sat upon my throne in my palace while my second, a typai demon named Gnaarl, pleaded his case. At his feet, a tiny figure trembled violently, her almost black hair hiding her face, her body curled up on the floor at his raptorial feet.

"... look at her!" Gnaarl was saying, speaking to me in his species dialect, "She is so... *cute*!"

I arched a brow at him, completely and utterly confused. Gnaarl, as my Second, was a frightening, intimidating demon who rightly earned his place at my side. He was taller than me unless I shifted into my full demon form. His head morphed into two long, uneven horns that arched straight up into the air, his skin a greyish colour with black, onyx armour that looked like it was made of tree bark. He was armed with long, black claws on each of his digits, as well as a long sickle-shaped one on his large toe, and his entire body was made of muscle. When he spoke in his

Mother tongue, it only made him more formidable, as the words were incredibly guttural, laced with growls and snapping from his overlong top incisors.

It was almost comical to hear him talking of this human girl with such affection, especially when I knew she likely assumed he was plotting her demise. The strangest thing about all of this was to hear him call a human 'cute' of all things. This was my lieutenant, one who liked to oversee the punishments that I don't personally dish out to sinners. He consistently reported back with glee that my instructions were being adequately carried out. Now, he was cooing at this miscreant like she was one of those creatures humans like to keep for pets.

"See how she shivers?" He gestured down at her. "She is cold! I can keep her warm. I have many pelts in my quarters that I think she would like."

"Gnaarl," I sighed, leaning my head into the palm of my hand, my elbow resting on the arm of my throne. I spoke to him in his dialect, deciding it was best to keep the girl in the dark for now. "You cannot be serious about this-"

"Hear me out, My Lord," he quickly cut me off but bowed his head apologetically when my fierce, green eyes narrowed at him for the interruption. "Look at what she does when I wiggle my claws at her." He leaned down from his great height, stooping over the figure, waggling his long, two-inch claws before the girl's face. She cried out and scuttled back, her shaking intensifying, and he laughed, "See what she did?"

I stared at him, struggling to understand what he was so excited about. "What?"

"She makes the sweetest little sound!" He was practically puffing up his chest, as if proud of her for almost shattering my eardrums with her shrieking.

"Bloody hell, take her outside before she defecates and makes a mess on my floors!"

"I'll clean up after her, I promise. Please, just... there's something about this one. She *needs* me. I'll make sure she is no trouble to you or anyone else." When I remained silent, Gnaarl shocked me by placing his palms together, as if in prayer! "Please, My Lord. Let me keep Kys."

"Kys?" I glanced down at the girl, who has since curled up into another tight little ball, sobbing softly to herself.

"Yes, that is her name."

"You *named* it?" I growled at him. "Never name them! It forms an attachment! Have you learned nothing from the others? We have too many cambion demons running around Hell as it is!"

"She told me her name. I think it's beautiful. It suits her, yes?"

My green gaze flicked to her again, and I curled my lip. The human peeked up at me for the first time, and seeing my more humanoid features, a flash of hope crossed her face, and she spoke up, "Please... I-I don't know how I got here." Her voice cracked as she tried to wipe her tears away. "I w-was just picking up some groceries, and m-my car swerved. I..." she furrowed her brow in confusion, "I don't understand what exactly happened after..."

"What is she saying?" Gnaarl demanded passionately.

I ignored the girl and continued to speak to him in his demon-tongue, "She is telling me that she is unsure of how she got here."

"Your waywraith's found her on Earth. She had been injured from one of those steel automotive devices they use to travel around in... kaw-rrs. The scent of her blood lulled them in, and they decided to bring her back here as a treat when I happened upon them."

It was not uncommon for demons to visit Earth or for them to take someone on the verge of death. My waywraiths served me. They were small creatures, about two or three feet high, with heads that were not unlike the anglerfish you see in the deep oceans of the human world. They had round little bellies that protruded and four crustacean-like legs, their skin a myriad of oranges, browns, and creams. They cared for my palace, prepared my meals, cleaned, did whatever I demanded. They were simple creatures and only wanted a safe place to dwell and food to eat. They lived in a dark, stone cave beneath the earth of my home, a spot that suited them perfectly. They often scavenged upon the remains of a human I'd obliterated from existence. Sometimes, the cheeky little things would go to purgatory, searching for a lost soul, or to earth in hopes of snagging a snack. A girl, bleeding on the road from an accident, reeking of death would send them into a frenzy of excitement. She was lucky Gnaarl seemed so taken with her. He had just saved her from being ripped to shreds.

In fact, Gnaarl had now gotten onto all fours and was crawling towards the human, obviously hoping to look not as frightening at eye-level, as he gently talked to her. Unfortunately for... *Kys* (I highly doubted that was her actual name, and more like a failed attempt to pronounce it with his overextended fangs), Gnaarl looked like he was stalking towards her as if he was about to attack. The girl screamed so shrill, I thought my eardrums would burst. She scuttled back again until she hit one of the pillars, but he was right on top of her. Before she could put up any semblance of a fight, he had scooped her up again and was nuzzling her neck, making an odd sort of purring sound from deep in his chest, a sound I'd never heard him make before.

Blast it... there was no way I could take her from him now.

"Fine, keep it. But I swear if it soils itself on my floors-"

"I'll clean it, I swear to you. She won't get underfoot or anything!" he said excitedly, cradling her close. Gnaarl wasn't the first demon to fall for a human, and most likely, he wouldn't be the last. Though it was frowned upon, as far as Lucifer was concerned, the demons simply used them as playthings, fucktoys... objects for entertainment, and used to vent their frustrations out on.

Although looking at my Second now, I knew that this human wasn't going to be abused in the way Lucifer would expect. I could see it on his face. Gnaarl, as terrifying and demonic as he may be, would care for her. He blinked down with his pure black, glassy eyes and grinned wide, showing off his horrifying fangs. I refrained from laughing at the sight of absolute horror on her face as she craned her neck back, tilting her head as far from him as she could before looking back at me.

"Please! Please, help me-"

"Silence, Kys!" I didn't even bother looking at her. She was nothing as far as I was concerned. "You may only speak when your new owner permits it."

"Owner? Kys..." Her voice trailed off for a moment, as though she was lost in thought, before it finally clicked in and she burst out, "Firstly, this guy is *not* my owner! I'm not a housecat! And second, my name is Alexis! Not Kys!"

"Kyssss..." Gnaarl crooned, nuzzling the back of her neck.

"*Stop* calling me that!" she snapped at him and swung. The moment her hand struck the side of his head, I grinned, eager for entertainment. This whole thing had been dull, really. But now, she had sealed her fate by striking him. I've seen Gnaarl tear limbs off of men as if they were a housefly's wings for simply speaking to him.

But instead, he roared with laughter, tossing his head back, and said jubilantly, "She is a fighter! I like that! But I'll need to train you, my Kys... Come, let me bring you to my quarters, your new home... Hoooome," he said slowly, the word odd and guttural on his tongue.

"What the hell are you even saying?!" she cried, kicking her legs as he turned to leave.

"That's right. Home! Good girl!" He peered gleefully over his shoulder at me, "She's a quick learner!" and disappeared out the double doors, leaving me alone.

I ran my hand over my face, my frustrations mounting it seemed with every passing day. It felt like there was some sort of a disease spreading through Hell, and one by one, demons were succumbing to it. I'd been calling it the Mortal Stroke. I stood by, watching in revulsion as demons latched onto a particular mortal, and noticed the shift in their behaviours. The fact that we had cambion demons running around, half-human/half-demon beings, was proof enough that they'd basically thrown Lucifer's rule about fornicating with them, straight into the fires of the Phlegethon.

You came so close once, Leviathan... a small voice whispered at the back of my mind. Sneering, I shook it off and stomped between two pillars that led out onto my open balcony that overlooked my kingdom.

I observed the misty plain, the haunting light from my Seekers casting ghostly luminosities through the fog. I found myself lost in thought, remembering the little soul that had caught my attention so long ago. When she vanished, I'll admit I went a little mad for a time. I actually went to the mortal realm, searching Earth for her, not telling anyone my whereabouts as I travelled to the places I figured a human such as her would dwell, but it was fruitless. If she did invoke envy, it was not enough to pull me to her, like it did other humans. After I gave up my hunt, I scolded myself for even bothering.

Why did I?

I couldn't answer. But seeing Gnaarl with his new pet, I felt that familiar sense of bitter jealousy. He looked so... *happy* to have her. I've never seen him react so strongly to anything before. I certainly never have. It was a side effect of the Mortal Stroke—odd behaviour like giddiness, signs of euphoria, acts of kindness... all towards their human companion.

But the demons affected didn't look like they were suffering. They appeared... content.

So why wasn't *I* content?

I was briefly tempted to force Gnaarl to kill her rather than keep her; my resentment stung me deeply. But he had not wronged me, and after I buried my ever-present pettiness, I had relented, deciding to instead use this as an experiment. I knew my Second better than my own brothers and sister of Hell. I was curious to see how this would affect him long-term.

As I stared off, seeing nothing, I thought about the restlessness I felt, the emptiness inside... I'd been given so much. Trusted with immense power and responsibility. And yet, I saw these demons, workers of mine, strolling around with their mortal concubines, and they appeared happier than I have ever felt in my entire existence. I let my head drop as I sagged against the railing, ignoring the distant sounds of screams as new souls fell into Hell to be sorted into the plane, which they would suffer for eternity. I sighed heavily, feeling a weight resting upon my shoulders.

Why couldn't I stop thinking about her?

The answer was obvious... The little leech infected me. I needed to be cleansed! I needed to be reminded of why I was here in the first place. I needed to see Lucifer, but that pompous ass would no doubt make me fill out forms in triplicate and make me wait for eons before granting a meeting, even with me.

Frustrated, I turned away, stalking back into the throne room. My familiar, Beast, hadn't been by as of late. I guess that meant there were no flight risks for the time being. I almost wished my great, serpentine hydra had another fool for me to vent my aggravation on. But no, all was quiet and peaceful in Hell. I collapsed onto my throne, sagging back, as I tried and failed not to think of her.

But then...

I felt it.

Somewhere on the mortal plane, I felt an intense pull. It was such a foreign feeling in my chest that for a moment, I thought perhaps I'd been stabbed, a vain assassination attempt on my life, perhaps... by a vindictive demon or idiotic human. I peered down to study my torso, but no, my charcoal grey tunic and bronze armour were in place, shining against the light of the room.

I didn't understand it, but somehow, I sensed something calling me. It was like somewhere out there, a thick chain was tugging at a spot at the centre of my ribcage, urging me to travel through the ether to... I don't know where.

I'm going fucking insane, I thought, gripping the arms of my throne. And yet... I was curious. What was going on? I raised my hand as I stood, a swirl of ash and smoke spinning before me as I opened a portal and stepped through. When I found myself on the other side, I scoffed and curled my lip in distaste at my surroundings, unable to understand why this call had brought me here.

I was in some shabby, stinking basement in the dead of night in the human world, of all fucking places! I hated the human realm and rarely, if ever, stepped foot here. I glanced around, unfazed by the darkness, and took in everything about this space. It's small, dungy, with plastic and patched-up furniture. The floor was uneven, the walls peeling, and the ceiling was open with pipes running overhead. Outside, it was pouring rain, setting the mood for how I was feeling. There was nothing in this shithole I wanted. Nothing for me.

I turned, about to raise my hand to hastily leave this place behind forever, when the sound of something shifting and creaking alerted me to the fact that I'm not alone. I spun back, finally noticing that a human was sleeping amongst the pillows and blankets upon the drabby fold-out bed. I melted into the shadows, my eyes never leaving it, watching as it hugged a pillow close. The bed creaked beneath their weight as they shifted again before suddenly, they looked up, staring around as though sensing that they, too, were not alone. Their gaze missed me, hiding here in the shadows, and feeling satisfied by their quick perusal, retreated beneath their blankets, but I did see the face.

It was *her*.

The very moment it hit me, seeing that lovely doll-like face again, I instinctively and unwillingly responded. My ability to shift between my humanoid form to my demon side was always something I had control over unless provoked by extreme rage. I wasn't the slightest bit angry at the moment, and yet, I changed. Unwillingly at that. I felt my muscles expand and painfully stretch as I grew. I could feel the horns cut through the skin of my skull, and I grimaced, bearing the pain. However, the part I hated most... my old wings...

I could feel them itching beneath the skin of my back, scraping beneath the surface to break free. *Please... no...*

They ripped through, splitting the skin, and I only just managed not to scream as they stretched and expanded. I could feel the horns sprouting from behind my pointed ears curl until they arched forward. My delicate wings shivered naked in the cool air, and I brought them close to my body, conserving the heat. Why had I shifted upon seeing her? Why, when I looked upon that face, did I feel such a strange sort of... *ache*... in my chest? I felt like I'd run for days at the sight of her.

For the first time in years, I saw her as she was meant to be. Big brown, doe-like eyes, with long dark lashes, a head full of shoulder-length, wavy chocolate curls, and even in this dim light, I could make out the tanned complexion of her lovely skin.

I licked my lips, my tongue scratching against one of my fangs, accidentally cutting myself. Seeing her, hiding beneath her blankets, as though they were offering her any real semblance of protection... I wanted to laugh. Humans were so foolish. Before I knew what I was doing, I'd taken several steps, prowling closer to her to... *wait, what? What was I doing?*

It was like I had no control over my body. All I knew was that I *wanted* her. I want to take her. I don't want anyone else to have her, and if she *did* belong to someone, I would fucking end them.

I was close to the end of the bed, my wings stretching out to the sides, shivering as though in anticipation rather than the cold, when a flash of lightning lit up the room, and she screamed bloody murder. What was I doing? I didn't even know she was awake again; I was so distracted. I snapped back as she threw herself from the bed and groped along the wall to her desk. The last thing I needed was this pitiful, tiny human to see me in my demon form. No, it was better she was left in the dark entirely and for me to forget about her. Before she could turn to face me, I'd withdrawn through the ether, returning to Hell.

Her body was completely wrapped around her blankets, having balled them up, and was now embracing them like they were another human to hold onto while she slept. For a moment, I was irate at the thought but reminded myself that the only one here with her was me. It was peaceful tonight, and despite the sounds from the distant sirens, she slept soundly. Her dark, wavy hair was tossed over one shoulder. Her eyes shut so that her long, curved lashes rested upon the tops of her cheekbones. I found myself wishing her eyes would open so that I could study their lovely, dark colour.

Why was I here again?

This was the third time I'd ventured to the mortal world to watch her. And why did I even *want* to? She was one of them... a creature that was so beneath me, I should either leave or find a way to lure her into hell so I could do what I do best... torture her soul. *Hurt* her.

At the thought of her in hell, weak, vulnerable, and at my mercy, I felt an odd stirring in my gut. Like... excitement. Was this excitement? It was similar to the feeling I had when I burned a human, guilty of attempting escape, guilty of sin, of... well, it didn't matter. As long as they screamed, I could feel myself get hard from it. But now, picturing this girl at my feet, in nothing but chains, I could feel that same stimulating rush flow through me, only it felt more potent than the thought of hurting her.

My hand moved, as though I had no power over it, reaching for her. I hadn't touched her before now, but I couldn't resist another second. During the past two visits, I'd hung on by a thread, disappearing back into my world before I could even get close to her. But now, the pull was unbearable, and all I wanted was to feel her.

One of my large hands lightly skimmed over her bare shoulder, the tip of my sharp, black nails running down its length. She shivered a little, goosebumps following the path I made, and I grinned in delight seeing her lovely skin react to my touch this way. How odd...

I edged closer, positioning myself so that I was practically prowling over her sleeping figure. I felt that urge to shift into my demon form, but I *just* managed to keep it at bay. The last few times I was here, it took a lot of restraint to prevent it from happening. It was a painful transition and took my back some time to heal once my wings retracted into the muscle beneath my skin. But what I wondered was, *why*... why does it seem like I have no self-control around this tiny, fragile human female?

She shifted beneath me, rolling onto her back, and sighed, the smallest of smiles curling up on her lips. I found it rather... pleasing... when she did that. I decided I liked it, too.

Strange, those were two things I enjoyed about her... the fantasy of her weak and at my disposal and her smile. It didn't make any sense. Without thinking, I leaned down, my nose barely skimming over her collarbone as I inhaled her fresh scent. My teeth gnashed together, my jaw quivering as a sudden urge to lick her crashed to the forefront of my mind, like a spell had just been cast upon me. My body shivered in anticipation, the same feeling I got when a kill was imminent... the anticipation, thrilling...

No! A small voice screamed from the back of my mind as I pictured tearing into her body with my canines like I would a victim or a meal. The thought of committing such violence against her made my chest constrict, and I furrowed my brow in confusion. What was happening to me? Why was I feeling such indecisiveness? I should just kill her now and end this uncertain restlessness.

But as this thought occurred, the little darling rolled her head to the side, her forehead touching my forearm, and her smile reappeared as though pleased by our contact. Before I could stop myself, I lifted one of my large hands again and carefully, gently, cupped her face. Her skin was so soft, smooth, and warm. I ran my nails cautiously through her hair, revelling in the silky feeling of her wavy curls. This was more gratifying than any kill, any triumph, or any trophy I've ascertained.

Wait, did I really just think that?

I held back a hiss as I snatched myself away from her, immediately summoning a portal to travel through the ether back to my world. Stepping through the swirling, black mist, I emerged in my throne room, which at this moment, was empty. Grateful for the solitude, I anxiously paced the room, running my hands through my long, caramel coloured hair, trying desperately to rid her from my mind. Everything from her scent, the feel of her, how she looked lying in sleep, nestled amongst the covers...

And I was hard *again!*

Snarling, I swung at one of the standing candelabras, knocking it over with a loud clang as it crashed to the floor, the candle's extinguishing. I stormed out of the room, bursting through the double doors that led into my entry hall, sending a flood of my demon followers and waywraiths to wildly scatter, leaving me a wide berth as I turned and headed through the winding halls of my palace until I found myself in my courtyard. It was a quiet place, one of serenity and where I could find peace when I found myself in a rage. But as I wandered, the sound of a female's voice, squealing in terror, followed by the deep chuckling of a male, had me freezing in place.

"Oh, Kys! Stop squirming, or I'll never be able to get these knots out..."

Gnaarl.

I peered around a rocky corner to find him and his new human pet seated upon a bench carved out of phaneritic rock. She was in his lap, struggling to free herself, while he raked his claws through her dark, thick hair. She seemed unhurt and cleaned up since I saw her last. There were no signs of starvation or mistreatment in any capacity. Gnaarl's patience was truly astounding. Why he wanted it around at all, I was still trying to comprehend, but...

Then I thought of the sleeping figure who nuzzled my arm, and I felt the spot she'd touched surge with warmth at the reminder. My confusion subsided as a strange feeling settled in my stomach. It didn't hurt, nor make me ill... I felt lighter, like there was a spark inside that's comfortable and that I found to be very... *amiable*?

A loud bout of laughter snapped me out of my reverie, and I found myself glaring at Gnaarl when I took in the look of pure happiness upon his frightening demon features. I was sure to Kys, he appeared as menacing and terrifying as he does to all humans, but I could see the difference. And I resented him for it. I had never felt anything that made me look that way. Not even when I had been rewarded a kingdom of my own for my loyalty. Not when I was trusted with the task as Gatekeeper, nor when Lucifer declared that I and very few others were a Grand Admiral. I carried these titles with gratification, momentarily content with my accomplishments and what I've ascertained since I was thrown from Paradise.

And yet I always carried this sinking feeling, stewing in my chest, making me sick when I looked upon Greed's kingdom and all that he has... or when I see Lusts' luxurious possessions and the refined extravagance of his domain. And Lucifer...

God, he was such an imperious prick. As much as I respected him as my leader, I always carried a spark of jealousy and animosity on my shoulder when I was near him. He had it all. He had been the favourite in Heaven before he fell. Now, he was the ruler of all evil and sin. Why was he so damned special? Why did he have the best of the old world and his new? Why couldn't I? What was so wrong with me that I always struggled?

"No, Kys. No! No hitting. Do you understand? *No hit*!"

Gnaarl's voice brought me out of my swirling mix of resentment and built a sense of yearning. Yearning for... *her*. No, it! Bloody hell... the *human!*

I felt like I'd been struck over the head as this realization hit. I wanted her. I wanted her *more* than I wanted what Lucifer had. I wanted her more than Riker's wealth and accumulated excess of possessions and grandeur. I wanted her so much that the very thought of another having their hands on her has me twitching with rage and longing. Realizing that the impulse, the desire, of having her was more alluring and stronger than owning all the materials and titles of my brothers, could only tell me one thing.

I was cursed with the Mortal Stroke! Oh fuck, no! No!

I spun on the spot, ignoring the loud squeal from Kys as Gnaarl draped her over his knee to be spanked for striking him, and raised my hand, summoning a portal through the ether. I knew Lucifer held days where his higher-up subordinates, like demons of his kingdom, generals, and princes, could come to him for a favour, though no one ever does, as his reactions to requests or complaints tended to result in death. However, I didn't think another Prince of Darkness had ever come to him for advice or a consultation. I hadn't spoken to him since before he destroyed my latest project, my attempts to mimic his palace still being a sore spot for me. But I needed to be reminded of why we were here in the first place. I needed reassurance that this was not my doing, that... that... this illness or sickness or whatever it was would pass. If anyone could help, it was him. No one else in Hell hated humans more than he did. Talking with him would refresh my palette, and then, that girl would be history.

The swirling smoke emerged from nothingness, and I stepped into it, knowing where it would take me. I could not travel directly into his private palace, but I could get close enough. So I wandered through the swirling mass of smoke until the gateway appeared, and I walked out into Lucifer's kingdom.

Chapter Four

Leviathan

I strode out of the ether into Lucifer's domain, an opening temporarily made for higher-ranking visitors to arrive for today only. Except no one came anymore. Why he even bothered to continue the charade of listening to his subjects' issues, or complaints, was beyond me. Everyone was too afraid. But I wasn't. I was more irritated by this human's presence in my mind, so much so that I'd risk a meeting with the Devil himself.

I looked up at Lucifer's palace, the structure a mirror image of home... *His* home. It was a massive castle of white marble, gold, and sections decorated with the most beautiful and refined jewels and riches.

And I could have had it, too... I thought bitterly before pushing that thought to the darker recesses of my mind. However, as I climbed the steps leading into the entry, I felt an odd sense of recollection, of the many times I'd walked up the ones that led to the Kingdom of Heaven, feeling like the moment I would enter, I'd be met with judgemental stares and contemptuous whispers. Only when I opened the doors now and stepped into the Throne Room, despite appearances, the atmosphere was significantly different. Though everything was decorated with white marble and gold trimming, the ceiling opened up to a skylight that gave the illusion that overhead there was the sun, blue skies, and clouds rather than the cavernous canopy of the Hellmouth; I could *feel* a contrast here. There was no false civility, hypocritical lies, or deception... it was what it was—the Throne Room of the King of Darkness, Lucifer.

The most significant differences were the fact that his little beastly *failed angels* were scattered here and there, cleaning the floors and wiping down the columns lining the path to the throne. The other was the large holding cell made of a Hydra's ribcage, which was fastened into the white marble wall, where he kept prisoners to question before his court. He had a flair for dramatics. And today, there were two trembling figures within the Hydra's bones, his throne was empty, and the King of Hell was standing before it in his angelic form, which he favoured.

His blond hair fell over his blue eyes, his white-feathered wings, which were so unlike mine, were alight with flame. He wore a simple pair of jeans and a black t-shirt as if he'd just recently arrived from the human world. I moved lightly, listening to their heated conversation. What would Lucifer be doing arguing with his captives?

"I think it's trying to say her name is Ashley!" the woman insisted. *A human!* I stopped and peered around one of the columns, getting a better look at the cell's occupants. It was indeed a human woman, with red hair and brown eyes, who was crouched along the back of the cage, right up against the marble wall, and with her was...

I blinked hard, staring. It was one of Lucifer's failed angels! The creature was cowering next to the human woman, both gaping up at the evil king with clear terror in their gazes. This woman was either incredibly brave, or stupid, to talk to the Devil that way. As if she were chastising him.

"I don't think this is a... whatever the hell you wanna call it," the woman went on, petting the creature as it snuggled into her side, and I have to say, I was inclined to believe her just from that interaction alone. I've never seen one of these ridiculous experiments behave with such emotion. "I think there's... well, a *person* in there. Her name is Ashley. But with her fangs, she can't speak properly."

"Afree! Afree!" The creature grunted, nodding enthusiastically.

Lucifer pinched his brow, muttering under his breath, as though this discussion had gone on much longer than he wished.

"Please, you have to help her-"

"Shut the fuck up!" he shouted, his scream echoing around the room, causing the two captives to tremble and cower once more. "If I hear another fucking word from either of you, and that includes you saying, *Afree, afree,*" he added, pointing to the creature, "I'm gonna feed you to my dragon or give you to my lieutenant to play with! I need to fucking think!" He turned away from them, wandering back to his throne, rubbing his temples with his fingers like he had a migraine. As he stood before the multi-step dais, in the ample open space in his angelic form, I couldn't help but notice the sharp contrast between him and his throne. The massive royal chair was gold, covered in hundreds of jewels and stones, one of the purple silk pillows made in Lust's kingdom resting upon the seat. Then, there was Lucifer with his t-shirt and jeans and fiery wings, looking all too innocent with his blue eyes and blond hair. It was beyond strange to see.

That was when I noticed one of the rubies that adorned the enormous chair was gone, a gaping hole left in its place. I had a habit of noting anything and everything extravagant in the palaces of my brothers and sister, secretly coveting any luxury or wealth, and this ruby had been incredibly eye-catching. I wondered what had happened to it, or if Lucifer even knew it was missing?

Enough of that. I needed guidance for my plight. Drifting away from the column, allowing my step to echo as I strode forward, his head snapped up in surprise, his irritation still evident on his handsome face before recognition took place, and he positively beamed at me.

"Leviathan!" He ran over, looking much too eager to greet me and, to be honest, was making me rather uncomfortable when he spanned his arms as if to embrace me like an old friend.

To avoid being awkwardly hugged by my king, I fell to a knee, bowing my head respectively, and greeted him, "Lucifer, The Great Red Dragon, Son of Perdition, Angel of Disaster, and King of Darkness and all Hell, I come to you seeking guidance and counsel."

Lucifer stood before me while I spoke, but the moment I finished, he touched my shoulder, signalling his approval. I rose only to be caught up in a hug that was much too tight and went on *much* longer than I preferred. In fact, I'd rather not be touched at all if I was being perfectly blunt. I stiffly pet him on the back, returning it with some semblance of brotherly affection that I could muster before he let go, only to hold onto my shoulders and grin up at me like I was an old friend he had missed dearly.

What the hell was wrong with him?

"Leviathan, it has been too long!" he said, motioning that I should approach the dais where his throne sat. He waved his hand, and two of his miscreants scuttled forward, pushing a golden chair forward for me to take while he climbed the steps and settled on his throne. I sat before him, though I would have rather stood, yet I knew it was better to play along and keep him in good spirits. "You are the first visitor I've had on this day for eons. I don't understand why, when I take the time out of my day to greet and offer assistance to my inferiors, no one comes to call?"

I can think of a couple... I remembered the time one of his lieutenant's captains came to him with a complaint about the forms Lucifer had captives of Hell sign out on... in *triplicate*. It was more work for the men to review and for seemingly no reason. The forms all ended up being disposed of in the end. The torment of filling them out for the humans doomed to Hell was becoming more of a misery to his own demons than those who he was supposed to be punishing. Well, that captain ended up disembowelled. His dick was removed and fed to Lucifer's dragon, Glazhale, as a "treat" all while the demon was still alive before he was thrown into the fiery lake that encompassed our plane beyond the black mountains.

"But here you are!" Lucifer went on, sparing me the awkwardness of trying to answer him.

"I am. I've been having an issue-"

"Please!" the red-haired human wailed, reaching between the ribs toward me. "Help us! Help!"

I cringed at the scream, actually shifting my chair back an inch, as if she could even reach from across the room. I rarely spent time with humans, save for when I was punishing them, but this one's screams reached a pitch I'd never heard before.

I gritted my teeth, averting my gaze, choosing to stare at the wall rather than the girl.

"I'll call for Gazaat! I swear to it!" Lucifer thundered at the woman. "If you are terrified now, pest, you will know true fear when you look upon his face!"

"I did nothing wrong!" she wailed, helplessly.

"Gazaat will remind you of that while he spends eternity torturing your sinful soul! Now, shut the fuck up and save yourself his punishable fury!"

The red-haired woman huddled back in the cell, sobbing softly while the creature called Afree made the most appalling blubbery groans. The creature's filmy layer of black flesh was wrinkled, its large lamp-like red eyes shining with unshed tears, and it waddled over to the woman, seeking comfort. Speaking of annoying little gnats...

My chair began to shift, the sound of it moving emitted a high-pitched *squeak-squeak*, as I found myself slowly pushed inch by inch across the space before the dais. Peering down, I saw one of those hideous little creatures cleaning the legs of the chair I was sitting upon, as if I wasn't already occupying it. When it moved on to my booted foot, Lucifer actually dropped his head in his hands and groaned in frustration, while I watched with a curled lip of disgust. These things were so unbelievably pointless and moronic I didn't have the patience for them. I gave it a little kick, but the creature just got right back up and moved on to my other boot.

"For fucks sake! His legs aren't part of the chair!" Lucifer shouted, his tone despondent, while his face actually turned red in frustration. "Get out of here! Get out! Get out!"

All of the creatures frantically scuttled about, some running directly into walls or each other. One even spilled a bucket of dirty, soapy water all over the floor it had just mopped, and took off through the little discreet door in the corner that led to the tunnels they used to get around the castle.

"You know... I could give you some of the minions that serve in my kingdom," I offered, though I actually didn't want to part with any of them. They were *mine*. They kept my palace running like a well-oiled machine. But a sense of compelled duty and loyalty had me making a bid to assist my dark king.

"Forget it," Lucifer groaned as he collapsed back in his chair, his face pointed up toward the deceptive skylight. "I've just been-"

"GAAAAAHHHH!"

The shriek had both my king and I jumping in our seats and spinning in shock toward the cage in the corner. The woman and the Afree creature were both huddled at the back, while one of Lucifer's remaining servants was attempting to clean them by sticking a rather mouldy looking mop through the bars, craning to reach them.

"That. is. *It*!" Lucifer rose to his feet, the muscles in his arms and neck flexing, as though he was fighting transition, his wings sparking, and roared, "Gazaat!"

Oh, for crying out loud... I moaned, rubbing my eyes in annoyance. I had hoped this visit would be brief and to the point. Now that Gazaat was coming, I knew

I'd have to wait even longer while his Second went to work. Gazaat was exactly as Lucifer described him. The demon took perverse pleasure in his tasks of torturing sinful humans, and to be honest, I was sure the lieutenant was partially insane.

At the call, there was a heavy rumble in the distance, like half the mountain had suddenly spurred to life and was storming through Hell. I remained in my seat, resting my head on the palm of my hand as I exercised all my patience while waiting for Lucifer to get control over his household.

Gazaat's thunderous steps could be felt by all as he approached, ducking to fit beneath the entryway of the throne room. The caged captives were too distracted by the little creature who still struggled to reach them with its filthy tool to notice his arrival. At the same time, Gazaat stormed down the pillared hall, that is, until one of his massive, raptorial feet crushed the servant with a simple step, flattening it in a second. Slowly, the human and possessed demon craned their necks, staring upward at the looming shadow that engulfed their cell, their mouths dropping open in silent screams as they took in the sight of Satan's Second.

Gazaat stood at nearly twelve-feet tall, his greyish, pale, purple-tinged skin stretched out over heaps of bulging muscle. His wings, which were similar looking to mine, batlike, stretched out with wicked claws upon the tips. I winced at the sight of them, remembering how *He* had forcibly transformed mine to them when He pulled me from the Abyss... *Now*, they were a scarred, ugly mess caused by the burning I'd suffered when I fell and from when I plucked the remaining feathers free.

Gazaat's bald head was adorned with two thick, massive dark horns which curled forward like a ram, and two more atop his skull, sharp and lethal, reaching straight up to the heavens. He preferred to walk in the nude, with his manhood dangling for all to see like the trunk of a giant bull elephant. I was so relieved that Gnaarl liked wearing his leather and armour when walking around my palace; I didn't need to see *that* much of my Second.

But it was Gazaat's face that was the most horrifying. His small white eyes were always fixed with a scowl, those small nostrils of his almost hidden above what I called, *The Chasm of Demise*. Gazaat stared at the two females for exactly two heartbeats before that dreaded mouth slowly began to open.

His mouth actually stretched open down the front of his throat, between his pectorals, to his sternum, the gaping hole surrounded by pincer-like teeth, and a long, blue forked tongue twitched and fluttered forward as though tasting the air before him.

"Gazaat, take one." Lucifer collapsed back on his throne. "I don't care which... just remove one from here to preserve my sanity!"

Gazaat ducked down to peer between the ribs, studying the two for only a second before he released a deafening roar, and with a single snap of one of his clawed hands, he tore away one of the ribs, throwing it over his shoulder where it bounced with a crash on the marble floor before sliding into the wall behind us. He reached in, the two prisoners scattering to avoid being caught up by his sharp lethal fingers, but he easily snagged the human girl and pulled her free. He held her up before his face with one hand and opened his mouth wide again. "Behold, petty human, your new master! For I shall inflict upon you physical suffering and pain, none like you have ever known!"

His deep, tenor-like roar of a voice echoed throughout the space, and the girl in his hold was staring at him, her eyes so wide I could see the whites all the way around. I thought she'd kick and scream or beg for my help again, but instead, her eyes rolled to the back of her head, and she went limp, her body slumping over his digits in a dead faint.

"It did not soil itself, as I prefer when threatening a new slave," Gazaat rumbled to Lucifer in disappointment.

"I'm sure it will comply later when it comes to. Just... remove it from here. *Now*!" he groaned, running his hands up over his face and into his blond hair, pulling at the ends in irritation.

"Very well, My Lord." Gazaat turned to leave, stopping when he finally noticed the squashed remains of one of his king's servants smeared on the bottom of his foot. He grumbled in annoyance as he wiped it off on one of the pillars before thumping away, the limp body of the human girl swinging in his hand.

We were *finally* left in solitude, save for the snivelling possessed creature that had curled up in a ball in the far corner of the cage. Lucifer sighed heavily and straightened, his anger vanishing as he grinned at me like he was now ready and eager for a chat with an old friend. Seriously... what was wrong with him? The King of Hell I knew was *not* this sociable, nor ever seemed to anticipate get-togethers. It was leaving me feeling incredibly uncomfortable and restless. But I knew better than to question Lucifer on anything, so I just accepted his overly friendly behaviour and decided it would be easier to just go along with it.

"So, what happened with that one?" I gestured to the one calling itself Afree.

"I have no idea... it fell into the River Styx and came out smart. I'm keeping it here because it keeps riling up the others and further distracting them from their duties."

And that was already one of the biggest issues in Lucifer's household. His staff was utterly helpless, but his pride kept him from seeking consultation from anyone else.

"Anyways, what has brought you here seeking my counsel, my old friend?" Lucifer leaned forward on his throne, his elbows resting on his knees as his piercing blue eyes stared down the steps to where I sat, his expression curious and eager.

"It's my Second-"

"He is failing in his duties? Do you need me to assign a new one to you?"

"No! Nothing like that," I said quickly, knowing that Lucifer's idea of "replacing" my most trusted companion would be similar to what he did to that captain. "It's... he seems to have become quite... ahem, *taken*, with a human female."

Lucifer's brows shot up, though his face remained impassive.

"He asked a favour of me to keep her as a pet, and as Gnaarl has been most loyal and dependable, I granted it. But his behaviour is... baffling and has given me reservations. I wonder if I should remove his pet from his care? I worry he is suffering from the Mortal Stroke."

He chuckled a little on his throne, sitting back as he took this news with surprising humour, which I had not expected. "He has become enthralled by the helpless defects of their kind. I've heard of such things happening to demons. I have often thought those besotted with them to be bewitched. But I also have considered that perhaps this phenomenon, of demons seemingly *falling* for humans, is nothing more than curiosity, one which will fade in time, I'm sure."

Again, that doll-like face came to mind. Is that all it was? A curiosity? I suppose, yes, that does make some sense. However, curiosity doesn't drive one to think incessantly about a subject, so much so that it interferes with their ability to focus on their day-to-day. Or drives them to visit the human world, a place they loathe more than anywhere else, just to watch them as they sleep.

"You seem perturbed, brother," Lucifer's voice broke through my reverie, the vision of a sleeping figure with dark curls vanishing in a second, and I'm transported back.

"I suppose we should discourage it before it escalates?"

He just laughed and shook his head. "Demons, as a class, are just a little above human scum. You can't expect that much from a demon. That's why it's good that we know better than to fraternise with mortals in any capacity. The angels call me the great deceiver, yet it is the humans who deceive. Your Second in Command has fought in wars, dismembered countless things, and yet this insignificant little human has him wrapped around her finger? What does that say to you? Who is the deceiver here?"

When he put it that way...

"Are you saying humans *do* hold some sort of magic? Illusions? Hypnotic abilities?" It wasn't until now that I regretted not learning more about their kind.

Know thy enemy. And yet, I never bothered. All I felt that I needed to know was how to break their bodies and minds, which came quickly enough. Why bother learning anything else?

"They fooled God, didn't they?" Lucifer said darkly, his upper lip curling at that mention of *Him*. "He loves them above all, yet half don't even believe He exists."

I thought about how I felt being close to my tiny human. No, not mine! Her. *It!* Whenever I was close to it, how it affected me. I wanted to be nearer, wanted to touch, wanted to explore. Odd feelings and impulses I've never felt before when I looked upon her face or the curve of her figure beneath her covers. He must be onto something here...

"I would advise you to keep an eye on your Second and his pet. Humans are not to be trusted, for they, above all living creatures, are the liars. Now! Stay a while! Let us entertain ourselves!" He snapped his fingers, and at once, four or five of his little hellions came barreling out from their servants' doors, all tumbling to the floor in their haste to respond to his command.

"Really, I'm fine. I must be heading back to my kingdom. Terribly busy-"

"I said stay." Lucifer's blue eyes narrowed, his nostrils flaring as he stared at his useless staff as one suddenly grabbed another by its ankles and used it to attempt to mop up the filthy water that had been spilled from earlier. "For the love of... Halt! Leave it! I wish you to summon that bar matron who passed two weeks ago... the one who killed her employer before she succumbed to her addiction? Bring her from whatever plane she was sent to. She makes a mean martini." He winked at me like he was including me on some special secret.

I smiled awkwardly, as it was not something that came naturally to me and sat as stiff as stone as his creatures raced off to do his bidding, wondering what a "mean martini" meant.

My dark king leaned forward then, looking suddenly eager. "Now, Leviathan... Riker tells me you enjoy Jenga..."

I always considered the Prince of Greed my closest confidant, but apparently, I must have offended him in recent years. Why on earth he told Lucifer I enjoyed this twisted, ridiculous human game where you move blocks on top of another is beyond me. Add in that you're supposed to fuck the life out of someone while you do it and consume a ridiculous amount of alcohol in the process; I couldn't think of a reason why Riker would say this was something I would seriously enjoy. My conclusion? I have wronged him, and this was retaliation. As Lucifer excitedly explained how you play, I stared in silent horror at the tower of blocks he'd set up, my feelings toward humans only souring further. Of course, they would think of something so depraved and vulgar.

It took me an hour to finally get Lucifer to pick another activity to pass the time, all while I was forced to listen to him brag about how he "kicked Riker's ass" when they had played Jenga together.

When the opportunity came that I was able to travel through the ether upon leaving Lucifer's palace, I took it, quickly returning home. He'd kept me for *hours*, coming up with one endeavour after another. After I talked him out of Jenga, he pressured me into consuming one of those "mean martinis" before forcing me to sit down to play Chinese checkers. Afterward, we went bowling in his gardens, using one of his little minions as a ball and several others as the pins. I had tried to escape then, but before I could think of an excuse, I found myself sitting with him in a grand, marble pool room, having our nails filed and trimmed while he talked on and on about... well, I honestly wasn't paying too much attention. I was much too disturbed by his behaviour to truly focus and was deathly bored. He enjoyed talking about his many feats and skills, going on about all the things he could do, showing off, etc. The demon working on my black, pointed nails appeared rather perplexed when they refused to file down. In the end, they simply massaged several foul-smelling oils into my skin.

It wasn't until I found myself lying on a table, a bland human vegetable called a cucumber cut into slices placed upon my eyes, with other incredibly off-putting smelling oils being massaged into my back by a particularly large, scaly demon that I took my chance to bolt, as Lucifer had fallen asleep during his massage. I shoved the demon away, dressed, and got the fuck out of there.

When I emerged back in my kingdom, where my own palace sat amongst the obsidian black mountains of Hell, I felt a rare sense of appreciation for what I had. My fortress was run like clockwork compared to Lucifer's. Though I still admired Greed's home, at this moment, it was enough, as all I wanted was peace and quiet. I staggered inside, heading up to my private quarters in the north tower, disgusted by the remaining slick feeling of oil lathered over my skin. I hurried up to my room, slamming the door shut behind me as I crossed to my washing apartments.

Under the hot jet of water in my bathing chamber, I finally felt like I could breathe. Despite how incredibly uncomfortable I'd been socialising with Lucifer, I did feel better about the situation. The little human female had obviously cast a spell upon me. That was all. She was a deceiver, a liar. There was *nothing* special about her. She was just one of many. Just another flawed being.

And yet, as I comforted myself with these thoughts, her face came to mind, her body, the curves beneath her sheets, the soft sound of her breathing, the pouty curve of her lips... and I was hard. *Again.*

FUCK!

Every. Fucking. Time! Every time I thought of her for more than thirty seconds, my dick would rise like a goddamn vampire from the coffin! I growled in frustration, refusing to do anything about it. It will go away soon. I just needed to stop thinking about her. *It!*

The more frustrated I became, the more my irritation and rage got the better of me. I could feel my inner demon flexing to be released, my skin tightening as my muscles threatened to grow, and in my upper back, I could feel the sting as my wings threatened to rip through the muscle and tissue to stretch free.

Ugh! No!

Clenching my jaw, pressing my hands against the wall, I fought for control. I wasn't known for having much of a sexual drive. That was Asmodeus's curse. I wasn't a loose cannon like Dai, that crazy bitch of Wrath. I was Leviathan... always controlled and respectful. But every time that little... *insect* of a human came to mind, I found myself lusting for her, craving her, while also conflicted with my feelings of confusion and a sense of inadequacy. The only others who have fallen to the hypnotic curse of humans were the demons, the lesser of us. Was it because I wasn't originally an angel? Must I also suffer the feelings of inferiority here in Hell as I did in Heaven?

That minute sense of reassurance I'd had with Lucifer was gone. And there was no way I would head back into that trap again. I needed to speak to someone else. Someone...

Riker!

Despite the fact that he must be upset with me for suggesting I enjoyed that block game, I knew he would listen if I came to him seeking advice. I felt a sense of hope as I shut off the water and dried myself with a towel. Riker was one I considered a very close friend... probably the closest friend I had besides the Devil himself... though given his behaviour from today, I was tempted to cross Lucifer's name off my small list of confidants. Waving my hand, the heat I cast dried my caramel-coloured hair into the waves that framed my face and rested on my shoulders, then readied myself. Whenever I set out to visit Riker, I made sure I was dressed in my very best. Though he preferred to linger in the human realm, he always surrounded himself with the very best riches, clothing, and women.

I never enjoyed mortal clothing. I favoured a wardrobe that embodied the divine being that I was. So, I dressed in an emerald silk shirt, brown leather breeches, a black cloak with a dark brown furred embellishment around the shoulders, clasped with a gold chain and gold serpent brooch with an emerald eye. The figurine looked remarkably like my familiar, Beast, and I touched it affectionately. It was one of my favourite pieces, one I wore often. Though I was powerful enough without, I always travelled with a weapon or two. So, I strapped my two silver, ornate blades to leather sheaths at my side. Slipping into a pair of dark boots made out of the skin of a Hell-dwelling creature that resembled a crocodile on earth, I then combed my hair back from my face with my fingers and closed my eyes, seeking out Riker's whereabouts.

The others enjoyed their modern conveniences of human technology. Texting, they called it. Not I. I liked the old ways. It was another way that I separated myself from those who stole His love from me. So, I searched, my senses taking me to the mortal realm where the humans lived. Not a surprise. But when it transported me to a remote farmland, far from the skyscrapers where Riker normally dwelled, I furrowed my brow in confusion. Why was he out there? No matter. I needed to speak with him. This human creature was tormenting my mind, and I needed to find a way to dispel her.

Raising a hand, I summoned a portal of smoke and stepped into the ether, to nowhere, my focus carrying me to my destination.

Opening my eyes, I found myself standing before a rather aged white farmhouse on a large plot of land. And there, sitting on a rocking chair on the front wraparound porch, was the Prince of Greed himself, Riker, and his closest companion, Shilo. Before fully comprehending the scene before me, a small weight hit my legs and I stumbled slightly before peering down. At my knee, a tiny human boy was hugging my leg, their little face beaming up at me like I was nothing to fear, and joyously said in a loud, squeaky voice, "Hi! I'm Max! Who are you?" His gaze roamed over my outfit with curiosity and then asked, "Are you playing dress-up?"

I glowered at the creature and raised my hand, ready to obliterate this thing from existence as I had Lucifer's failed angel and all other sinners who try to escape Hell, when Riker snapped, "I wouldn't do that, if I were you..." I glanced over to see he had risen to his feet, his golden gaze fierce as he looked between the child and me. I hesitated, sensing the distress and fury in his voice, but then, why should he care? I looked back and forth between him and the little one, and what I finally saw disturbed me greatly. The similarities between them were indisputable, save for the ocean blue eyes of the boy, they had the same golden blond hair, comparable features that they share...

It *was* mortal, no question, but I could sense something else about it. Something... *more*. At this revelation, I glared at my friend. "You have procreated with a human?" So, the rumours were true.

Riker ignored me, quickly storming over to scoop the boy up into his arms. It's then that Shilo, a demon who has been to Riker what Gnaarl was to me, rises. The human, Max, or whatever its name was, is passed off to him and Shilo disappears into the house, leaving Greed and I alone. Riker turned to me, his expression guarded, wary, and snapped, "Why are you here, Leviathan?"

"Was it *that* human?" I pressed. "The one Lucifer and I saw you pull from Styx? How? How is that possible? She moved on to Heaven. She is dead! That was years ago..." I remembered that day. Lucifer had brought me to The Last Stop for a drink when we caught sight of Riker flying over the Styx, searching. We stared, completely baffled, as he pulled a soul from the river so they could talk on the embankment. Even through the thick, foggy glass of the windows, we could see them conversing, their expressions full of pain, but I hadn't heard a word. I never asked him about it, as the soul returned to the Styx and moved on to Heaven. I assumed the matter had been closed.

"Why are you here?" Riker asked again, crossing his arms over his chest.

I glowered from where I stood. For now, I'd let this go, as I had more pressing matters, but I wasn't done. I sneered at the old farmhouse and the enormous, empty plot of land where I found him. "I have come to speak with my brother. I assumed you would be in one of your penthouses. You can imagine my surprise when I find you here." I gestured at our surroundings, not bothering to hide my displeasure and confusion. "Of all places, never would I have imagined Riker, Prince of Greed, here in this stinking, dilapidated shack." I let my eyes wander as I took in his appearance, now completely at a loss when I saw the pair of tight jeans, plaid shirt, and scuffed-up cowboy boots he wore as his attire. "Did you lose a wager?"

Riker snorted and rolled his eyes. "Yeah, that's exactly what it is."

His sarcasm was not lost on me, and I did not appreciate it. Finding him this way was unsettling. It's like he had gone and lost his mind. Did he genuinely expect any other reaction from me? Though I could also detect the defensiveness in his words, I reminded myself of why I was here in the first place. "I had hoped to speak plainly with you, brother to brother. I seek your counsel-"

"First of all," he said, cutting me off, "you gotta cut out the formalities. Take it down a notch. Would you like a beer?"

A beer? Yes, he has definitely lost his mind.

Before I could even respond to his ludicrous offer, he disappeared into the house, leaving me to stand alone in the yard. I stared up at the structure, feeling like it might keel over at the slightest breeze, but decided my plight was urgent enough to brave it. So, I followed.

Inside, it was as plain and unseemly as I imagined. The wallpaper is a faded cream with tiny flowers, the floors wooden, which creaked under my step. I don't even bother removing my boots, as I'm sure they are cleaner than the floor. To the left beyond the stairs, I heard Riker move around and I trailed after him down the hall. On the way, I noticed the framed family portraits and immediately recognized him and the boy, but there was a young baby in a few and a woman who was clearly the mate he chose. She had raven black hair, large blue eyes, just like the boy, and pale, snow-white skin. I cannot tell if she was the soul he pulled from the Styx or not, but either way, I couldn't help but wonder what Lucifer would think if he found him like this. As confused as I was by this situation, I still considered Riker to be my closest brother, and so, I would keep his secret.

In the kitchen, he's seated himself at a small table, a bottle in hand, and another opened and set before the chair on the opposite side. He gestured for me to sit, which I did, but not before I made sure my cloak was guarding my leather and silk against the dusty and grimy-looking wood surface. I ignored the open beer before me and fixed him with a hard stare.

"Don't," he warned me.

"I've said nothing."

"No, but I can hear your thoughts. Just don't."

I shrugged, choosing silence while he settled back in his seat. Evidently, my presence here has unsettled him, and I can see how nervous and guarded he is. I suppose the fact that I rarely entered the human realm was one factor, that I'd risk coming here to find him probably had him thinking some dire circumstance was at hand. Perhaps he feared that I was here to announce Lucifer had decided to wage war again.

"What counsel do you seek?" he asked, in an undoubtedly mocking tone, but there was an edge to it. As much of a jackass as Riker could be, I could always tell when he was deflecting.

"It is a personal matter... and though I first sought Lucifer's advice, I still find myself... torn." I thought about my little human female and immediately cringed. *My* little human female? I shouldn't be thinking of her that way! This was why I needed help from my brothers. Only it seemed as though Riker had fallen under the same spell.

"That's your first problem, is that you went to Lucifer for advice or help of any sort." Riker took another long sip of his beer and shook his head. "That guy is completely fucked in the head."

While I was surprised to hear him speak this way, I silently agreed. After that visit, I wished nothing more than to stay far away from Lucifer. Now I was questioning everything he had told me. Did humans have some sort of power that could lure in demons? I thought of Gnaarl and his little female... how crazed and absolutely besotted he was. This was the demon who took pleasure in torturing the damned, who punished those who failed me or the escapees when I couldn't be bothered. He was terrifying, a monster in the eyes of humans, someone who others trembled before. Yet the other day, I caught him feeding Kys by hand a particular sort of food he'd acquired from the human world. He'd crooned at it, calling it a 'good girl' when it took each bite nicely from his hand. Even later that day, I found him running his clawed digits through its hair, brushing it back as it prattled on about something about working at a bank... a human place of business where I knew money was stored and traded. Though he couldn't understand English, he sat there while it went on and on, like its voice was the most beautiful thing he'd ever heard.

Yes, I was absolutely certain he was under a spell.

But, myself? I had no idea.

"Lucifer said something about human's casting spells upon demons... and a demon friend of mine has been acting most peculiar since he took one for a compan-"

Riker choked on his beer, banged on his chest, and started laughing. "Spells? What in the fuck?"

"You know what I mean. You've clearly fallen under one. I mean, look at you." I gestured at the worn jeans, cowboy boots, and the drab surroundings. "In comparison to your kingdom in Hell... I mean, to quote you, brother... what in the fuck?"

Riker caught his breath, his chuckling subsiding some, but the bugger still looked like he was enjoying this too much. "Humans are lesser beings, and demons are not capable of falling under a lesser being's spell. I am the Prince of Greed. You are Leviathan, the dark, powerful demon of Envy. Do you think we are capable of succumbing to any sort of magic such pitiful beings possess?"

"I never said I had befallen..."

"Okay, I apologise. Your "demon friend" then, is still too powerful and considered too divine to succumb to a human's level of..." he snickered, "Magic."

"But..." I was frustrated, hating how entertained he was by all of this. "The behaviour he's exhibiting is completely different from his usual."

"Have you ever wondered that maybe, it's not a matter of spellcasting and more like an... awakening?"

"An awakening?" I stared at him incredulously, now wholly frustrated by how casual and unconcerned he was by all of this. That look of smug superiority had me silently seething in my seat. Who was he to be all judgemental of me when he's been affected by this human girl, he's flipped his life upside down for? "Are you mocking me?" I practically snarled.

"For once, no," he said simply, unfazed by my pure exasperation. "I'm very serious."

"I don't believe it," I scoffed, still ignoring the human beverage sitting before me. Riker tilted his head, that little smirk of a smile of his fading ever so slightly. I didn't like the way he was staring, like he felt some sort of pity for me. I glared at him, "Don't."

"I didn't say anything."

"No, but whatever you're thinking, stop it now." Every muscle in my body tensed, my insides twisting uncomfortably. The judgement, the condescension... triggered that side of me that always felt inferior, lacking.

Unworthy.

"Leviathan... when was the last time you were ever happy?

Riker's question caught me off guard. I froze, staring at the tabletop, thinking about what he asked. Happy... was I ever? Or was I always feeling like I had some challenge to overcome? Someone to outshine? To prove myself to? I was the one Prince of Sin who felt no satisfaction from their curse. I didn't believe I'd ever really known happiness. The feeling was rather foreign to me.

"Leviathan... when was the last time you gave in to your instincts? And I'm not talking about how concerned you are about what others are doing-" my eyes snapped to his face at that, hating that that part of me was something he was so aware of, "I'm talking about something that only involves you, and what you want. Not what I want, not what Lucifer has, not what any of us. What do *you* want?"

It... her, I thought. I craved *her* like I've never craved for anything else in my long existence. For some reason, I wanted that little human. I didn't know for what reason, why, or how to even care for her (did I even want to care for her?), but all I knew was that I needed her close.

As if reading the thoughts in my head, Riker leaned over the tabletop, his expression candid, open, serious. "Go get her."

I stepped out of the ether and halted at the sight before my eyes. I'd been seeking out Gnaarl, intent on giving him my list of instructions and demands now that I've made a decision. I fully expected to find him with his human, yes, but what I did not expect was to come across him with Gazaat. What was more, to come across him, Gazaat, and *two* humans. The female Lucifer had given to his Second in Command was leashed at the enormous demon's side; arms crossed like it was irritated, no longer afraid. Gnaarl was off at the other side of the room, his own female leashed, standing there with her face in her hands, like she had just witnessed something truly humiliating.

"No, no! Ronka, you must heel. Heeeeel!" Gazaat snapped at the human standing by his side.

To her credit, the girl kicked a leg out to the side, shifting her weight to one hip, and glared up at him like she was ready to take him on head-to-head. "Listen, asshole, if I have to say again that I'm not a dog, then we're going to continue having a problem here."

"Don't you snipe at me!" Gazaat lowered his massive form to crouch before the woman, face to face, the breath wafting from his enormous, gaping mouth blowing her hair back. "I may not understand you, human, but I know when one is being difficult! Do you want to be punished again?"

"I don't speak... whatever the fuck you're speaking!" She began tapping her foot on the ground, like she was becoming even more irritated. She leaned right into his face, waving her arms as she pointed at her own ears. "I... don't... understand... you!"

"What the fuck is going on here?" I half-shouted to make myself heard over the racket that tiny person was able to make. The two demons spun to face me, eyes wide, looking instantly chagrined to have been caught doing... whatever the hell it was that they were doing.

Gazaat's dwelling is large to accommodate his size. It's like a giant dome built into the rocky obsidian mountain. Usually, I'd find it filled with his favourite weapons, chains, and fresh meat to cook over his fire pit, that sort of thing. Instead, he has two cages set up, like the ones humans use to store their furry companions in. Some squeak toys littered the floor, feather-tipped wands, and he had a bowl of raw meat set on the crude, wooden table where he ate, the chunks cut up into tiny little bits. Gnaarl, however, had a bright pink pouch with daisies on the front, a bag from the human world, wrapped around his waist, and from inside of it, he brought out a chunk of dark brown... whatever the hell it was, and handed it to Kys, who took it gratefully and munched away. Human food, then.

"Beg pardon, My Lord," Gnaarl said, moving forward, bowing his head to me in respect. "We were just... ahem, training our new companions. Kys is doing *very* well!" He beamed at her with pride, his sharp, fanged teeth flashing in the firelight of Gazaat's home. To my surprise, she didn't recoil at the sight. Obviously, this little human had adapted quickly to Gnaarl's behaviour. *Interesting...* that gave me hope. "You had said you didn't want her making a mess, so Gazaat and I decided that we might see better results if we worked together with training." His explanation was rushed, his voice laden with guilt and uncertainty. He probably thought I was going to punish them or remove their pets from their care. I might have, had I come across this several weeks ago. To see them both, despite the arguing that was going on still in the background between Gazaat and the fiery redhead, so visibly content and happy, would have soured me. I would have probably made some excuse to remove the humans from their care, maybe even killed them in front of them.

Seeing them so happy when I am not, absolutely crushes me. I would have taken it away from them, because they had something I didn't. Petty, Leviathan.

"As long as it obeys you, then I am unconcerned of what methods you choose to... train. I glanced over Gnaarl's shoulder to see Gazaat lift his female by her ankle, holding her upside down before his face, both of them still arguing back and forth, both claiming to not understand the other, and yet, he did not choose to crush her as he would any other creature that riled him up like this.

I suppose he had been, how did Riker put it? Awakened?

I sighed heavily and turned back to my Lieutenant in time to see him applaud Kys when she took a seat on the floor, her expression now filled with boredom as she waited, watching the ruckus between the other demon and human like this had been going on long before I arrived.

"Well done, Kys! Yes, sit! Good girl!" He hurried back over to her, reaching into the pink daisy pouch, and withdrew another small chunk of that human food, eagerly pressing it against her lips, despite the fact she twisted her face away. "No, Kys, reward! Treat! Treeeeeat. Eat!"

"I'm not hungry for chocolate!" She pressed her lips together, twisting away. "I need something else besides sweets!" I wondered how much of this chocolate he had given her. Apparently, it was not enough to sustain her health if this was her complaint. I made note of that as I cleared my throat, earning his attention back.

"I have a request," I said, my voice steady and severe. At the tone, he immediately snapped into work mode and approached me, both of us moving some distance away from the other demon, who was now trying to reach around his backside to grab the female, who had managed to cling to his broad shoulders, staying just out of his reach.

Gazaat whirled in frustration, shouting, "Bad girl! Bad girl, Ronka!" as he struggled to grab her from the awkward position. I shook my head and refocused on my second.

"I have several requests that I wish to be fulfilled as soon as possible."

Gnaarl nodded eagerly, leaning in to listen to my rather lengthy list. If I was going to take my human, I wanted to be prepared for anything. This creature had infested my mind, and so, I would do as Riker suggested and delve into my curiosity. Perhaps I'd discover why the human had such a hold over me and I would free myself from the incessant fantasies that have been plaguing me. I could dispose of her after... *it!* Humans were just pitiful, unholy creatures after all. She was a thing, nothing significant nor important. Just a disease that has infected my thoughts. Regardless, for once, I would be taking and there was nothing in my way that could stop me. Not even *it*.

The frail, little human female with the wide, brown eyes, and dark waves. The one whose luscious figure had my body stirring with unfamiliar desire, but it was her pretty face that was at the forefront of my mind.

And mine it would be...

CHAPTER
FIVE

Evangeline

I woke up in a pool of my own sweat, crying out as my eyes flew open. I frantically gazed around my room, as if the monster stalking my nightmares would actually be there. But I was alone. I dropped my head, running my shaking hands through my hair as I focused on my breathing and reminded myself that it wasn't real. It's not. It was just a bad dream. That was all they were. But why was I having them? And almost every night?

It felt like sleep paralysis. I was in my bed, dead to the world, exhausted from a day of classes, homework, and running my business. It was always late and in the complete darkness, that I felt it. That same... *evil* presence. I was frozen in place as this dark figure manifested in my room. I wanted to scream when it neared my bed, to run, but I couldn't. I couldn't because it was as if I'd been frozen in sleep. Whatever this thing was... I could feel the unnerving, inhumane, *wrong* aura radiating off of it in waves. I could do nothing as it sat at my side, and though I could only see the shift of shadows, I could *feel* it watching me.

But then, it all changed.

I felt a chilling, feather-light touch skim over my face and down my neck. The shadow seeped beneath my comforter like a mist, a slithering, ghostly caressing of my curves. My fear began to shift, my breath caught in my throat, and even though I was as still as stone beneath its touch, I felt a build in my belly, a sense of wanting. The musky, woodsy scent mixed with a hint of the sea filled the space, and I breathed it in like I wanted to devour it. As it filled my senses, I licked my lips, and it wrapped around me like an embrace, making my nipples painfully harden. I wanted it. And I could feel how much it wanted me.

Then, as quickly as it came, it was gone and I awakened with my heart racing, and my mind whirling with conflicted emotions of confusion, fear, and craving. I was terrified of it, and yet, I *desired* it. But I didn't even know what *it* was.

Why these dreams had become more and more frequent in passing months was honestly starting to worry me. Perhaps my mind was conjuring up some eerie shadow that came to hold me because of an underlying issue? For a moment, I felt my mouth go dry at the thought of my Non-Hodgkin Lymphoma returning. That scared me more than the idea of a ghost.

I ended up having to change my pajamas and the bedding that I'd soaked through with my sweat before I could go back to sleep. I decided that, when I woke up in the morning, I'd call my doctor for an appointment and get checked out. Perhaps my night sweats, fatigue, and weight loss were more than just a lifestyle? My heart raced at the thought while I snuggled up beneath my blankets. I've fought so hard to get here. To have it ripped away would destroy me.

I was so tired today, but I needed money, so I had to suck it up. I made my way around campus, delivering my homemade kits to the Wiccan group, the Gamer's Club, and the Sports Medicine Facility, carefully pocketing the cash before heading home. These nightmares were seriously affecting my sleep. I'd called my doctor just this morning to schedule an appointment. The moment I told him how I was feeling, he booked me in, which was a relief knowing I wouldn't have to wait very long. I was trying to be optimistic about all of this, but I had a sinking sensation that my mind was warning me... things were going to get bad.

Please just be stress. Please just be stress. Please, please, please... I begged over and over again in my head. My lack of sleep, the fatigue I was feeling, the nightmares and night sweats... please just let it be stress from school, from work. I could handle that. But the return of my Non-Hodgkin Lymphoma? No, I couldn't bear going through that bullshit again.

When I got home at the end of the day, I found myself sitting on my fold-out bed, staring at the contact I had open on my phone... Mom.

Do I tell her how I'm feeling? Or keep it to myself?

My first instinct was the latter; however, I knew she would be terribly offended if I kept her in the dark. Though my parents weren't exactly there for me the last time I went through this, it wasn't because they didn't love me. They just couldn't handle watching me slowly die.

But they should have been there for you regardless, Evie. You're their child.

I sighed wearily.

Ever since I got better, I felt a distance between my parents and me. A mistrust. After they abandoned me at the hospital, I felt like I couldn't rely on them anymore. How could I, when at my absolute lowest point, they left me because they put their own feelings first? They did what was best for them. They only came back when they were told I was pulling through, that there was hope. So as soon as I graduated high school, after my health finally pulled together, I took off. I left my hometown and came to New York, wishing to start over. And I have. *Without* them.

But *Mom would still want to know...*

I sighed, casting aside my self-doubts, my own personal feelings on the situation, and pressed the 'call' button. I waited, wondering if they were perhaps out? Lately, they liked going to local bars and fancy lounges together, like date nights. That was one thing I did love about my parents... was how much they loved each other. Even if that meant it was more than they loved me.

"Evangeline!" My mother's voice floated through the phone on the other end, sounding like she was having the time of her life. There was music in the background, the sounds of people's voices, and here I was about to burst that bubble. "How are you, darling? Hey! Hey, you all! My daughter is calling me from New York! She's attending business school. She's so gifted. Look, that's her on the mantle-" She went off, getting lost in her discussion with her friends. I put together that they had a few over at their house, maybe a dinner party? My guilt began to churn in my stomach. "So how is school?" she asked finally, after several minutes of showing off how "pretty" her daughter was to all her friends. I knew what pictures she was showing them; the ones before I lost my hair, and the more recent ones, as it is now, shoulder-length. I doubted her friends even knew I had been so sick once.

"School is great." I didn't mention the hours I spent studying, feeling like I was killing myself to keep my grades up. I also didn't mention how some days I couldn't afford anything other than packaged mac n' cheese or soup in a

Styrofoam cup and what little fruit and veggies I could find for my health. She wouldn't want to hear it. She would spin the reality of it into a false optimistic opportunity, then accuse me of being a pessimist. I wasn't. I was just realistic.

"Are you dating?" she asked next. Textbook. She wanted to know if I had snagged some rich, preppy boy.

"No, I'm not. I don't have time-"

"That's an excuse. You need to get out more and socialise. I'm sure many lovely people there would be just dying to take my beautiful daughter out to enjoy New York city's nightlife!"

"It's expensive-"

"I'm sure there are boys at that school that are more than financially comfortable to treat you to a meal and dancing." She insisted, not at all fazed.

I sucked my bottom lip into my mouth, refraining from snapping and giving her a serious reality check. But honestly, what was the point? She lived in her own little world where she was happy and safe, and if anything penetrated that bubble, then she would cast it out. She'd done it before. I had no doubt she would do it again.

"Okay, Mom, I'll do that. I'll keep my eyes and ears open for a rich Trust-Fund socialite to dig my claws into... mwa-hahahaha!" I laughed dramatically into the phone.

When I stopped and pressed it back to my ear, there was nothing but silence for a moment before my mother said, "What is wrong with you?"

I shrugged and rolled my eyes, knowing very well she couldn't see me. She could be very dry sometimes. My Dad was a little more of a jokester, but he tended to be very quiet, more comfortable watching and listening in the background than being at the centre of things, like Mom. "Nothing. Just being my normal self."

"Hmmm..." she murmured, clearly not sure if she believed me or not. It was kind of sad how little my mother knew about me as a person. "Well, is there anything else you wanted to update me on?"

Yes. "Nope."

"Are you sure?"

No. "Yup!"

"Okay, then. Get some rest, honey. Don't work too hard. Remember to get out and have some fun, alright?"

I could always rely on my mother to remind me to let go of the serious side of things. It was a gift of hers, I think. "I'll remember that. Say hi to Dad for me."

"I will. Love you, honey!"

"Love you," I hung up and stared at the 'Call Ended' screen.

Why didn't I tell her?

That was simple enough to answer. I didn't want to be a burden again, a dark part of her life that she didn't care to acknowledge. Hearing her so happy and enjoying herself, with no worries, only reminded me again that even if I told her I was seeing my doctor because I was worried for my health again, I would still end up dealing with it alone. She wouldn't come down here to keep me company during appointments or treatments, if it came to that. She would turn a blind eye and pretend it wasn't happening.

Telling my parents wouldn't change anything on my side. I'd still be alone. I'd be cast aside while others put their own needs concerning my situation first. Telling them would just penetrate that bubble of perfection they needed to be happy.

Besides, I didn't even know if I *was* sick again. For all I knew, I'd go in and find out I was anemic or something and be told to take an iron supplement. Or prescribed some sleeping pills. Why make a fuss over what could be nothing?

Because you've been through this before, and you know what this feels like...

I shook that bleak and scary thought away. I was a realist, yes, but worrying about it now wouldn't help me. Not until I heard definitive proof from my doctor would I then think about the next steps.

Right now? All I knew was that I was exhausted, so much so that I wasn't even going to bother making myself a bowl of soup made of those plastic-tasting noodles with chicken broth, which was all I had in the cupboard at the moment. Instead, I changed into a pair of pink cotton sleep pants, a lavender tank top, and curled up under my comforter. For a while, I lay there with the light on, watching the shadows in the room, my heart thudding hard as I thought about that terrifying presence. Would it come back tonight?

Please, God, no. Just let me rest. I just needed to rest...

Summoning some courage, I reached over and yanked the chain to my old lamp, immersing myself in the darkness, and huddled beneath my blankets, staring around in the dark for some sign of movement. Except nothing happened. There was no sense of being watched, no strange, unnatural shift of the shadows, nor the cool touch of mist brushing my face. I was alone. I was safe.

Breathing a sigh of relief, I wearily let my head fall upon my pillow, and drifted into a dreamless sleep.

I mean, at first, it was dreamless... just a peaceful dark void of nothing. But then, it shifted. In my dream, the shadow had come back, moving faster and with more deliberate actions than it had any other time. It rose over the side of my bed, casting a large shadow over my still form, and while I wanted to scream, I was frozen where I lay, incapable of moving or even calling for help when it reached for me. I felt it grasp my ankles, and slowly, inch by inch, I began to slide beneath my covers, down the length of the bed, until my ass was resting at the edge. The shadow enveloped me, snaking beneath my back, then lifted me into a sitting position. My head rolled back, my body limp like a doll's, unresponsive to my will, yet inside my mind, I was absolutely losing my shit. I was shrieking, yelling at myself to move, fight, do something!

But it was fruitless. I could do no more than watch as I was lifted into the air, the shadow's form solidifying some, but not nearly enough for me to make out any definitive features. I found myself suspended in the air, a strange sort of buzzing sound filling my ears as a swirling mass of black smoke manifested from nothing, growing larger and larger until it was nearly the size of a door.

Oh my God... no... NO! Whatever that thing was, I didn't want to touch it. I didn't want to go anywhere near it! The feeling I got from simply looking at it was chilling, foreboding, promising nothing but terror and horrors from my worst nightmares. Somehow, I managed to twitch my fingers, which were resting on my stomach, ever so slightly, the slightest sign of rebellion. When I moved, the shadow beast stilled for the briefest moment, as though I'd startled him. I felt the mist swoop over my face, neck, and chest, making me feel like I was being studied closely. I shivered in response. The second movement only seemed to spur this evil being on as it turned toward the black smoke and glided toward it.

NOOOO! I screamed in my head. *Fight, Evie! Fight back! Move your arms! Move your legs! Something!* But whatever power this mystical shadow of evil had, it wouldn't allow it. I remained immobile, cradled in their hold, and next thing I knew, it carried me into the black smoke.

The air around me whirled like a gust of cold wind. I could see nothing, hear nothing... I just felt. The air was rushing, compressing, and I thought for sure my head was going to implode. It smelled metallic, coppery, leaving a bitter taste in the back of my mouth. I felt dizzy like I was spinning uncontrollably, and though I tried to fight it, that overpowering sensation seemed to click some magic 'on/off' button in my head, and I passed out cold.

I could feel myself slowly coming to. Though my eyes were still closed, I knew I was waking up. Everything felt like it was moving slowly, my senses turning on one by one. First, I could feel the soft blankets cocooned around me. Whatever I was lying on was pure heaven, much softer than I was used to. My fold-out mattress wasn't ever this comfortable. I could make out an assortment of material beneath my arms and fingertips... silk, velvet, what I think was cashmere or fur, and the softest, warmest wool.

I blearily opened my eyes, my vision blurring ever so slightly as I slowly came to from my deep sleep. Overhead, I was looking at what appeared to be a golden spiderweb.

Wait, that wasn't right. A gold spiderweb? I blinked hard, reaching up to rub my eyes and clear my blurry vision. Looking again, I saw it was actually a metal, barred dome high over my head.

What in the hell?

I sat up, everything now hitting me at once.

I was in a cage, like... a giant, golden, ornamental birdcage. It was well over six feet tall, its circumference about six feet across. I was lying upon a makeshift bed of velvet and silk pillows, a fancy, emerald throw tossed over my figure. I sat up, staring around the space, my brain sluggishly registering one thing at a time.

In the half of the floorspace of this cage, there were cat toys, a fancy, decorative fern set up along the far wall by the door, which had a giant, gold lock on it, sealed from outside the bars. There was even a bowl of water and one filled with what looked like an assortment of random food... a banana, a chocolate bar, a pile of crackers, a can of tuna fish, and a jar of strawberry jam.

What in the ever-loving fuck?

"Good morrow, human female."

I stilled at the sound of that piercing, growl-like voice, the feeling of absolute terror enveloping me when I realized that whoever had taken me was here now, watching. My heart was pounding, my skin crawling and prickled with goosebumps, as I slowly turned to crane my head back, way back to take in the sight of my abductor. But what I saw versus what I expected could not be farther from each other. I thought I'd find some skeezy drug lord, a human trafficker, some crackhead who had broken into my tiny home in the middle of the night and taken me because he was on some insane high. Instead, what I found myself looking at had my cheeks flushing and my mouth dropping open in shock.

He was huge, somewhere between six and a half and seven feet tall. Though he wasn't skinny, he wasn't hugely muscled either. He was leaner but still had a definite threatening presence, promising nothing but brute strength. As I tilted my head way back to see him, I took in his clothes, moving from the feet up. His boots were made of black leather, as were his pants. He wore a black silky-looking top, the open collar at the shirt trailing down to show just the hint of his muscles at his chest. He wore an insanely decorative emerald cloak made of velvet, the silver clasps draping over his chest and pinned with a silver brooch in the shape of a serpent, a glowing emerald in its eye. He looked like he belonged in a different time, the style very old-fashioned, reminding me of princes and knights and castles.

His hair was a beautiful caramel colour, dropping to his shoulders in waves, loose and messily tossed to the side over his head. But the moment I locked eyes with him, I found myself suddenly lost as though trapped in some sort of hypnotic trance.

His eyes were a bright, acidic green, entrancing and eerily unnatural, framed with dark lashes and brows that were pulled down over his gaze. He had a square face, sharp features, high cheekbones, and a look about him that gave him a cruel edge. And yet, I found myself incredibly enthralled, stupefied by his rather androgynous beauty.

It hit me then that he had just wished me good morning. However, in a rather Shakespearean-esque way, and all I'd done for the last thirty seconds was stare at him like an idiot, mouth hanging open, eyes wide, probably looking like I'd lost all my brain cells in the last half a minute. Really, it wasn't my fault. I've never seen someone so... well, insanely and unnaturally beautiful. I had to respond to him. He was waiting! But my tongue felt thick, my brain oddly blank, and as I began to panic the more prolonged the silence between us stretched on, I quickly said the first thing I could think of.

"I'm wearing PJs."

Inside my head, I could hear my brain giving me a slow clap. *Well done, Evie. You wake up in a giant-ass birdcage, you're physically attracted to your crazy hot kidnapper, and you announce that you're in nothing but a pair of sleep pants and tank top. Was that the cleverest thing you could have said at this moment? No. Not at all. How are you in school?*

"This is true." Instead of looking at me like I was a complete moron like I expected, he simply bowed his head, acknowledging my idiotic statement.

Try again, Evie. "I'm in a cage."

Ding-ding-ding! We have a winner for The Stupidest Most Obvious Observation Award! Hands down, it goes to Evangeline Kelly!

"This is also true," he agreed, his unblinking stare unmoving. In fact, the longer he went without blinking or looking away, the more self-conscious I became. I pulled the blanket up to my shoulders, hiding myself from him, the truth of my situation now becoming clearer to my sleepy brain.

"You kidnapped me." *Evie, c'mon, longer sentences, please!*

"Kidnapped..." He tilted his head slightly to the side, like the word I'd used wasn't one he was familiar with. "I took you."

"Yeah, that's what kidnapping means."

"You are not a child. You are fully matured."

I could feel my face shift, which had been one of admiration of his looks for the last two minutes but was now morphing to incredulity. Was he serious? "No, I'm not a child," I agreed, "But the term 'kidnapping' means taking someone against their will and moving them elsewhere."

"Ah, I understand now," he agreed, looking all too pleased by this discussion. He moved closer to the cage, bending at the waist and resting his hands on his knees, and he studied me between the bars. "Then yes, I agree. I *kidnapped* you."

Was this guy for real? My brows rose high on my forehead. I could feel my confusion etched upon my face, seriously baffled by every part of this situation. "Why?"

"Because I wished it."

"You wished it?" I confirmed, thrown by his peculiar way of speaking.

He nodded, looking much too eager with every affirmation made between us. It was like he was glad we were getting on the same page of understanding. I've never been kidnapped before, but even I knew that this wasn't typical behaviour given the situation. I squirmed on the giant pillow pile I'd been sleeping on, re-examining what he'd given me. A bed, blankets, *cat toys?* Really? Why the hell were those here? Did he have a cat? And the food... the random assortment of food that made no sense together was actually piled in what looked like a doggy bowl, judging by the cartoon milk bones painted around the side. Then there was that fern, set in a huge pottery vase like it was some decor piece, and my confusion only increased.

"Wh-what are you going to do with... with me?" I stammered, now dreading his response. This was the question I should have asked from the start, but it was also one I was terrified to hear the answer to. What was this unnerving person going to do with me? Rape? Torture? Did he have some sick fantasy to abduct a girl and try to force her to become a sex slave? What if he planned on selling me to the highest bidder? That looked to be the most likely reason, given how refined he was dressed and my elegant cage. "I'm not a virgin!" I announced, keeping up the pattern of humiliating myself every time I opened my mouth.

What I meant by that, was that since I was *not* a virgin, I wasn't as valuable to him and therefore wouldn't fetch a reasonable price at an auction. I knew how these things worked. But of course, my random declaration finally had the result

I expected, complete bafflement on his part. His brows rose high, clearly taken aback by my statement, before he suddenly glowered, as though learning that my value being tainted seriously pissed him off. Great, hadn't counted on that. This *is* the twenty-first century. Was he genuinely that surprised to learn this?

"Who has touched you?" he thundered, his eyes beginning to glow. Glow! What the... how was that possible?

"Uh, a few guys-" I started to say, but the moment the words left my lips, he absolutely lost his shit. He turned and flipped over a bench that had been innocently sitting at the end of the massive bed, sending it flying. He moved on to the curtains draped across a set of floor-to-ceiling windows and tore them down, revealing an archway leading out onto a balcony. He roared, his muscles beneath his clothing flexing so much, growing in fact, that they strained against the fabric.

"I shall tear their phalluses from their bodies! I will feed them to Beast! I will make them scream and beg for mercy before I set them aflame!" He raved.

"Whoa! Whoa! Easy!" I cried, cringing back against the bars of the cage, now terrified of how quickly and over-the-top his reaction had been. "It's okay! They're long gone!" I didn't know why I said that... maybe because I had sensed that these threats he was vocalising were no joke, that he really would hunt down the poor, innocent men I'd carelessly slept with months ago and make them suffer. This guy was clearly a lunatic... talking about ripping dicks off, feeding them to a strangely named dog, and then venturing into pyro territory to finish it off. Yeah, nothing good would come from me giving him names or expanding on the fact that I'd lived a little.

To my relief, when I had shouted that they were "gone," he suddenly stopped his rampage and turned to look at me closely, like he was suspicious as hell, peering through the bars at my trembling figure. "They are deceased?" he confirmed.

"Uh, yeah. They're out of the picture." A half-lie, but all for the greater good.

His chest was heaving as he panted, slowly coming down from his hissy fit. I gave him a minute to settle before tentatively asking again, "So... what are you going to do with me?"

"I don't know?" he said without hesitation, sounding as baffled as I was.

"You... don't know?"

He shook his head, his look of confusion intensifying. "Do you do any tricks?"

Tricks? My mouth fell open again as I stared into the genuine intrigue on his face. This guy was actually serious. "What do you mean?" I narrowed my eyes a little. "Tricks?"

"Like, what can you do? What do you do better than all others?"

Okay, this was clearly this guy's first kidnapping attempt, and he was doing a real original job of it. I can guarantee that no other person on this earth has found themselves in this situation, which made me doubt this was real. Perhaps I was having some trippy dream? I thought about what he'd said. *What can I do better?* But he had also said *tricks*. For some reason, even given how scared and thrown off I was by this whole thing, I couldn't resist a little smart-assery.

"I can sit. I can lie down. Rollover..." I watched his reaction, waiting to see if he'd flip again.

However, all he did was nod along, watching me intently, as though cataloging all the things I could do off a mental checklist in his head.

"I can clean myself-"

"Oh, thank fuck." He sighed with relief, holding a hand over his heart. "What else?"

Did he worry about cleaning up after me? Holy crap, this guy was NOT *all there.* "Uh, I'm good at fetch-"

"Oh really? Like what?"

"A newspaper," I snapped sarcastically, wondering if he was fucking with me.

He tilted his head to the side again, not registering that word. "A newspaper?"

"No! A fucking stick!" I snapped.

"Watch your tone," he warned me. "I don't appreciate backtalk."

"Well, I'm not a dog, asshole!"

He mused on that for a minute, though his expression was unreadable. Again, he watched with that unblinking stare, and I remembered how little I was actually wearing and pulled the blanket back into place.

"I don't know why you would proclaim such a thing, as you are obviously a human," he said at last. "But I assume that my treatment of you reflects that of your furry companions on Earth."

Slowly, I turned my head in his direction. I understood everything he'd just said, and at the same time, it didn't make any sense. So, I just repeated, "I'm not a dog."

He nodded, now deep in thought, considering, and it made me uncomfortable. What was he going to do with me? He didn't know, apparently. Would he let me go now that he knew I couldn't do anything special? There was nothing special about me that stood out over all others. That was impossible. No matter what you're good at, there is always someone better. That level of perfection is impossible to reach, and if you live thinking that way, you'll never be happy.

"Good," he said at last. "Those tricks of yours are boring anyway. I didn't take you to simply watch you sit and lie down." He rose to his full height and moved over to the lock. I didn't see a key, yet when he waved his hand over the massive gold device, it clicked open.

Holy shit! How did he do that?

"Come."

My head reared back in alarm. "I beg your pardon?"

"Come. Heel. Approach. Exit your cage so I may get a better look at you."

Nope. I didn't like this at all. "Or... you could come in here?"

"You are in no position to make any demands of me, little human." His sharp green eyes, which by this point had stopped their eerie glowing, narrowed, and his upper lip curled. Okay, so he didn't like being told what to do. Noted.

Just be sweet and obliging, for now, Evie. But at the same time, I thought that I blurted out, "My name isn't 'little human'. It's Evangeline Kelly."

"Evangeline Kelly?" One of his brows rose as he tested the name out, repeating it over and over for a minute. "Evangeline Kelly... Evan-geline... Kelly. Evangeline Kelly..." He began to smile, as though he enjoyed saying it.

"Or Evie," I added, not even knowing why I bothered. This dick *did* kidnap me and lock me in a cage, after all. "Evie is what everyone else calls me."

"I would rather not," he said, the moment I told him how others addressed me.

"Okay, then Evangeline. Kelly is my surname. You don't need to add it on every time you talk to me. It's a mouthful. As long as you aren't calling me 'little human'." Which, let's be honest, was weird as fuck to begin with, and was just another perplexing thing he'd said in the last five minutes.

"Evangeline," he practically purred it, extending a hand into the doorway of the cage, slowly curling his fingers in beckoning. It was then that I noticed his fingernails were completely black, short, but sharp, thick... *unnatural!* "Come to me."

For some reason, when he said this, I felt my body shiver, not with cold, but with something else entirely. I actually squeezed my thighs together in reflex. He grinned as though sensing my response to his demand. I wanted to wipe that cocky grin off his face. Determined to show him that I was unaffected by everything about him, I got to my feet, shaking slightly at the knees when my body was exposed to the cool air wafting through the open archway leading outside and strode forward, ignoring his hand. Instead, I stepped out of the lavish, gold cell and into the room, looking everywhere but at him and his smug expression, taking in my surroundings instead of letting him distract me.

We were in a bedroom. No doubt, given the enormous bed that was pressed against the opposite wall. The space was circular, the ceiling peaking in the centre, the floor made of smooth river rock. As my eyes wandered, the walls appeared to be made of rough stone, like the walls of a cavern, only made out of a blueish-grey colour. At random sections, there looked like what appeared to be fossils embedded into the rock, an anemone, strange skeletal fish, some with fangs, and what looked to be a massive twelve-foot eel running along the wall over the bed. The frame of the bed was made out of a smooth granite in cobalt blue, with streaks of white, black, and flecks of gold swirled into swirling patterns. The bedspread was gold, shimmery under the lights above. Then I caught sight of where the light was coming from in this space, and it was from what looked to be floating, glowing jellyfish drifting overhead like there was some invisible barrier between them and us that kept them there. How the hell was that possible?

The cage I'd been held in was set close to a gigantic desk made out of the same granite as the bed, the chair luxurious, pillowed, with gold cushioning. There was no computer, no sign of any sort of work there, only a silver, hammered metal bowl sitting at the centre of the surface, its contents not visible from here. Now that I studied them where they lay upon the floor, the curtains he'd ripped down were another strange feature. They were hazy, like they were made of mist that you see floating over cold water on a freezing winter's day. They didn't even look solid, and yet, he'd torn them down, and they lay upon the floor in a heap... a strange, white, smoky heap.

It was all beautiful. Stunning. I felt like I was in a cave under the ocean. But the little things, the strangeness to them, the ethereal way it was all put together, told me that this wasn't right. This wasn't normal, and it was more than just special effects and cool technology. The back of my mind was screaming at me that this was all off. *Abnormal. Impossible.* Yet it was here.

I slowly peered up at my captor, who had been watching me look around his space the entire time without moving an inch. There was a tightness to the way he held his jaw like he was clenching it together, his brows slightly furrowed. Why did he look so nervous?

"What's wrong?" I asked, eyes wide, wondering what the hell could be bothering him when I was the one who was abducted here.

"I just... I know it is not as fine as some dwellings here. I am lacking in my collection of riches and finery." He scowled at the room, like it truly bothered him.

"Are you serious?" I asked, incredulously.

"Why would I not be?"

I gaped at him. "Did you *see* my home? I have plastic patio furniture for my kitchen setup. I sleep on a fold-out couch. My clothes are piled into a suitcase under my bed-"

"Your impoverished ways mean nothing to me, human,"

"Again, not human. Evangeline. But that's not the point-"

"I did not take you because I thought your wealth would add value to my home."

"Clearly not." I rolled my eyes at him, still having a hard time processing the fact that I was arguing with my kidnapper about wealth. "But this... *this!*" I gestured around the room, staring in awe again at the floating, soft glow emitting from the jellyfish overhead, "This is amazing!"

His head jerked back at that, now looking to be incredibly vexed and stunned. "You jest."

"Speak current day English, please." I sighed and shook my head at him. "And no, I'm not kidding. This is absolutely stunning. I can't believe this even exists!"

"Other palaces have greater splendour-"

"Who *cares?*" I snapped at him. "Look at what you have! I would give anything to have a room like this! My God... just the walls themselves, the fossils, the stonework... that in itself is amazing enough. Then you throw in that big, beautiful bed, your desk, the gold embellishments, and coverings..." I sighed, frustrated that this douchewad had zero appreciation for all of this. "Are you truly unhappy with all of this?"

He peered around the room, studying it as though he was seeing it for the first time. The corner of his mouth, his lovely, full mouth with that perfect cupid's bow... *pull it together, Evie!* He seemed to be considering what I was saying. But instead of addressing it, he turned to face me again, his hands folded behind his back. Those unblinking green eyes bored into mine in a way that sent a flutter through my body, making me very aware of how scantily dressed I was. I crossed my arms over my chest, realizing that my nipples were pebbled beneath my tank top, poking out against the thin, cotton material.

But his gaze never left mine, and his decision to not be a perv and check out my body while I was vulnerable and open to him made me feel a little safer.

So far, he hadn't hurt me, touched me (from what I was aware of, anyway. Who knows what happened while I was passed out), and instead seemed to be more or less figuring out exactly what he wanted to do to me. I wondered if I could appeal to the humane side of him, if that would protect me if he decided to go the opposite direction and suddenly attack.

"Sooo..." I let my voice trail off as I tentatively peered up at him from beneath my lashes, feeling very nervous and on the spot. "What is your name?"

His lips pursed slightly like he was deliberating telling me anything about himself. Any information he gave me I'd just hand over to the police anyway, but I needed to call him *something*... fake name or not.

"Leviathan..." he said finally. The way he dropped his voice several octaves as he rumbled the name seemed to reverberate through my body. *Leviathan.* Not a name I'd heard before. The way he said it, I felt like I could taste warm caramel on my tongue, the name sounding much too sensual given who he was to me.

"Levi-a-than?" I sounded out the name slowly, to which he slowly nodded in approval. "Leviathan... Leviathan..." I repeated, testing out the foreign name on my tongue.

"Evangeline," he whispered, his voice reminding me of a caress by how he spoke. Whoa, that actually had me forgetting how to breathe for a minute there. I sucked in a breath between my teeth, struggling to find the ability to wrench my gaze from his. It felt like when I had been lying in bed, paralyzed, unable to move while my mind screamed and thrashed and...

"You took me from my room," I said to him, my voice hushed.

"I did."

"How did you... how did..." I struggled to focus, trying to remember exactly what had happened last night when he took me. How did he get into my space? Was he the mysterious shadow that has been lurking in the dark? Was he behind my immobility? What about the smoky doorway that appeared magically in the air? Was he some sort of an illusionist?

No, a voice whispered at the back of my mind. *Wake up, Evie. This is* not *natural. Trust your instincts. Look at him... LOOK at him!*

The longer I stared into that green gaze, the more my feelings seemed to fuse together. The answer dangled before me, but it was so out there, I was having a hard time believing it. "Where are we?" I asked, my voice cracking slightly as I began to tremble.

"In my home."

"And where is that, exactly?"

He hesitated for a moment, as though he really didn't want to tell me. Seeing as I was taken against my will. But there was more to it than that. The otherworldliness to everything was too glaring, impossible to just ignore and brush off with excuses that made me feel comfortable and safe. They were lies I was telling myself, even though lying to myself wouldn't save me here.

"Elsewhere," he said finally.

For some reason, the weight of that word knocked my breath from my lungs, and I needed to sit down. Instead of retreating to the bed, the chair behind his desk, or even the soft cushions inside the golden cell, I plopped down on the ground, my legs stretched out before me, my hands resting limply in my lap as I felt the blood rush from my head. This was too much. Too much. How was this possible? I didn't know where I was still... but a part of me knew that 'elsewhere' didn't mean... well, home. Earth. Whatever the hell. Wherever I was, this was something new, something entirely out of my depth of understanding, and honestly? It terrified me.

Leviathan crouched down, resting on his haunches, his fingertips pressed together as he studied my shocked expression. "You will take a minute to accept this," he said to me, his tone serious and clipped. "And then you will accompany me as I have many errands to run. Do not stray from my side and follow my orders without hesitation. Do you understand?"

I thought I had responded to him, but I guess I was still in a state of shock, my mouth parched, because he snapped, "Do you understand, Evangeline? My home is a dangerous place, and a misstep could result in fatal injury."

When my eyes widened in alarm, he nodded as though pleased to see the fear on my face.

"So, you understand?"

"Y-yes... yes. I understand," I whispered, feeling like my entire body had gone numb.

"Good. Your minute starts now."

CHAPTER SIX

Leviathan

I cannot comprehend any of it.

Everything from the way I spoke to her, her reaction to me, to my palace, all of it was very strange and new...

As we descended from my private tower, she slowly started coming out of her thoughtful reverie and began to rave about the way the circular staircase was made and decorated, her excitement building the farther we went. She pointed out the turquoise tiles that mixed with the iridescent dark blue, the pattern making it look like waves lining the way down, going on and on about how beautiful and extraordinary its artistry was. I suppose it *was* nice. I never really thought about it when I designed it. I just needed a stairwell, and seeing as I was Ruler of the Chaotic Oceans, it made sense to pay homage to that in the construction of my palace. She *really* liked the lighting, which at this point, the hanging chandeliers resembled massive pearl clusters in colours of cream, white, lilac, pink, and black.

As much as I didn't care for it, to hear her get so excited over my home was actually quite... well, pleasing. I felt a flicker in my chest at her admiration, an alien feeling that had me puffing my chest out proudly at every compliment she made in her observations.

I thought she'd get over it soon enough, but the moment we stepped through the archway into the halls leading us from my private wing to the rest of the palace, her excitement only heightened.

"Oh, my Gawd!" she practically hollered. Her choice of words, rather than pitch, made me wince. "I feel like I'm walking through a coral reef! This is amazing!"

The walls curved overhead, closing in above to block out the ceiling. The array of rock I'd used to decorate made a sort of tunnel through my castle, the random breaks overhead through fan coral and small openings, casting blueish rays of light down into the space, the anemones that clung to the rock around us glowing to guide our way. Again, it was nothing compared to the riches of Greed's golden kingdom, or Lucifer's, which represented the Kingdom of Heaven itself. Mine was just... convenient. All supplies that had been available to me when I needed to construct my new home. That's all it was to me. Convenience.

But as I peered over my shoulder at Evangeline (*Evangeline...* I could not get enough of that name), she excitedly ran from one side to the other, inspecting an elaborate shell or one of the purple-coloured long tentacle anemones that swayed back and forth in an invisible current.

"Caution, female," I snapped before she could poke it, "That species is aggressive. It will sting you."

Obediently, she listened, retracting her hand, but glared up at me, looking like a very angry, cute little doll. "What did we say about you calling me that?"

"You had said 'human'. I said 'female', which is what you are."

"Yeah. However, we established that I have a name. I'd appreciate it if you used it."

"But you *are* a female. So I am not incorrect." I turned to face her, amused by how she seemed so irritated by what I was saying.

"And *you* are kind of a dick. But I doubt you'd want me to call you that, am I right?" She raised a brow in challenge.

I smirked. "I have a dick. So, you are not wrong."

She sighed in frustration, and I felt a strange sense of satisfaction at having gotten under her skin in some way. "Well, congratulations!" she said finally. "That's awesome. Kudos to your penis. But my name is Evangeline, and since you've brought me here against my will to your weird, underwater-without-ac-tually-being-underwater kingdom... would you at least do me the courtesy of addressing me by my actual name?"

I thought about what she said, and that wicked part of me wanted to tell her no that she could not demand anything of me. Although, at the same time, I very much enjoyed saying her name. It suited her. I took a step in her direction, my stride so much longer than hers, that it lined me up directly before her, our bodies barely an inch away. Being this close, I could feel the heat from her and see how she shivered at my proximity. Her pupils in her wide, chocolate-coloured eyes grew, almost blacking them out, and her pouty mouth fell open in shock. It was comforting to me to know I had an effect on her, physically. I hadn't quite figured out why that mattered yet, but so far, I wasn't bored.

I slowly leaned down, bending at the waist to reach her ear, and whispered, "Evangeline..."

Seeing how her skin pebbled, her pert nipples poking at the flimsy shirt she wore, sent a thrill through my body, right to my groin. Fucking dammit! I did not need this right now. I thought having her close would cease that reaction, but apparently not. If anything, I felt an even stronger yearning to yank her against me, closing the gap between us.

That's a dangerous thought, Leviathan...

Before I could do anything to compromise myself, to go too far that I wouldn't be able to come back from it, I spun on my heel and strode away, each step deliberate and firm. She was still a human. Still one of them. Though I wanted her and took her, I was still hesitant around her as I've spent nearly my entire existence loathing her very kind. I'd get close enough to appease my curiosity but not enough to allow any sort of real bonding, especially when I didn't understand any of my feelings and reactions to her.

When I made it to the open foyer before the grand staircase, I turned to look back at her, only to see her standing in the same spot, stunned into a state of paralysis.

"Evangeline! Come!" I barked, and she let out a little squeak before she hurried to my side. I felt a sense of pride at that. Two times now, she followed my command with perfect obedience. Those fools, Gnaarl and Gazaat, attempted to train their humans with rewards and treats, while mine just did as I bid. Clearly, my selection was superior to theirs.

When she made it to my side, I began to descend the grand staircase while the entire time listening to her exclamations about how beautiful it all was. Again, that little alien spark that I found to be immensely pleasing flickered each time she gave some positive observation or compliment about my home. I was finding myself rather eager to show off my throne room, despite the fact I didn't care much for it. Again, it was all just convenient to me. Nothing like the other kingdoms and their lavish decor and substantial wealth. And she did not disappoint.

Her large, doe-like eyes nearly popped out of her skull, marginally reminding me of a human I'd done the very same thing to some moons ago. I'd squeezed and squeezed his temples, slowly pressing in, watching as his eyes began to protrude from the pressure. The filth had attacked one of my guards in the plane he'd been cursed to. I wouldn't have it. So I took it upon myself to punish him personally. The man had slobbered like an animal, spittle flicking out from his blubbery lips, soiling my shirt and the floor. He'd looked like vermin, smelled like it, the way he soiled himself. His pitiful, choking cries were more annoying than anything, the rattle of his voice sour to me. Everything about him had been offensive.

But Evangeline...

Thus far, everything she did I found to be very enjoyable. It was... different. Strange. And not in a bad way. I suppose this might be how Gnaarl felt when he first took Kys under his wing. Yet, how long could it possibly last? I suppose if worst came to worst, she would help pass the time, to entertain me, and when I'd finally be through with her, I could either dispose of her or throw her back to Earth.

The thought of hurting her, of doing what I would typically do to a human in this scenario, gave me the most peculiar feeling in my chest; a tightness that I didn't like. I quickly pushed those thoughts away and focused again on the human girl as she stared in awe at my place of business.

"What is this room for?" she whispered, staring around.

"It is where I work."

At this, her attention returned fully to me, which I knew I definitely liked. I much preferred it when her focus was centred on me. "Your work? What kind of job do you have? Do you have employees?" The trivial tilt of her voice, the hope, at her last question had me sneering. She thought my people would betray me and help her? She was mad. I stormed toward her, catching her off guard as I backed her up into one of the pillars that lined the aisle toward my throne and towered over her. The thought of her escaping, of someone turning traitor on me to get her out, had me as furious as the thought of another man touching her. I wasn't upset by the fact she was not a virgin, but more that I had to accept the fact that some human filth had sought pleasure with her.

This time, however, I managed to control myself. My skin had rippled painfully as I forced down the urge to transition to my demon form. The sharp prickling at my back, my wings scratching painfully against the underside of my skin to break free, was just a way to remind me I needed to get a grip. She wasn't gone. She was here, and I was going to make something *very* clear to Miss Evangeline Kelly.

"Listen to me carefully, Evangeline... because I don't like repeating myself, and I think you need to hear it now before you make any mistakes that will only provoke me." One of my hands snapped up, enclosing around her throat, not hard, something I had to remember to be cautious of. My strength. But it was enough to send a tremor of fear into her. Good. She needed to fear me. "You will not try to escape. Nor will you conspire to, by hoping to enlist my servants and loyal followers to aid your plight. You do not leave here until I wish it. Do you understand?"

Her tiny body trembled under my hold, and for a brief moment, I felt a flicker of something unfamiliar to me. What was it? Her expression flashed with a series of emotions, pain, sorrow, and lastly...

Shame.

I scoffed. Surely not. It didn't matter. The important thing was that she nodded, too stunned to speak and too intimidated to counter with her fearless, open candour. I released her, though my fingers paused on her slender neck, feeling how her pulse jumped beneath my touch. I let my hand slide away, dropping it to my side, ignoring the heat from her body that seemed to cling to me like some part of her had seeped through my skin. I ignored it and headed to my throne, beckoning her to follow. I could hear her soft steps as her bare feet carried her across the stone floor, her movements careful, like she was afraid of upsetting me. That was good. It would save me the trouble of having to break her in. If she complied right away, then I wouldn't find myself having to go through endless "training sessions" like Gnaarl.

As promised, at the base of the stone steps where my less grandeur throne was arranged. Though I couldn't help but compare it to Lucifer's, I grinned wickedly when I remembered his was missing a ruby, shattering its sense of perfection. I was pleased to see that my Second in Command had my waywraiths set up a place for my new... *pet*, human companion, whatever she was. There was a large golden pillow, surrounded by silk and velvet throws and smaller cushions on which she could curl up on, a thick, dark grey metal chain attached to the wall, and a new collar. It was about two inches wide, and I loved the detail Gnaarl had my followers decorate it with, an image of Beast carved around the entire loop. It was this I picked up and held out for her, waiting to put it on.

But at the sight of the thick, brown leather restraint, Evangeline stopped in her tracks and stared, her look of horror quickly turning furious. "And *what* exactly is that?" she spat, crossing her thin little arms over her chest.

"It is where you will sit while I conduct my business," I explained and shook the collar at her, "Now come."

"I don't think you understand when I say I'm not a dog... but, well, I'm not a fucking dog!" Her voice rose a little into a piercing shriek, the sound actually hurting my ears a fraction. Fucking hell... were all humans capable of reaching that pitch?

"This has been established and agreed upon!" I snarled back. "Why do you keep bringing that up? Desist!"

"Because you keep treating me like one! *That* thing," she pointed to the leather in my hand, "Is a bloody dog collar, and I absolutely refuse to wear it."

I straightened to my full height, and wouldn't you know, the little female didn't wither in response, even after I'd frightened her into submission mere minutes ago. "You *will* wear this collar, not because I think you are a... *dog*... but because it keeps you safe."

She raised her brows at me in disbelief for several heartbeats before finally, she tossed her head back and laughed. *Laughed*! Right in my face!

"Is this so amusing to you?" The idea of her laughing at me hit me in a way that reminded me of the angels in Heaven who whispered about me. Leviathan, the tainted one, the dark monster pulled from the abyss. Inferior, inadequate, impure. I was a joke to them, and I refused to let anyone, even her, make me feel that way again. If she thought I was some idiot, that I was someone she could humiliate, I would correct that opinion right now!

I was about to storm over to her, my hands shaking as I prepared to punish her like I would anyone else dragged before me, when she faced me and smiled, wiping a tear from her eye. The only time I'd witnessed a human crying was because they were in pain, and yet, as far as I could see, she was unharmed. I furrowed my brow, now completely lost and alarmed. For some reason, the way she shook her head, now bending over at the waist as she laughed almost uncontrollably, made me pause. She waved her hand at me like I had misunderstood something. My flash of anger slowly began to dissipate. "Have you gone insane?" I asked, trying to figure out what had her behaving so strangely.

"N-no!" She giggled, looking up, her face flushed, her lips spread into a wide smile. My eyes were drawn to it, finding I rather liked seeing her white teeth and the spread of her pink-tinted lips. The sound was not nearly as grating as that shriek from when she'd been scolding me before. "I'm sorry, just-just the idea of... of *that*... of you keeping me safe... given the circumstance..." She shook her head again and broke out into a fresh wave of giggles.

Yes, I was certain she had gone mad.

Nevertheless, she wasn't arguing, so I suppose the fact that she was slightly mentally unstable wasn't such a bad thing. Especially if it meant she was filling this ample, empty space with the lovely sound of her laughter, which I enjoyed the more I heard it.

I still didn't understand what was so humorous, though, but she wandered over, wiping her eyes and waiting as I clasped the collar around her neck.

"Anyone who visits me here will see this as a sign of possession," I said as I magically sealed the leather closed. "They will not harm you. If one of my followers thought you were fair game, they would take you and inflict whatever they wished upon your body and mind."

She coughed at that; her brief moment of joy now shattered as I 'fessed to the very real dangers of the situation. Her wide, chocolate eyes stared up at me in shock, like she didn't quite believe me. "What, you have a bunch of psychopaths working for you?"

The corner of my mouth twitched at that. "Not exactly, Evangeline. Though I suspect you will find out soon enough." I moved the chain so that it pooled on the stone floor behind her, giving her space to settle on the pillows, before I climbed up the few steps to my throne, where I took a seat, getting comfortable, before checking down on her. She had a blanket wrapped around her shoulders as though she was cold. I felt a small bubble of displeasure swell in my chest. I didn't want her covered up. I wanted to show off my newest possession to all coming to see me. But, as this bitter thought came to mind, I suppose the plain clothing she was wearing when I took her was not exactly protective, but soon, I'd have what I ordered from Lust's domain, which should better her comfort.

Who gives a shit about her comfort? A voice snapped in my mind. *She's here for you. No other reason than that.* But at the same time, I couldn't shake the thought of her dressed in a luscious silk dress, accentuating her curves. As I pictured it in my head, I felt another rush of blood flood to my groin, and I quickly shook that thought away. Fuck, I didn't need a rock-hard dick saluting the demons who came to call.

Repositioning my legs to cross one over the knee of the other, I rested my hands upon the arms of my throne, faced forward, and nodded. The double doors that led from the entrance hall to the throne room opened at my command, and my first issue of the day was pushed through by one of my followers.

Chapter Seven

Evangeline

Wearing this collar was seriously putting me on edge. I didn't like it. But...
Leviathan's apparent strength and the weird magical power he could wield, put
me in my place fast. I was his captive, in *his* world, elsewhere... I wasn't the one in
control here. If he could make a hallway out of living coral, seal a band of leather
closed, have a crazy beautiful throne room and people he called followers and
loyalists, then I was seriously out of my element.

Even though I was intimidated as hell by it, the idea that magic even existed
had me thrumming with excitement, eager to see more. He was something other
than human, no doubt. And just wrapping my head around that very fact had me
reeling. Magic exists, beings that are more than human exist, and my abductor was
one of them. I just hadn't figured out *what* yet. A wizard? No... I wasn't getting
that type of vibe. Some sort of necromancer? Possibly. I even considered a vampire
at one point, given the sharper appearance of his canines. But the way his green

eyes would glow when his mood heightened, or how his body would vibrate and grow before shrinking back when he was infuriated, had me doubting that theory, too. Which didn't leave me much left to go with.

But this was why I didn't put up a fight against him chaining me to the wall. The irony that my captor wanted to protect me had me rolling, but his explanation of why only further instilled my sense of vulnerability. So, I obeyed like a "good girl" and let him collar me and then took a seat on the pillows, glad that I wasn't sitting on the river rock stone floor. It was drafty in here, and though I had a blanket to wrap around myself, I couldn't stop shaking.

This room was incredible, much like every other space I'd seen so far in his home, which I was beginning to think was more of a palace, judging by the side and the setup. I mean, this room had a freaking throne in it! Like he was some sort of king! Again, another tally added to his intimidation factor.

While the floor was that same river rock, the walls were made of green and seafoam sea glass. They were thick enough that you couldn't see through the other sides, but with the floating jellyfish lighting bobbing overhead along the arched ceiling, it brightened the space. The ceiling itself reminded me of stained-glass windows, only the pattern didn't create an actual picture, but a random spattering of sea glass colours of pale purples, blues, whites, greens, and occasionally, a rare red one. The pillars that lined the pathway towards the throne were made out of dark green granite, with shimmery bits dotting the rock. The wall to our left from the throne had three open archways leading out onto what looked like balconies, but the curtains were closed like the ones upstairs. Their misty sort of transparent appearance obscured my view, so I couldn't get a real grasp on what it looked like beyond.

Leviathan cleared his throat, catching my attention, and I stared up at him on his throne, where his green gaze studied me closely. The throne itself looked like it was carved out of a giant labradorite crystal, the shimmery greens and blues shifting in the drifting light from overhead. The silk cushioning was made of emerald green, and behind it, the wall was decorated with a blue abalone scalloped tiled wall, and a sizeable, strange symbol carved into a bronze plate was set over the peak of the throne's back.

It was all incredible and jaw-droppingly gorgeous, and either this guy had no idea how lucky he was, or he was just so used to it.

"Stay quiet, Evangeline," he warned me as the doors at the end of the throne's path banged open. "Make no remark during proceedings."

Yeah, cuz I have any idea what's going on, I thought, but nodded in promise. I was way too nervous and jittery at this point and kept trying to hold it together. As terrified, confused, and overwhelmed as I was, I didn't want to break. It was safer to just go along with things than freak out, cry, kick, and wallow. If I didn't pay attention, I'd be stuck, unknowing and confused. Understanding and learning would be my key to possibly getting the heck out of here.

At my nod, he settled back into his grand chair and turned his gaze to whoever was approaching.

I heard them before I saw them.

There was a strange growling like a huge, burly animal was coming our way, accompanied by the whimpering and snivelling of someone crying. I craned my head a bit to peer around the pillars, but I was not prepared for what I saw.

A giant-ass snake was drifting towards us, but it wasn't slithering across the floor. It was *floating* through the air! My breath caught in my throat as it neared us, and the longer I stared, the more detail I could make out about it.

It wasn't a snake, exactly, more like a hybrid of that and a dragon. It had no legs but a set of leather wings that didn't honestly look like they had a specific function. They were not what was helping this thing float like a nightmare several feet off the ground. Its face had a long snout, the end sharp and pointed, with an array of white teeth poking out from under its leathery blue lip. The scales on it were a mix of deep-sea blue, black, and white and shimmered under the low, comfortable light of the space. Its head was wide, its eyes on the sides a freaky, glowing icy white that swirled like a snowstorm in its sockets. The creature had webbed flaps behind its gaze, which twitched, fanned open and closed, flickering at every sound in the room like a pair of ears. I think this creature was about twenty feet long, its round body thick and muscled, and as my eyes travelled down, I caught sight of the sobbing human man clutched in the scythe-like arms that were about halfway down its body.

The creature dropped the man to the ground and floated up, its movements graceful as it flowed through the air like it was swimming, straight to Leviathan, who was unfazed by this monster's appearance and proximity.

"Well done, Beast," he murmured, stroking the creature's massive head like it was a cat, even scratching behind one of its webbed flapped ears. The animal leaned into the touch, its milky eyes closing in appreciation of the praise and head massage.

I shall tear their phalluses from their bodies! I will feed them to Beast!

This was Beast?!

Holy fucking shit! I almost started crying with the man who had been dumped on the floor, my heart pounding at the thought of this thing viewing me as dinner. However, at the sound of the small gasp I'd made upon connecting this, the creature's eyes snapped open, its head whipping in my direction, nostrils on the end of its long snout expanding as though smelling the air. Leviathan cupped the side of its head and murmured to it in a strange, deep hissing growl like he was speaking a secret language that the creature understood. But before I could even fathom what this meant, the monster, or Beast, whatever the fuck it was, made a beeline down the steps right toward me.

I cried out in horror and lurched backwards from my pillows, the chain holding me to the wall yanking my head sideways when I moved too far.

Fuck! Fuck! Fuck! I thought, pulling on the cold metal hard as though I had a chance in hell of ripping it from the wall. I stared at the dragon-snake as it swooped down the steps, its body moving in a wide arc to the side as though trying to herd me back to the wall, which I did, as there was nowhere else to go. I thought I was going to pass out. My heart was pounding so hard, my breathing was uneven and quick, and I could feel my lips and fingertips going numb as I unwillingly began to hyperventilate.

Beast swooped low, his face at level with my stomach, and rushed me, moving so fast the only thing I could do in response was brace myself and press my back against the smooth sea glass wall, eyes squeezed shut as I prepared to meet my death in the most horrendous way possible. But as I waited, tears squeezing out of the corners of my eyes, all that happened was a soft bump against my belly.

Nervously, I cracked open an eye and peeked down to see the thing nuzzling my stomach the way a cat would. *What in the ever-loving...?*

"Uh, hi?" I said to it, wondering if it was trying to tenderise me with its nose as its rubbing became a little more insistent.

"He wishes for affection. Grant it to him while I deal with *this...*" Leviathan sneered at the poor man sobbing before the steps.

Okay, I had no idea what was going on, but if I wasn't going to be eaten, that was a plus. Tentatively, I gave Beast a small pat on the head, to which it hummed from deep in its throat, though the moment I stopped, so did he. I pet him again, a little harder this time, letting my nails run up the length of its snout and between its eerie-looking eyes, and the humming intensified. I guess that meant he enjoyed it? Heart still racing, I continued to rake my nails lightly over his head, and he pressed back, demanding more attention.

Okay, I was doing this. I was befriending some crazy giant snake, dragon thing. I wasn't its next meal. Though I felt like I was clinging to life by the tips of my fingers, I couldn't deny that the longer this went on, the more relaxed I felt around it.

"Human!" Leviathan's deep voice boomed from above, echoing throughout the room and back again, sending a deep tremor through my body. "Beast has brought you here because you are guilty of seeking escape." It wasn't a question.

I guess that meant the verdict was absolute. I glanced at the man, who was still blubbering on the floor. Was he like me? Forced here and in some desperation, he'd tried to leave? Would this be me if I made any sort of attempt to get away?

"I-I..." The man's voice was thick and raspy like he'd smoked one too many cigarettes. "I was doing nothing wrong. The creature is mistaken-"

"Beast is *never* wrong!" Leviathan snapped furiously at the accusation against his pet. In retaliation to the remark by the man, Beast turned his head to stare at him with one of his swirly, milky eyes and narrowed it, like it understood everything he'd just said. "What's more, you were found outside of your plane! Why were you climbing the Black Mountains?"

"I was... lost," the man insisted, but even I could hear the lie.

His plane? I thought. *Black mountains? What did that mean?*

Leviathan leaned forward, his elbows on his knees and fingers pressed together before his mouth as he glared down at the guilty party. Beast gave my hand a slight, but insistent headbutt, and I went back to stroking him, letting the hum vibrating up his long throat calm my nerves. "You are a sinner. That is why you are here. That is why you have been punished and sentenced to spend eternity in the eighth circle, for your crimes of fraud are by far, your greatest offense when you were alive."

Uhhh, what? My head whipped back and forth between him and the guilty party. I knew what he was saying, but at the same time... *your greatest offense when you were alive?* Then did that mean... Was I...?

My hands began to shake, my knees starting to buckle as the thought smashed into me. That one time when I'd... when I was sure I'd passed... I remember that haunting feeling of being stalked by something evil and terrifying.

Leviathan...

Sound faded out into a buzzing sort of vibration in my ears, and my feet felt like they'd fallen asleep. I began to sag, only to find myself suddenly bundled up in Beast's scythe-like arms and carried back to my nest of pillows. As I sat there, reeling, seeing, and hearing nothing, I felt his body shift, narrowing. In my deaf and dumb stupor, I glanced down to see he'd shrunk in size, now fitting in my lap like a house cat, his body curled up in a ball, head resting on the top of his snake frame, eyes shut, and I was absentmindedly petting him.

"... millions from those of your kind!" Leviathan was shouting. "You put those vulnerable into poverty and ruin because you stole from them. You took and destroyed and did nothing to right your wrongs. You *belong* in hell. But your lack of penitence and remorse has only earned you alternative discipline..."

"No, no, please!" the man begged. "Please! I cannot go back there! I cannot! The-the demons... it hurts. It hurts all the time. I have suffered. I have paid my price!"

Leviathan's sharp face looked like it had turned to stone. The display of pure loathing, the rage, the burning hostility was evident in his glowing, narrowed eyes. His hands were gripping the smooth arms of his throne as though he was holding himself back from lurching out of his seat to throw himself at the man.

I felt a small, wet stroke on one of my fingers and looked down to see Beast's tiny tongue giving me a small kiss, as though reminding me to keep doing what I was doing. Resuming the careful strokes, I watched, now wholly terrified of Leviathan as he leaned forward, like a hunter, his muscles flexing and pulsating as though they yearned to grow beyond plausibility.

"This is what I hate the most about you humans..." he hissed between his teeth, the ones where his fangs were actually longer than a normal person's, and it only added to the ferocity in which he spoke. "... is that you are so vain. You are all so entitled and reprehensible, yet you are favoured by Him, and for what reason? Why?"

The man shook his head, cowering on the floor as he wrapped his arms over the top of his head like he was trying to hide.

"But what I *love* about humans like you," I could hear the cruel joy in his voice as he changed his tone, "is that I get to take you away from Him. I get to inflict what is deserved upon your damned soul and deny you His love. Each painful torment inflicted upon you is agony for Him, and *that* is something I relish every Earth day." He lifted his hand, and I watched in silent horror as the man was magically lifted into the air, suspended off the floor by a foot or two. At first, nothing happened, like everything had frozen in time before the screaming began.

Leviathan twisted his fingers, and in response, the man began to wail. His bawling increased with every passing second, shifting from one of agony to utmost torture. He flailed in the air, seizing his stomach as though there was some sort of unbearable pain there, his face red and sweating, like the temperature in the room had gone up. When Leviathan suddenly closed his fist tight, his hand shaking as though he was trying to squeeze something, the man's breath hitched, catching in his throat like he was choking.

"Stop... stop it!" I cried, forgetting that I was still holding Beast in my arms. I set him down and lurched to my feet, straining against the collar at my throat, watching the scene unfold like the worst kind of horror movie. "Leave him alone! Stop, please!"

But it was like my voice triggered something in him. Leviathan's shaking, quivering fury unleashed, and without removing his eyes from the poor soul before him, he slowly rose to his feet, and his body began to change.

"You are *nothing*..." His voice began to quake, deepening to a tenor-like rumbling drum as he shot up, his body expanding in every which way. His muscles bulged, ripping through his shirt and pants, the cloak falling from his back as his pale, white skin began to change in colour, turning a grey tone. Two spots in his back began to protrude, like something was pushing against the underside of his skin until finally... they ripped through. Two enormous bat-like wings, with sharp, black claws on the thumbs, flexed and stretched, the fleshy membrane of the skin wrinkled and pockmarked.

Leviathan's height was unfathomable, taller than any human by far, his lean figure transitioning to a bulky, muscular form that promised immense strength.

But his face...

The handsome face began to morph. His caramel-coloured hair darkened to an inky black while two thick, onyx horns ripped out of his skull behind his ears, looming forward like a bull's, in two sharp points. His eyes became that bright, fluorescent, vivid green I'd seen before through his fury. His ears pointed, his face turning that same, greyish colour as the rest of him, still human-like, but harder, meaner, with a wild edge that was inhumane. His nose sharpened, elongating to look like Beast's snout. The upper fangs in his mouth stretched, elongating into lethal-looking incisors, like a lion's only... sharper.

He looked like... a monster. A demon.

I cowered back at the sight of him, his extended, clawed hand still flexed tight, only now, a bright green light was emitting from the cracks between his tense fingers, and the man began to shriek and writhe in pain.

Beams of bright green light shot out from his eyes, nose, and mouth as his head tilted back in a long, gut-wrenching scream. His veins began to glow like they were filled with some sort of radioactive fluid searing through his body.

"You are nothing!" Leviathan boomed again, his tenor now a heavy bass voice that vibrated through my body. "Nothing but a leach! A waste! Undeserving! You are not remorseful, filth! And have proven untrustworthy... for *that,* you shall now face the suffrage from The Great Devourer!"

I scooted back in a ball on the floor, trembling against the wall as my chains rattled together. I felt Beast's long, twisting body as he grew a little, wrapping around me to hide my body entirely from view, leaving enough space between his coils so I could still see. I wish he hadn't because I found myself trapped as I continued to watch, like a car wreck.

Leviathan's fanged mouth suddenly stretched, opening wide, but as it kept growing and growing in size, I screamed at the sight of the burning, green inferno swirling from the depths of his throat. His teeth multiplied and lengthened into sharp points, like hundreds of needles, the rest of his face disappearing as his massive mouth stretched to the side of my own body, and the screaming, flailing man found himself drifting closer, heading straight for that gaping hole.

Slowly, the man was tilted so that he began to float headfirst into the mouth nightmares were made of, and I could do nothing but watch as inch by inch, Leviathan consumed him whole until nothing was left but him, me, and Beast. Leviathan closed his mouth, his demon-like features returning to... well, I guess what normal would be for him in this state.

I just watched him swallow someone... Now was *not* the time to faint, but holy shit, I was close. He turned toward me, his wings flexed irritably, his green gaze still malicious and glaring, and he descended the stone steps to where Beast was still wrapped around me. Each time his foot stomped upon the ground, I swear I felt the palace tremble. When he stepped off the dais, that was when Beast abandoned me in favour of his master, the long serpent body growing back to that long, more dragon-like size. Without him wrapped around me, I felt open and vulnerable, and as Leviathan closed in on me, I cowered back, though it was not lost on me that doing so would not save me from his ire.

My eyes were squeezed shut, my body trembling, as I waited to be devoured like the other human. But when his stomping stilled, the silence stretching out, I couldn't help but peek up over my arms at him. He still looked like a demon, though his face still bore some resemblance to his former self, the sheer size, and extra sharp additions to this side of him had me shutting right the hell up. Not to mention, he was now completely nude, and before I could get a good look at his... ahem... other appendage, I craned my neck back to hold his green, glowing scowl.

"Evangeline..." he rumbled, stooping to one knee before me. One of his huge, clawed paws reached out and even though I flinched back, hitting my head against the wall, he didn't stop until one of those lethal nails was touching the bottom of my chin, holding my face in place as he ducked his head mere inches from mine. His breath was hot, wafting, sending my shoulder-length waves flying back from my face, and it smelled of death. "Do not ever... *ever* intrude upon business matters. Ever again. Do you understand me?"

I'd broken my promise. But honestly, how was I supposed to know that "business" to him meant eating a person alive! Seeing that and the weight of my understanding for my predicament settling in my mind, had me feeling almost catatonic. I was despondent, numb, empty. All I could bring myself to do was mutter, "I do."

"Good," he growled before releasing me, storming back up to his throne, the massive size of it now made sense as his demon body took a seat. "Next!"

CHAPTER EIGHT

Leviathan

As I'd gone through the rest of my appointments, I was pleased when she obeyed my command and remained silent in her little spot. That first human was the only one guilty of an escape attempt, and most of the other issues were more household-related, personal requests from my loyal demons or to settle a dispute between officers. Talking with my followers calmed my earlier fury, and slowly, I began to shrink down. My body painfully forced the muscles, bones, skin, and joints back in on themselves. I'd ordered one of my waywraiths to bring me a change of clothes, as I had a sense of self-modesty. But when I was ready to take some time to investigate further my complicated and confusing feelings toward this little human, I found she hadn't moved from her spot on the floor by the wall.

From what I've seen of humans, they are fidgety creatures, and it is unnatural for them to remain in one place for such a lengthy span of time. As I dismissed the demons I dictated over, I stepped down from my throne to see Beast wrapped around her, fast asleep, his head snuggled beneath her chin as he perched it upon her shoulder. He'd shrunk his size down to comfortably fit around her without crushing her. I could tell that he was taken with her, as the only other living thing he's ever done this to was me. As much as it pleased me to see my familiar behaving so comfortably with my new... whatever the hell she was, time was up.

"Beast, go," I growled in one of the many demonic languages I knew he understood. He let out a huff like he was irritated with me. Raising a brow at him, I settled my hands on my hips. "Are you really going to be a brat about this? Go to! Resume your task!" Beast was one of the few creatures in Hell that could wander practically anywhere undetected. His ability to shift his size helped, and the fact he could silently move through the air gliding along, his wings never making a sound. The moment I stomped before him and Evangeline, he reluctantly uncurled himself from around her figure, and floated away, his size expanding as he went on the hunt for more unruly souls. I turned back to her, and that's when I realised that something was terribly wrong.

Evangeline stared off seemingly at nothing. Her eyes were unfocused, her body tight and rigid from where she was sitting pressed against the wall. Perhaps she was just bored by the proceedings?

I stood before her. "Stand," I demanded, fully expecting her to follow my instructions like before. But she didn't move. She didn't even blink. I furrowed my brow in confusion and barked loudly, "Evangeline! Get on your feet!" But it was like she had suddenly gone deaf. Had she? I crouched on my heels before her and snapped my fingers sharply by her ear. She winced slightly, so no, her hearing was still intact. When I moved my face closer to hers, she shrank away, ducking her head like a frightened animal.

This threw me off. Up until now, even though she's had moments of fear, she hadn't behaved so timidly. Her blunt honesty and frankness when she faced me straight on seemed to be very much a part of her, but now, she wasn't making a sound. Nor would she meet my eyes.

She must be broken.

Well, certainly, I could fix whatever was wrong with her. Scooping her up into my arms, her body shivered like she was chilled, and yet, at this close proximity, she still refused to look into my face. I frowned at that, finding that I wished to see her large, innocent eyes. But they hid from me. Puzzled by this, I stalked out of the room, heading up the stairs in the direction of my private wing. I would get to the bottom of this myself. If not, then I would summon Gnaarl to take a look at her. I wondered if his pet had had a similar, almost catatonic reaction to him at some point during their time together.

Once I barricaded us into my sleeping quarters, I put her back in her cage, settling her carefully on the cushions, and waited for some change to take place. But when she refused to move or make a sound, I found myself starting to panic slightly. Desperate, I found one of the toys I'd put in her space and dangled it before her face, the bells chiming prettily, but she only curled up on her side, hiding amongst the pillows. I threw the toy aside and grabbed the food bowl I'd ordered one of my followers to collect from Earth for her. I held out the strange yellow fruit under her nose. Nothing. The can of... whatever it was, was next... still no reaction.

You must have broken her, Leviathan...

Oh no, no, no! How? How had that happened? Now feeling thoroughly alarmed, I began riddling through the rest of the food, but she turned away from it all.

"Evangeline!" I bellowed, trying to get her to snap out of it. "Enough! Stop it, now."

Nothing. No sassy remark or shift in her expression.

"I said, stop it! Enough of this!" I demanded and gave her a little shake. I could feel her cringe from my touch on her body, that slight reaction to me was now making my chest tighten and compress together. She hadn't retracted from Beast. Just me. *I'd* done something to spark this wallowing. This understanding made me uncomfortable. Whatever I had done, it had changed her personality completely. Though she was quiet and non-combative, she wasn't... the same. It didn't feel right.

Desperate, I rushed to my washing room and filled the enormous tub sunken in the centre of the floor with hot water, trying one final attempt to wake her from this strange stupor before I caved and ran to Gnaarl, seeking his assistance. That would be humiliating, and the thought made me feel awkward and uncomfortable. For some reason, *I* wanted to be the one to fix her. And I bloody well would!

I snatched her up from her spot and carried her into the steamy room and, without ceremony, dumped her into the water. For a few agonising seconds, there was nothing but the bubbles from the impact of her body when it had touched the water, and silence. Until...

Her dark head popped up, her hands wiping her eyes furiously as she sputtered and gasped, coughing the little bit of water that she'd swallowed. I sighed with relief. Thank fuck! I don't ever remember smiling so wide. I felt like my cheeks were cracking. The look she cast me, however, would make even Gnaarl tremble. I swear the fury in her eyes was so evident, I almost laughed at the sight. To see such a tiny, frail, little human such as her give such a look of frightening rage was rather humorous. But, despite the fact she seemed to have snapped out of her daze, she moved to the other side of the tub, which could easily fit twenty beings within. Although, I'd never had such a number in here, it took her only far enough out of my reach that I knew the move was intentional. And she still didn't say a word.

I narrowed my eyes at her and glowered, not liking this attitude and shunning that she had been giving me.

Her hair was plastered to her head and neck, her clothes soaked, and for a brief moment, I could make out the swell of her breasts and nipples through the pink shirt. It caught my eye almost instantly, but she immediately wrapped her arms before her chest, blocking my view. The sight had my cock stirring, again, something that only seemed to happen with her, but I quickly quashed that unfamiliar impulse down as I wanted to get to the bottom of this.

"Why do you shrink away from me, female?"

When I addressed her so, her glare became even more pronounced, and I smirked again. She really did dislike being called what she was, for some reason. I didn't understand why. To my disappointment, she did not answer but simply moved again, turning her face so she could look everywhere but at me.

"Human!" I barked. "I'm talking to you!"

She flinched at the loud, snapping shout, and I saw how she cringed again at the name.

"Female human! When I address you, I expect you to answer. Now enough of your pouting. Why are you removing yourself from me?"

When she still refused to turn to look at me, I decided I had enough. I stepped into the tub, forgetting that I was still dressed in my spare clothing. At the sound of my splash, however, Evangeline whipped around, staring in surprise as I stormed over to her, the water waist-high on me. With a frightened yelp, she struggled to pull herself out of the tub, but my hand reached out like a whip, and I snagged the back of her shirt. I pulled her back with a sharp tug, causing her entire body to submerge again. When she shot up, coughing and wiping her face, I took advantage of her momentary disorientation and wrapped my arms around her back, crushing her to my chest. Being so close to me, her face inches from mine, she raged. Her body began thrashing about with such violence and frenzy that I almost lost my grip on her wet figure. Growling in the back of my throat, I heaved myself up to sit on the floor at the edge of the tub so I could try to maintain a better hold. Though she kept fighting it, at least I could sit somewhat comfortably as I waited for her to tire herself out.

And that didn't take long.

She was so tiny in my arms, her body so thin and frail. I wasn't surprised when she sagged after only a minute or two, even though her face was still craned as far from me as possible. Her chest was heaving from her effort, and my eyes unwittingly drifted down, drawn to the sight of her figure beneath her sodden coverings.

"Look away, asshole!" she snapped. Hearing her scold me so, actually made me giddy. I did enjoy teasing this one.

"I will, if you'll explain to me what has you acting like a Trictep."

Her head reared back, eyes wide as she stared up at me, "A Trictep?"

"A species who follows m-" I began to explain, but she held a hand up before my face, like she didn't want to know. When my breath brushed over her fingertips, she squeaked and quickly yanked it back, withering away like she was frightened. "What makes you so nervous, female?"

"My name is-"

"I will address you as such once you explain yourself to me!" I quickly cut her off, hoping this promise would appease her.

She was quiet for a moment, considering, before she whispered, "Will you please let me go if I tell you?"

No, I didn't like that. But I was frustrated with her silence and desperately wanted to know what had suddenly made her so lethargic. Reluctantly, I released her, and she drifted to the other side of the tub, lowering her body beneath the hot water's surface, hiding herself from my roaming eyes. Evangeline was still silent but judging by the way she was rolling her bottom lip between her teeth, it seemed more like she was considering what she wanted to say. I waited, my patience wearing thin, but found myself entranced by the sight of her bottom lip.

"Am I dead?" she whispered at last.

My brows rose high on my forehead, caught off guard by this question. Did she believe I killed her? "You are not," I said, my voice firm. I *could* kill her so easily, but in doing so and bringing her here had such permanence to it, that I hadn't considered it. I was more curious than anything. Trying to figure out why I was so drawn to her. I fully expected this all to pass once I became bored with her. If she were dead, then I wouldn't be able to send her back. I'd be stuck with her, that is, if I did not allow her soul to venture to Heaven where it likely belonged. So no, I had no plans on ending her life as of yet.

"Then... how am I here?" she asked, her voice lilting slightly, as though she was on the verge of crying.

I stared at her, wondering what she was thinking by that. "Where do you think you are, Evangeline?"

She blinked, her face turning ghostly white, despite the fact she was sitting in a hot tub of water. "I'm-I'm in Hell. Aren't I?"

I held her gaze for several seconds before I gradually nodded, mindful of her reaction.

But she only seemed more confused. "H-how am I here, then? If I am not dead?"

"I brought you here."

"But, how is that possible unless you killed me?"

"Many things in this world are possible. You just have to open your mind to them... the thing is, you humans are so closed off, so ignorant and short-sighted that you miss so much. You are unwilling to see what is beyond your basic understanding of your world and so absorbed in yourselves that you shape the impossible into what you *want* it to be. To suit what you want, what you need, rather than accepting things as they are."

"And how have I done that?" she hissed, obviously offended by my perception of her kind.

"By ignoring the possibility that you can move between your world and the others outside of death."

"Just because I didn't know that was possible doesn't mean I'm absorbed in myself, or that I'm short-sighted. How can I be aware of something I had no knowledge of, to begin with? Not unless it was explained and shown to me?"

I sighed, irritated. It was *such* a human thing to say. "Sometimes, darling, you just need to expand your mind and *believe* in something."

"I don't understand why my being upset about the fact I'm in Hell has anything to do with lack of belief." She glanced around the washroom as though searching for something. "How long have you been holding this hatred in you?" she asked, sliding her gaze back my way.

"What hatred?"

"The obvious hatred you have towards... well, humans. Seems like you were just itching for an opportunity to completely insult me and my people. Why?"

"Tell me why you shrink away from me."

"Why do you hate me?"

"We aren't discussing that. Now tell me."

"I feel like I'm in a conversation with my mom. We've jumped several subjects off-topic, and now I'm lost..." At the mention of her mother, the corners of her eyes tightened, and she quickly ducked her head to rub her eyes. I could see the moisture building up in them, yet she didn't cry.

"Why do you evade me, Evangeline?" I asked, inadvertently amending my tone, gentling it at the sight of her so clearly distraught, despite the fact she tried hiding it.

"You-you..." She sucked in a long, shaking breath, like explaining this was more difficult than she thought it would be. "You... changed..."

"I shifted," I corrected.

"Shifted... into a..." She glanced at me nervously, searching for help as her voice trailed off.

"Into my other form."

I could see that my answer did not satisfy her by the way her lips pressed together, but she accepted it for now and, with a trembling voice, whispered, "You... *ate* that man."

"I punished him," I corrected again.

"You ate him," she insisted, eyes wide, the fear evident in her stare and by the way her voice shook. "You... you ate him and..." Her voice trailed off.

"The soul I consumed was guilty of many things, Evangeline," I explained and got to my feet, disliking how my wet clothing clung to my body. I began to undress, leaving my grey silk shirt on the floor, along with my belt, before turning back to her. "He was not remorseful for anything he had done prior to his escape attempt. Even as he cowered on the floor before me, he was not penitent. He deserves to suffer for eternity."

Her gaze flickered to my stomach like she fully expected to see something there. A small breath escaped her lips, and she quickly looked away.

"I am the Great Devourer... The Gatekeeper... The Dragon of the Abyss. I protect the worlds outside of Hell from the sinners who have earned a place here."

"That man-"

"Was damned." I felt my lip curl at the very thought of him. "Do you want to know what he was guilty of?"

Evangeline winced at that but didn't answer. She appeared... torn.

"Perhaps not. Your innocent ears might not be able to-"

"What did he do?" She had the audacity to roll her eyes at me, but I'll forget about that for now. I wanted her to continue engaging with me. I stepped closer to the edge of the marble floor where it gave way to the deep basin of hot, swirling water and stared down at her. My face was a void, figuring it would be best to explain this without emotion so that she could take in the facts.

"What are your thoughts on those who... what is the word you would use? Scam? Yes, those who scam others? Who deceive?"

She shrugged. "Like those guys that call saying you owe a bunch of taxes or some shit? Yeah, they're annoying dickheads and need to get a life and stop leeching off others."

I arched a brow at her words, a rushing feeling swirling inside my veins at the acidity in her voice. Why did I feel aroused by her venom?

"But I don't think that warrants being eaten alive-"

"He was already dead."

"Fuck it, *eaten* then... I don't think that warrants being eaten!" She shivered again, her eyes leaving me as she curled up on the other side of the tub.

"That man planned fraudulent schemes which robbed many who were more vulnerable than he of millions of dollars," I snapped, hating that she still clung to some remorse for him. "The consequences of his actions left many penniless, lost their homes, their life savings. Some took their own lives after he was through with them, leaving their lives in ruins. Seniors who were unable to make up for what he took, unable to pay for care, their own homes. Those who were widowed, sick, ignorant of the prowling hunters of their kind who would suck their last hope from their hands and leave them with nothing. That human," I spat, thinking of the waste that had sullied the floors of my palace. "Deserved what he got. He deserves to suffer."

Evangeline was shaking hard, the water rippling around her. I waited for her to say something, but instead, once she seemed to collect herself, she pulled herself up over the edge and stood before me, her body bared to me from beneath the transparent, wet clothing she wore. The look she cast at me was strange, questioning. I could see the war she was struggling with within herself. Unwillingly, I softened at the tormented look twisted upon her face and sighed, "There cannot be good without evil, Evangeline," I said, finding myself hypnotised by the chocolate gaze boring into me. "There is always a choice."

"And what choice did you make that you ended up here, as you are?" she threw back at me, her words sharp and piercing. Accusatory. The implication that I was responsible for some fault of mine had my skin crawling.

"I was always here," I hissed between my teeth. "I was always one with the darkness." I fisted my hands, trembling slightly at the thought of her sneering down at me. *Just like the rest of them...* "I have not changed! It is no fault of mine that I am what I am!"

"I never said you were at fault." She tilted her head slightly, drops of water slowly falling from the tips of her wet hair. She appeared utterly bewildered, like she genuinely had no notion of what I was referring to.

"Everyone is a sinner," I spat, turning away to grab a towel hanging from a hook on the wall. I began to wipe my arms and chest down, my movements a little rougher than I meant to. "Humans being the worst of them."

"Worst of what?"

"Of all beings under *Him!*"

"Him who? Do you mean-"

"Do not say his name!" I flashed my teeth at her, and again, my body rippled as my demon wished to tear my body apart. At the sight of my body pulsating like a dying star, she took a giant step back, pressing against the far wall. I spun away and pressed my face into the tile by the mirror, trying to calm my emotions. I sucked in one breath after another, trying to think of something that would calm me.

"You're right..." she said softly.

At once, that angry, vindictive fuel halted its poisonous course, and I glanced over my shoulder at her, surprised.

"Humans *are* sinners. But..." She tentatively let her body relax, standing firmly in place as she watched me, her expression concerned. "Where you're wrong is that you lump us all together. You forget that while everyone is capable of sin, we are also capable of good. The question is, to what degree?" She shook her head at me. "I'm not perfect. I've lied. I'm pretty sure everyone has in some way or another. Hell, when I was eleven, I once took a necklace from my mother's jewelry box because I loved looking at it." The corner of her mouth tilted up a little as though she found the memory of her feeble "crime" humorous.

"That is a petty thing," I said to her. I could not see Evangeline swindling elders or hurting someone. She wasn't capable; I knew it deep down in my bones.

"Still a sin. I stole from her. And that's my point. There are different degrees of it in everyone. That man who you... *punished*... he deserves to suffer for the crimes he committed. He was guilty. I won't compare my stealing my mom's necklace to being on par with him. Yet your obvious hatred to humans seems to paint us all with that same, tainted brush that marks us *all* to be as guilty as he was."

I stared at her, my forearms and forehead resting against the wall, her words repeating over and over in my mind.

"And humans are not the only ones who are guilty," she added, staring at me. "Can you honestly say that you yourself are so virtuous? Like you said... there cannot be good without evil. And that applies to each individual. Human and... and... whatever the hell you are. Pardon the pun."

I could feel my nostrils flare at her words. My rage was simmering away in my gut, while at the same time, I felt oddly off balanced. When she turned and began to walk away, heading back into my private room, however, I snarled and stomped around the tub towards her. "Where do you think you're going?" How dare she try to just leave me? She really was mad!

"I need space, please." She automatically stepped back, keeping distance between us, a flash of fear in her gaze. "My whole world has just been turned upside down. I just watched you... What you did to that man..." She shuddered. "It's not an easy thing for me. I feel sick."

"You cannot leave!" I snapped angrily, reaffirming that fact. She was not leaving! I made that clear. Not unless I wished it.

"I wasn't going to." She sighed, now appearing exhausted and shaken. "I just need to lie down." And without looking back, she walked across the room and climbed into the golden cage, curling up on the pillows, soaking clothes and all, and turned her back to me.

CHAPTER NINE

Evangeline

That whole talk with Leviathan had been very weird. I kept getting the feeling that he was associating whatever I was saying with something not at all related to our conversation. But in his twisted mind, he'd found a connection and became incredibly irritable and offended by it. I decided it was best to put some space between us, not to mention I was still freshly mentally scarred for life from the scene in the throne room. Add in the fact that I had been literally dragged to Hell by Leviathan, who just so happens to be some sort of member of the nobility or high standing demons in this place for... for... I still didn't get *why* exactly he brought me here. It didn't make sense, especially since discovering that he unequivocally *loathed* my kind. Regardless, though, I was in Hell. Demons existed. *Monsters* existed (I'm looking at you, Beast). Oh, and I was physically attracted to my demon-man abductor.

It took a lot for me not to stare at him as he stood there on the opposite side of his miniature pool of a bathtub, shirtless, his muscles shining from the water, his terrifying, monstrous features now back to the humanoid version of himself. Luckily my fear, my confusion, and our argument helped work as a distraction, but when he stormed over to me, I had to quickly think fast and step back, keeping space between us. I could feel something deep inside myself yearning to reach out and place my hand over the sculpted lines of his stomach, to slide it up, and then rest my palm over his chest, curious if there would be a heartbeat there.

But the fucker had made me so furious that it, luckily, had helped keep my sanity in check and stopped me from making a complete fool of myself by reacting before thinking, a bad habit of mine that seemed to get worse the longer I was around him. Just like the word vomit. Not only was I seriously offended by what he was saying to me, but his rage, the pain in his eyes, frightened me. Remembering what he was, what he could do, I knew I needed to just get out of the same space as him.

Hoping to preserve my dignity, and to let all of this information sink in, I needed to be alone. The only place that I had? Well, that was my cage.

My cage...

How stupid was that?

Shaking my head, I shivered as I crossed his luxurious bedroom and stepped inside, still dripping wet, hating that the only clothes I had were now soaked, not to mention my hair was plastered to my head and neck. The selfish bastard hadn't even offered me a towel after throwing me into the massive bath. I stared around at the pillows and blanket, considering using those to help dry myself just a little, when Leviathan suddenly stormed after me, towel and robe in hand, the one he'd been using to dry himself off with was now wrapped around his bare waist.

When he spotted me reaching for the blanket I'd woken up under, he actually hissed, grabbed the back of my sopping shirt, and hauled me out of the cage.

"What is your problem?" I cried indignantly as I tried to rise to my feet.

"My "problem" is you!" He had the nerve to sound annoyed by *me*, when he was the bossy one. "You've made a mess on the floor and were about to ruin the bedding I've had especially accumulated for you!" Before I could even defend myself, the next thing I knew, he pulled my shirt up over my head.

"What the fuck are you doing?!" I shrieked, trying to cover myself.

"Getting you out of your wet things so I can dry you off and change you," he grunted when I flailed wildly, one of my hands managing to hit him straight on the nose. Remembering his ability to dislocate his jaw and how all those insane teeth grew in his demon form, I instantly retracted it and turned away. Wrapping my arms around my chest, I hunched over and tried crawling out from between his legs, all while trying to hide my nudity. Before I could get more than a few feet, he snagged my ankle and dragged me back, my front falling forward onto the soft, fluffy rug, which eased the fall.

"You humans and your stubborn-"

"*I'm* stubborn?" I snapped over my shoulder as he took a seat on the edge of his bed, dragging me to the floor before his spread legs. I averted my eyes from the opening beneath his towel and rolled, twisting my foot free from his hold. I lunged forward again, trying to escape so I could shut myself in my cage, but his fingers snagged the waistline of my wet sleep pants, his fingers with their creepy black pointed nails brushing over the top of the swell of my ass. He pulled me in with an easy tug, so I was standing between his knees, still fighting to run, while he effortlessly held me in place.

"Yes, very," he remarked. "Stubborn and irritatingly impulsive."

"Says the prude who literally decided to snatch up a human girl in the middle of the night for seemingly *no* reason, whatsoever!" I swung back and blindly slapped, hoping to hit some part of him, but only just managed to hit his shoulder. "Now, let me go!"

"Just because I don't know why, it does not mean I acted impulsively." He shoved my hand away. "I had been thinking about it for some time. Now stop your squirming! You're as bad as an imp!"

"A-a what? *What*?!"

"Be still!" he scolded, making me feel like a child before I heard the loud rip of my sleep pants as he easily tore them and my underwear apart. I squealed and threw myself to the floor in a ball, trying to conceal my body. He scoffed. "You have nothing I haven't seen before," he almost sounded bored. "I care not about the exposed human form." Maybe that was true, but just because *he* was used to the nakedness of humans, doesn't mean I was comfortable with it. He took the extra towel and began ruffling my hair with it, helping it to dry, his touch much gentler than I expected, especially since he sounded so pissy.

Tentatively, I peeked out from under my arm as he moved on, patting me dry as he ran the towel down my back. But with the angle I was at, where I was lying on the floor before him, my gaze zeroed into that opening of his towel. He lied. Seemed like his body cared... *a whole freakin' lot!* His hard-on pushed up the towel, tenting it in his lap, hiding the bared length of his dick from my eyes, but from what I could see, it was definitely intimidating as fuck. I quickly ducked my head as he tried turning me over.

"I can do it myself!" I squeaked from my huddle.

"I have taken you under my care. I am responsible for your-"

"Yeah, but I already told you before, I know how to clean up after myself. That includes drying my body off after a bath. So, do you mind?"

He was quiet for a moment like he was deliberating. What was there to think about? He hated me, I annoyed him, and from what I gathered from his earlier reaction to me confirming I could tend to myself, he seemed relieved. So why the hesitation? When I lifted my head slightly and caught his expression, I could see the mixed feelings warring on his face. He looked torn. But the moment he caught me staring, he just rolled his eyes, tossed the towel over me, and shielded his raging hard-on by rising to his massive height and walking away. "I care not, human female," he threw over his shoulder, making me cringe. "It is better you can fend for yourself, for I haven't the time to deal with you and your basic hygiene. Dress yourself in that robe I've left behind. I need to change." And he left me, heading through a narrow archway leading... well, I didn't know where.

Ass. I thought to myself as I quickly took the towel and wrapped it around myself.

I gotta say, though, all of this helped ease my earlier trepidation after seeing his demon form. As much as I apparently bothered him, at least he hasn't morphed into that monster and threatened to eat me like...

I stopped, gagging a little at the memory. *Nope! Too soon, Evie!*

So, I quickly dried myself off and grabbed the rich, plush royal blue silk kimono robe and tied it closed around my waist, my hair damp, but at least not dripping down my back any longer. It fell in ripples around my face, which I brushed away with my fingers, since there was no comb available, and wandered back to my cage, having nothing else to do. And I still wanted alone time.

I stepped in, kicking one of those stupid feathered cat toys out of the way, and curled up on the giant pile of pillows, my back to the room, and zoned out as I stared at the rocky wall, fossils of scallop shells trailing up the wall at the back of the golden bars. I still hadn't really had a moment to process everything that's happened to me in the past several hours. It was all so surreal and unbelievable, but there was no doubt in my mind that this was actually happening.

As the silence extended, everything began to slow and settle in my mind, and I felt what I probably *should* have the moment I woke up in this place.

My heart started to wrench in my chest, my throat tightening as tears stung the backs of my eyes. My mother and father's faces came to mind. I mean, even though they drove me up the wall, their sense of selfishness often left me feeling hurt and conflicted; they were still my parents. I thought about friendly faces at school, my education, my business... I thought about my health. I had been in the midst of trying to figure out my night sweats and fatigue. But I tried to console myself that all of that was probably because there actually *had* been a dark shadow visiting me at night... Leviathan.

As though I summoned him by merely thinking his name, the weight on the pillow beside me shifted. I hadn't expected him to come in here, but I didn't bother looking his way. I stayed where I was, staring at the wall, quickly wiping my tears away, but it was no good. He saw.

"What is this about?" he asked, accidentally poking my cheek harder than he intended, I think, just by the way he carefully stroked the skin before carefully sweeping the corner of my eye to inspect my tears.

"I'm crying," I told him, wondering if he even knew what that was.

"What for? Are you injured?" he questioned, his other hand sliding down the curve of my body, its weight over the silk of my robe shifting the material slightly so that where it crisscrossed over my boobs, it pulled away a bit. I quickly clutched it with my hands, holding it closed and ignoring how hot my skin felt when he moved his hand, now resting on my lower back.

I laughed, but even to me, it sounded hollow. Of course, he would think that the only reason one might shed a tear would be because they got physically hurt.

"You find my inquiry comical?" He sounded genuinely confused, and a little hurt if I wasn't mistaken. But it was just barely. I could be totally misreading his tone. I didn't know this... *demon*... at all.

"Just... typical," I murmured, wishing he'd go away while ignoring that small, teeny-tiny voice at the back of my head that wished the opposite. Almost like, it was enjoying the attention he was lavishing on me. How fucking lonely am I that my subconscious is drawn to a Royal Monster from Hell? Sad, sad, Evie.

"Typical?"

"Nevermind. It's not really that funny." I kept my eyes on the fossils, ignoring the burning feel of his hand on my body, hating how I was stupidly responding to this psycho-dickwad-demon.

"Well, if you are not wounded, why do you shed these tears?" he probed.

"I wish to be left alone, please," I said flatly, ignoring him.

He tensed beside me. Huh, I wonder if anyone's ever really told this guy what to do? I tried to stay relaxed under his hand, which was pressing down slightly, as though he was bracing himself. What if my simple plea was met with raging hostility? Did I inadvertently seal my fate with such an innocent request? I shut my eyes, deciding that I'd rather not see that mouth full of teeth and frightening green light when I met my end, and waited.

But finally, after an unbearable length of stony silence, his posture relaxed the slightest bit, and the fingers on my back absentmindedly stroked my body over the silky material. "Very well, Evangeline. If you wish to rest, I will leave you be."

I was shocked by his accommodation, and even more, by him calling me by my name again. For the past hour, I'd been 'human, or 'female'. I suppose this meant he was no longer angry with me.

He retracted his hand, and I could feel the pillows beneath me shift as he got up and quietly moved away.

"Leviathan? I called, peering slightly over my shoulder. I caught him stepping halfway out the doorway of my cage, his green eyes staring back at me, an endless void and carrying no emotion whatsoever. I couldn't tell if he was just a master of controlling his emotions, if he was bored, or something else. But either way, I appreciated him giving me this, at least. "Thank you."

Though I turned away, not waiting for his response, I did catch the way his eyes flared, his brows rising ever so slightly. I'd caught him off-guard with that. But I was so weary, drained mentally and physically, that I felt like I was about to pass out if I didn't rest my head on the pillows and close my eyes. Because he had been so quiet, his footsteps light as he moved around the room thus far, I couldn't tell if he had left or not.

"You're welcome..." he murmured at last, his voice sounding soft and very far away. But the clang of the cage door told me he was still close by, now locking me in so I could have a moment alone. Though I wanted nothing more than to weep and wallow in self-pity, my body seemed to give up completely, and soon, I was drooling away on my pillow, the blanket pulled over my body, as I passed out into a deep sleep.

The past few days had been frustrating. At least, I thought it had been a few days. For all I knew it has been over a week since I first arrived here, but there was no way to tell the time. There were no clocks in this room, which I hadn't left since that first day. In fact, I'd barely left the cage, except to wander to the washroom from time to time to relieve myself. Other than that, I've remained curled up on my pillows, sleeping, crying softly to myself, and wallowing in self-pity and lamenting.

I was still waking up with night sweats, still tired, and even though at the back of my mind I was feeling slightly terrified of the possibility I was sick again, I brushed it off to the overwhelming and unbelievable predicament I was currently in.

Leviathan, meanwhile, went about his business for the first day or two. Initially, he'd left me alone, locking me in my cage before leaving, however, I noted that he only left the room a handful of times. And even then, it was only for maybe an hour or so. At night, he'd wander over and peer through the bars at me, saying nothing, before he climbed into his huge, luxurious bed to sleep. I'd peer through my lashes at him as he raised his hand, dimming the lights in the room so that the hovering jellyfish overhead cast off the faintest blue glow. The curtains he'd ripped off the windows had been replaced with the same strange falling fog, and when he dimmed the lights, the swirling white mist would turn black, cutting off the warm, fiery glow from outside. In the near darkness, I'd watch as he restlessly turned one way, then the other in bed, as though he was struggling to sleep himself. He would also periodically get up and silently tread close to my cage, crouching on the other side of the gold bars so he could watch me. I always feigned sleep, and whether he was fooled or not, it didn't matter because he said nothing.

I wondered if he got bored with me, would he send me back?

However, instead of getting bored, he got frustrated.

When he saw I hadn't eaten anything in the doggie bowl, he held up the now brown banana before my face, snapping at me to eat it. When I refused, he threw a handful of the stale crackers onto my lap, but I just brushed them off, shaking my head and rolling over. He started acting panicked, then grabbed the can of tuna and thrust it at me, encouraging me to open it and to quote him, "Consume the sustenance within."

I didn't even bother telling him that there was no possible way I could open the can without the help of an opener or a knife or something. I didn't have the will or the energy to fight him or explain. So I just ignored him. In his frustration, he threw another fit, tearing his blankets from his bed, and actually ripping the cloth before throwing it all through the archway leading onto his balcony outside. He raged, further insulting me and my kind, before he stormed out, slamming the door at his back. By now, his temper didn't scare me as much as it had that first day. Though a few times I saw his body flex and pulse, like he was about to transition into his monstrous form, he didn't, nor did he threaten any sort of physical pain upon me.

I simply remained quiet, listening to his unreasonable and crazed scolding, often going completely off-topic to curse humankind, constantly rambling about something to do with being disrespected. His ranting sounded more bitter and resentful to someone else rather than just being discouraged with an unruly pet.

But by now, whatever day it was at this point, I was done with my wallowing.

I was never one to allow myself to get lost in my feelings of self-pity, even when I was really sick. All it did was make me feel worse about myself. All the time spent laying about, feeling like shit mentally on top of my physical deterioration, never sat well with me. And that hasn't changed, even now.

So when I woke up to the gentle prodding of something against my arm, I was ready to get the hell out of this god-forsaken cage.

Rubbing my eyes hard, I stretched, my joints in my arms and legs cracking as I yawned hugely, wondering if I could sneak in a bath in Leviathan's extravagant tub? If he weren't around, I'd feel more comfortable enough to actually enjoy it this time, rather than spend it with him watching me and arguing over proper social etiquette, like *not* staring at a girl while she's trying to bathe.

Thinking about him ripping my clothes free from my body suddenly had my face burning with heat, the memory of it making my stomach jump like I was a ten-year-old girl, and the boy she was crushing on had just said he liked my special pencil.

Leviathan...

Just thinking of his name had me irritated. We hadn't stopped squabbling since I arrived, but it was different. Not outright fighting. It felt more like... teasing? Nah, that wasn't the right word. It's more like bantering or bickering, but I feel like he almost enjoyed it. *Sometimes.*

Again, that little prod at my arm.

"I know, I know... you want me to get up off my ass..." I muttered, my eyes still closed as I lazed on my back, trying to summon the energy to get up. But when I draped my arm over my face, the prodding jabbed me right in my armpit, sending me flying upright in shock. My eyes flew open as I spun around to confront him, only to find Beast next to me.

He was smaller, maybe about the same length as me, his body curled up like a ball python, his serpentine face staring up at me with those milky eyes, reminding me of a cartoon character when it's trying to be super cute and endearing. He pushed his nose into my stomach now, giving me a gentle, nuzzle-like push, like he desperately wanted attention.

I couldn't help but smile and roll my eyes as I reached out and ran my hand over his smooth, scaled body. "You're as persistent as your owner, you know that?" I said to him. Beast simply hummed, the sound deep, melodic, with a hint of an animal-like rumble blended with it. "You know," I said to him as he tilted his head to the side, leaning right into the touch of my nails raking behind those strange flap-like ears of his, "I never thought I'd find a giant snake-dragon thing cute... but you're pretty damn sweet for something so terrifying."

Beast's lids closed, hiding his eyes from view as he hummed louder, pressing back into my hand, and let out a groan like this was absolute bliss.

I laughed and shook my head. "Yep. Cute as hell." Oh God... the puns were non-stop. "Where's your owner?" I asked, now scanning the bedroom, searching for some sign of the brooding figure that was Leviathan.

Beast's eyes opened, and I didn't know it was possible for something with eyes like his, but I swear, by the way his lids arched themselves, it looked like he was cross-eyed, so lost in the head scratch he was receiving from me. Well, it's not like he could talk to me, so judging for myself, it seemed we were the only two here. A perfect opportunity for me to clean myself up in privacy.

I removed my hand from Beast's head, making him sway at the loss of my touch, and got to my feet, my steps shaky with going so long without exercise and little food. Lucky for me, the cage door was open, which made me wonder if Beast was able to open the lock or if it had been intentionally left this way in hopes that I'd be ready to come out? Either way, I wandered over to the bathroom, prepared to wake myself up and possibly explore a little of this place.

As before, Leviathan's private bathing quarters were stunning. The walls were made out of scalloped shaped white mother-of-pearl tiles, the floor a cream marble, and the chandelier overhead was a mix of gold ironwork, pearl clusters, and shining aquamarine stones. The bathing tub sunken in the middle of the floor was massive, the colour a pale mix of blue, green, and white swirls, lashed with glinting lines of gold, the stone smooth and a perfect oval.

I turned the gold taps, the tops decorated with a giant red ruby on one and a blue sapphire on the other, indicating which was cold and hot water, which helped. I guess even in hell, some things are just universal, like the symbols for temperature. And surprisingly, even though the tub was huge, it wasn't long before it filled up enough for me to sit in it without the worry of drowning. I disrobed and climbed in, sighing as the hot water relaxed my muscles and joints. Yes, I definitely needed this.

Sitting on a small, seated ledge in the tub, I relaxed with my head hanging over the edge onto the floor, staring in the direction of the lonely window on the opposite wall; an arched one made of white and aquamarine coloured glass. The shape reminded me of Beast, who, by the way, had joined me in here, curling up on the floor beside the tub, hiding his head beneath his scaled stomach and closing his eyes like he was gonna fall asleep from the steamy warmth of the room.

After a few minutes, I submerged myself completely, soaking my hair, before I found three crystal bottles on the edge, sitting on a gold tray. They looked like they were filled with fancy cream-coloured gel-like soap, so I tried one, pouring a little out onto my finger first to make sure Leviathan didn't bathe in acid or some shit. I mean, he *was* a demon. Who knows that they used to clean themselves? It might not be "human-friendly," but all the gooey substance did was bubble on my hand, the smell reminding me of the ocean, and so I used it to clean my body and another one for my hair.

I found I loved the smell so much that when I rinsed my hair out in the water and found that it lingered, I smiled, happy that I'd have it clinging to me. It wasn't until I realized that it smelled like Leviathan that I crinkled my nose in annoyance. What was wrong with me?

"Enjoying yourself?"

"Holy fucking shit balls!" I screamed, lurching to the opposite side of the tub, my arms wrapped around myself as I spun to see the very ass I'd been thinking of, standing in the open archway and leaning against the stone, as though he'd been watching me for some time. "Don't you knock?" I snarled, scowling at him.

He raised a brow, the corner of his mouth twitching slightly. "In my own rooms? I think not."

"Well, you're sharing with me now, evidently. It would be appreciated if you knocked, so I don't die of a heart attack!"

His eyes tightened fractionally at that, the movement so slight, I wasn't positive that it had even happened, but he frowned at my words like he didn't like my attitude or something. "Well, if you died, you would just end up here anyways. And I *still* won't knock."

"Are you saying I'd go to Hell if I died?" My mouth dropped, this insult hitting me harder than I thought it would.

He shrugged. "Either way, your soul would start here before it would move on to purgatory, and I wouldn't let it leave, even if you *are* meant for the heavens."

"I-I... you..." I gaped at him, his selfishness actually rendering me momentarily speechless. "You are *such* a dick!" I said finally, not managing to find a more classy insult I had planned in my head, and instead sputtered the one I could come up with. "Are you kidding me? You would curse me to Hell even in death? For all eternity? Even if I was meant for Heaven?"

"Yes," he said simply, arms crossed over his chest. His green eyes moved down to the water, which just barely hid my lower torso and privates from sight, but I still crossed my legs, further obstructing the view, just in case.

"Yo, this isn't a free peep show," I snapped, now seriously pissed off. "Can you please go?"

"I can... but I won't."

Correcting my grammar? Oh hell no... "Please leave!"

"No."

I gritted my teeth and glanced around, searching for a towel, as my silky, blue robe had mysteriously vanished. Beast had awoken during our argument, and his broad head was peering back and forth between us like he was watching a tennis match, his gaze somehow managing to look mildly entertained. "Would you please pass me a towel or something, then?" I asked through my clenched jaw, hating that I had to ask Leviathan for any sort of help.

"Certainly." He wandered over to a tall, narrow golden door by the white marble sink and opened it, pulling out those large, fluffy white towels. He held it between two fingers, far out from his body, as he wandered over to where I was in the tub, standing just out of reach, waiting.

"Uh, would you please look away?" I asked him, not budging from the water.

"No."

His one-word answers were starting to get on my nerves.

I sighed hard, reminding myself that hitting this guy probably wasn't the best idea. Plus, I've never been one to react with violence. Not intentionally. I mean, if you tickled me or something, yeah, I'd flail and kick, but that was involuntary. With Leviathan, however, I constantly felt like we were butting heads like he was pushing me to see how far he could go. "Would you do me the courtesy of closing your eyes, then?"

To my surprise, though he hesitated, he shut his lids, still facing my way with the towel held out, unmoving. I think this was as good as it was going to get, so taking the opportunity, I quickly pulled the plug at the bottom of the tub, squeezed the water out of my hair and climbed out, hurrying over to snatch the towel from his light grip, and wrapped it securely around myself. He remained there, eyes still closed, though he dropped his hand to his side, he didn't leave. He just waited.

I couldn't help but stare at him. His androgynous features were just so perfect and beautiful, the colour of his hair unusual, the paleness of his skin flawless and smooth like the marble of his washroom. He really was stunning—a shame that his personality was like... a zero.

"Okay, I'm good," I said finally, watching as his vivid green eyes slowly opened, immediately moving to my face to stare unblinkingly at me. For what felt like an age, we stood there, eyes locked, even as I shifted my weight from foot to foot, feeling suddenly nervous by the heat of his gaze. I couldn't bring myself to look away. Was he hypnotising me? Did he have that ability? "So..." I muttered quietly, finally managing to let my eyes drift away, taking in the sight of his outfit, which was as old-fashioned and stunning as the last one he wore. Black leather pants that looked like they were made out of crocodile skin or something but were probably from the hide of some poor creature here in Hell that I've never heard of. His shirt was a charcoal grey silk, the sleeves rolled back to his elbows, showing off the muscled forearm, the veins running down to his hands catching my eye. Holy crap... who knew that an arm could look so sexy?

The neck of his shirt was unbuttoned some, revealing the collarbone and very top of his chest, the complexion as flawless as his face. He had no jewels, brooches, or other adornments today. I guess for him, this was casual, but he still looked elegant and sophisticated, even with his shoulder-length hair loose around his face.

"So?" he prodded, prompted, and I realized I hadn't continued with my thought, as my mind had zoned out entirely as I blatantly checked him out.

"Uh, my robe..." I tore my eyes away from him and glanced around once more, hoping it would magically reappear, but there was no sign of it. "Do you know where-"

"I have sent it to be cleaned."

I stared up at him, wide-eyed. "Oh... uh, well, is there something else I can put on in the meantime? I'm not picky. I like sweaters and sweats and stuff, if you have them."

"Sweaters... sweats..." His voice trailed off like he was confused. "You wear sweat as apparel?"

"What? No!" I baulked. "It's just what we call clothes we lounge around in. Have you honestly never heard of sweatpants or sweaters?"

"I do not prefer human commodities," he said simply and turned, leaving the room. I guess I should follow? Having no real other option, I did, all while holding my towel securely to my chest. He led the way into that narrow archway he'd disappeared to on that first day, and when I stepped in after him, I froze, too stunned to say or do anything.

This room was freaking magnificent!

It was a walk-in closet, but... it was so much more than that. The room was the size of his bedroom, the walls a black onyx, and it was just filled with crap! And by crap, I mean endless amounts of clothes, jewels, and various accessories, way more than one person needed.

One wall was lined with just shirts, all hovering neatly in the air lining the shiny black stone, arranged in colour and textile. Then there were pants, endless, endless pants, what looked like cloaks, mantles, and wraps. There was a round, gold carousel about two feet in diameter that spanned from floor to ceiling, which peaked high like a domed tower. It was covered in about a hundred belts, leather holsters, and baldrics.

There were glass cases with velvet cushions and cloths laden with hundreds of rings, bangles, embellished cloak clasps in gold and silver, brooches, crowns, and laurels.

One wall was decorated with about a hundred different swords, axes, blades... just weapons. All sheathed or held in decorated scabbards, all arranged so that they framed one sword in particular, a beautiful silver one with green emeralds on the hilt, the blade almost glowing with light. I was no expert on weaponry. In fact, I wasn't even at the beginner level. I had zero concept of what made an excellent blade versus a bad one, but when I saw that sword, I knew it was something special.

Leviathan, however, sauntered in, barely acknowledging any of it, as he wandered over to the clothes and began to scan the endless swaths of hanging material.

"Uhh..." I was vaguely aware that I was shuffling forward, my arms at my sides all limp, forgetting that I was only wearing a towel, as I stared around myself in awe. The floor was decked with a soft, fluffy fur that reminded me of the down hair from a dog's undercoat, the colour a soft grey. "This is... this..." I turned on the spot, taking in every article and richness.

"My closet," he called over his shoulder, his tone as bored as his expression. He finally found what he was looking for, a section near the back of his clothing that looked much finer and more delicate than anything else he owned. In fact, the colours were softer, like pastels, and the material had a gauzy sheerness to it that made me wonder if it was see-through. I couldn't help but wonder if these were his nightshirts, though I hadn't seen him wearing any such thing in the past few days.

It wasn't until he snagged a lilac coloured one and held it out to me that it clicked... these were dresses. They were sleeveless, scoop-necked, fitted gowns that fanned out from the waist, the material much looser around the legs than the chest area. It was also mysteriously my size. I cast him a suspicious glance, wondering how long he'd had these in his closet while I'd been wandering in a bathrobe for days on end.

"Change into this, and then you will eat," he said, as bossy as ever as he thrust the gown into my hands.

"No socks? Shoes?"

He shook his head. "They are not needed. You will not be wandering in areas where your feet will be at risk of injury or trauma."

"Oh... okay?" *Hypocrite,* I thought, glancing at the smooth, black leather boots he was donning. I glanced around, looking for a screen or something to change behind, but there was nothing. And Leviathan didn't budge. I was about to head out into the bedroom to change there when he sighed heavily and theatrically made a show of closing his eyes again, like my sense of self-preservation was bothersome.

I quickly dropped the towel and pulled the dress on over my head, sliding my arms through. The material was so soft and smooth it slid around me like water, cupping my chest and upper torso snugly before dropping loosely around my legs. I thought it would be see-through, and though I could make out the shadow of my tanned skin beneath it, any physical detail was hidden beneath the purple tint. I ruffled the towel in my hair, getting it damp-dry before combing it out with my fingers. By the time I was done and turned back to Leviathan, his eyes were open as if he'd been watching me the entire time.

"Stare much?" I said with a huff.

"Pardon?"

"You're staring. Stop it, it's rude."

"Well, I could say the same for you," he said softly.

"Huh? What? What do you mean?"

"I mean, you were staring in the washing quarters only a few minutes ago. So, if it's so rude, then maybe you should apply that same practice to yourself."

I felt my cheeks burn. He wasn't wrong there. "I'm sorry about that," I muttered, shame-faced.

"Don't be." When I glanced up at him curiously, he just said all nonchalantly, "I enjoyed it. Because then I could stare back without concern of rebuke from you."

Okay, my cheeks were already burning before, but now they felt like they were on fire. "You... enjoy looking at me?"

"I do." He nodded, his green gaze slowly trailing down the length of my body, like he was studying me rather than making me feel like he was checking me out. Maybe that was just his way? "I do find pleasure in staring into your eyes."

Okay, wow. Usually, I'd gag at such a cheesy line, but because of the casual way he said it, I knew he meant it.

"They are lovely eyes, you know," he said, taking a step forward, his gaze now on mine once more. His head tilted slightly, his stare narrowing slightly like he was speculating. "Wide, with long lashes, the colour intriguing."

"They're just brown," I said, my voice sounding oddly hushed.

"Not just brown, but a mix of the shade, with a golden crest around the middle." Suddenly, one of his large hands was cupping my chin, tilting my head toward the light from the black ironwork candelabra nearby, as if he was trying to see better. "Innocent, doe-like... so expressive and reflective of your consistent mood changes."

At once, that lighter-than-air feeling in my chest evaporated, and I came crashing back down, arching a brow at him as I glowered at him.

"Like just now," he smirked, "So easy to read."

"Well, thanks!" I snapped.

"'Tis, not an insult, Evangeline." Ugh, why did he have to say my name like he was savouring it on his tongue? "I find it rather endearing and... entertaining."

"I'm not a toy."

"No, you are certainly not. We have already established that you are a human."

He really needed to stop being so literal.

His thumb suddenly stroked along the curve of my cheek, almost absentmindedly, like he wasn't aware he was even doing it. His green eyes drifted to my mouth, settling there, and stared and stared until I felt my knees begin to quake. Leviathan licked his own lips, his feet shuffling forward ever so slightly, bringing him so close our bodies brushed each other, the heat from him warming me. He turned my face back, angling it toward him, his eyes never moving from my lips, his expression shifting from one of speculation to intrigue.

Before the moment could proceed, I had no idea, but I wasn't even sure I wanted to find out, there came a loud, trilling hum. We both snapped out of our moment and stared as Beast joyously floated through the air towards us, his size now larger than earlier. I swear, the way his body bounced through the air, he might as well have been skipping, and he looked like he was actually smiling, pleased that he found us hiding in here.

"Why are you not guarding the hellmouth, you pest?" Leviathan sighed, rolling his eyes as he released my chin.

Beast didn't seem the least bit fazed by his owner's indifference to his presence and merely made his way over to us, wrapping around our bodies and tightening, lovingly crushing us in his coils; the action therefore also forcing Leviathan and I pressed completely against each other, my chest to his lower sternum. My entire body felt like it was flushing red now, and I struggled to put some space between myself and the hard planes of his body. As I fought to free myself from Beasts' forceful hug, Leviathan firmly planted his feet and sighed. "You are the neediest familiar in Hell! I swear!" he lamented, letting his head fall back, staring up at the ceiling in agitation. "You are the guardian of the gates, and here you are begging for affection! You are supposed to be a hunter! Terror! A devourer!"

At the mention of devouring, I was reminded that Leviathan had called himself the Great Devourer, and I immediately thought of his large, unhinged mouth littered with hundreds of needle-like teeth, all of which were momentarily absent. But the memory itself sent me into a wave of panic as I now desperately tried to free myself, to put as much distance between us as possible, but Beasts' great head came around and rubbed against my chin, humming, and chirping.

Leviathan's hand slid around my waist, holding me still as he reached out and gave Beast the head scratch he had been looking for. The coils relaxed, slowly loosening until we were free and his long, blue scaled body was lying in a lazy heap on the floor, like he'd overdosed on gratification from his owner's attention. I tried to step back, but Leviathan held me fast, refusing to let me put any space between us as he finished giving his familiar the love it had been seeking.

"There, now away with you." He gave Beast a final pat, and the great serpent rose up, heading out the archway with determination, like only now it was ready to resume its duty.

Left alone with him, I went to step away, but once more, Leviathan refused to allow any space between our bodies.

"Why do you suddenly shirk away from my touch?" he asked me point-blank, something I hadn't expected.

"I just... I like my personal space," I said, placing my hands on his chest to push away again, but the moment I felt the defined muscle beneath my palms, I inadvertently shivered. I couldn't help it. It was like some part of me was constantly aroused by the bugger. It made no sense. It was like some weird pull seemed to be reaching for him.

"I don't believe you," he snapped, "Do not lie to me. It does nothing but hinders any sort of understanding between us. Now explain. Why do you suddenly wish to distance yourself?"

"Because you scare me," I blurted out. I don't know why I did. Maybe because I did agree that not telling the truth just left a confused void between people. I didn't like dishonesty, but it seemed necessary at times, like when talking to my parents about my health. With Leviathan, however...

He was right.

"I scare you?" His eyes flared at that, and he seemed... appalled. "How have I frightened you?" He actually did release me then, and I staggered back several steps, crossing my arms defensively over my chest.

"Um, maybe because you're a demon and you've brought me here to Hell for some unknown reason, even to you? Or because I watched you eat someone whole, and now I wonder if you'll do the same to me if I make you mad enough?"

For a moment, he stared at me in absolute shock before his features twisted, and he rolled his eyes, looking more offended than anything. "Please, Evangeline... I have done nothing to you personally to make you think I would curse you for eternity in such a way."

"Uh, I don't know a thing about you. So how do I know that?"

He bit his bottom lip, the sharp glint of his fang digging into the flesh, and for a brief moment, I wondered what it would feel like to have him bite me with those incisors?

Holy crap, Evie! Get it together, you harlot!

I really have no idea where that thought came from... it just popped into my head. I even surprised myself because I've never wanted a guy to bite me during sex or when we were fooling around. I've been given hickeys, yeah, but that wasn't something I asked for or craved. But with Leviathan, the mental imagery of him lying on top of me, his lips pressed to my throat, his teeth scraping over my skin... I felt my flesh prickle excitedly at the thought.

Seriously, Evie. You're becoming a little too "friendly" with your thoughts. Lock it up!

"I suppose this is true," Leviathan said at last, as he pondered over what I'd said, "You don't know anything about me. Although, in my defence, you have been pouting for days on end in your cage-"

"Pouting? *Pouting?*" I asked, incredulously. "You call me being upset about the fact that I've been kidnapped by a demon and brought to hell unworthy of a little need for some alone time? Are you kidding me?"

"Yes, pouting," he said, blamelessly, and that did it.

I marched right up to him, my chest brushing against him as I set my hands on my hips and glared up at him, having to crane my neck nearly vertical to see his face. His green gaze flickered to my breasts momentarily before settling on my face. "Listen here... you can cast blame on me. Seems like something you have a habit of doing. You blame others for any wrongdoing. But have you ever considered that maybe, just *maybe*, you're dodging responsibility for the harm that *you* have done?"

His nostrils and eyes flared at that, and I felt like I saw a spark there, a fury raging in his green orbs that had suddenly been spurred to life. But I didn't care. He needed to hear this.

"You blame humans. You blame *others* for your current circumstance... who they are, I have no idea, but perhaps it wasn't all of them, hm? Maybe your actions, or lack of action, resulted in the way you've been treated. Ever think of that? The idea that everyone else is wrong and that you are the only one right is laughable." His body began to vibrate at that word, and I realized that I was pushing him to the brink of control. Well, you'd think I'd have the sense to stop now, but no. The word vomit kept coming.

"I tell you that you've caused me hurt and a reason to be afraid, but then you spin it to blame me, rather than just accepting that perhaps a human seeing a creature from Hell as terrifying as you would be a staggering revelation. You ask for understanding, patience, and acceptance while giving none in return. Can you not understand my frustration here?"

Leviathan said nothing. He silently fumed, his eyes never leaving mine, the inner conflict in his head clear as day on his face. I felt like he was on the brink of losing his mind or transforming into that other version of himself, but instead, he held it together, taking some time before the shaking ceased, and his breathing calmed.

"Very well," he rasped, his words stilted like he was struggling to speak. "I will... try to amend my... behaviour, so that I may be more understanding and... patient. Is that agreeable to you?"

Huh, I hadn't expected him to actually have listened to me. But the fact that he even agreed to try to be more cordial was a win, in my opinion. So I grinned wide. "Very much appreciated."

"Good, then in return, I ask something of you."

I hesitated, now nervous. I'd heard of the phrase, "making a deal with the devil", but Leviathan wasn't the devil, as far as I knew. So I nodded my chin at him, encouraging him to go on.

"I wish for you to speak plainly to me. It will help me... *understand*, I think. Humans are not something I've spent time familiarising myself with, and I fear I was not as prepared for your arrival as I thought I was." I could hear how hard this was for him to admit. He didn't like saying it, and the tight way he spat the words out made me feel like there was more to this than just saying that he was unprepared for me being here. I wondered if he felt like he had failed in some way? That seemed to be an ongoing underlying indication I was picking up from him each time he ranted about those he disliked.

"Of course, I will," I said easily, "And... I suppose if the roles were reversed, I would feel the same way. I have no idea what demons eat or what you do for fun." I laughed at the very thought of me trying to keep Beast happy in my New York apartment. "So, it's okay."

My words had a profound effect on him. Leviathan's face softened, his brows furrowed, looking both hopeful and contrite. I don't think it was easy for him to admit he wasn't perfect at something, but he sure seemed to appreciate my understanding.

I took his hand, smiling up at him and wagging my eyebrows. "Now, I'm gonna be completely honest when I say that, if you don't feed me in the next hour, I'm going to hunt down Beast and eat him myself."

Leviathan paused for a second, eyes wide in alarm, before tossing his head back, laughing so loudly, it caught me off guard. His smile stretched across his face, a true, genuine smile, and it indeed was a beautiful sight to behold. For a moment, he didn't look remotely demon-esque. He looked... well, like any other man, only a much more handsome one.

"Well then," he chuckled, giving my hand a little squeeze. "For Beasts' sake, let us find you something to soothe your ravenous appetite, hm?"

CHAPTER TEN

Leviathan

I honestly thought that after being around my human for several days, the strange pull I had for her would wane, but instead, it only became stronger. At first, when she'd been sulking in the cage, silent and non-combative, I was relieved. The effort it took to mind her was more than I had anticipated, so I was willing to let her sit there quietly and wait for my intrigue to die.

But the opposite happened.

Her silence and disinterest became worrying, then infuriating. But as days passed, my anger shifted again to concern, and I ended up summoning Gnaarl to speak with him about her behaviour. Thankfully, he reassured me that his Kys had a sort of "mourning stage" when he first brought her to his home. In time, she would want to eat, bathe, and explore. Humans had an innate drive for survival, which would eventually trigger her to care for herself. He advised me to leave her cage open, go about my business, and let her decide for herself.

When I returned to my rooms to find the golden cell empty, I cannot remember ever experiencing such a feeling of... alleviation. Following the sounds of water sloshing about, I soon found her bathing in my washing quarters, looking like some sort of a siren or nymph coming to entrap my soul. The sight of her naked body, wet from the water, eyes closed and face tilted up to the light; I lost my breath as I sagged against the archway, my mind going oddly blank as I drank her in. She hadn't noticed me as she used my oils to clean herself with. Watching her lather it over her form, I couldn't remember the last time any sort of individual body held such a physical attraction to me. In fact, I could feel the blood rushing through my body, heading straight to my groin, the impulse to abandon all self-control and just bury myself in her.

When she began to breathe in the scents of my oils, however, I couldn't help but feel quite a different sensation wash over me at the sight. The little smile she gave as she breathed in the smell, even holding a lock of her freshly rinsed hair close to her face to inhale the seaside fragrance that I was known for, I felt a sense of complacency fill the centre of my chest. This was new. To see someone revel in something that was so clearly a part of me, to seek it out and savour it, I couldn't help but wonder if this is what it felt like to be enough for someone?

I've never been the first choice.

I've never been one whom others sought out, admired, or coveted. So to see this beautiful female relish such a personal part of me, who I was as a being, moved me more than I thought it would. And with that feeling, all I wanted was to interact with this little human after so many Earth days of silence.

As I brought her downstairs to search for some food she would be able to consume without getting sick, I thought about the scolding she'd given me in my dressing rooms.

Maybe your actions, or lack of action, resulted in the way you've been treated.

Was there something there? The stubborn side of me refused to believe that. So I let her preach all she wanted. I reined in my displeasure with her accusation that

I was at all at fault for my treatment in Heaven, hoping she'd tire herself out. If I agreed to be amiable, she'd desist, and we could move on. But I'd underestimated how complex a human could be. With her easy agreement to continue to be honest with me, I would hopefully have more success in figuring out why I was so drawn to her and ending this silly charade.

I'd requested for lunch to be arranged in my courtyard, deciding that a change in scenery was in order. As we stepped outside, her mouth dropped as she turned her head this way and that, staring all around as she took in her first peek at Hell. I was hoping she would behave as she had with my other rooms in my palace, but instead, her reaction was the opposite.

"Holy shit!" she cried, pulling her hand free from mine as she stared upwards at the rocky canopy overhead. I studied her face, noting how distressed she appeared by how her brows furrowed and how she practically clawed her nails into her cheeks. I didn't like that. It would damage her pleasing facial features. If there was one thing I knew about humans, they didn't heal as demons could. I snatched at her wrists, pulling them away from her face before she could harm herself, and followed her gaze.

She was staring at the hellmouth, the large, carnivorous opening lined with thousands of fanged teeth, a red light radiating from it, the warm glow from the fiery Phlegethon only adding a rather daunting effect to the sight. From the opening, humans fell.

Bodies of the damned, of the sinners on earth, tumbled out of the mouth, their bodies defying the laws of gravity as they rolled along the rock of the cavernous dome that shrouded the royal kingdom of Hell. They tumbled along the wall, down, down... where they would disappear in the space lining the black obsidian mountains and the fiery river that surrounded our dimension, and then would be sorted into one of the nine planes to suffer for all eternity.

I'd never really thought much of it in all the time I've been here. It was just that—the hellmouth. But I suppose... being a human, such a sight would be somewhat disconcerting. Perhaps bringing her outside wasn't the best course of action.

I looped my arm behind her head, bringing my hand around to press over her eyes, shielding the view from her sight, and called to my waywraiths, "Please move our luncheon to the Temple." I figured if any spot outside worked, it would be my sanctuary. The temple was a circular cella, with Corinthian columns lining the outside. Her view of the hellmouth would be obstructed by the roof, but she would be able to see the gardens around us, the walls blocking out everything outside of my kingdom.

"Wh-what the hell is that?" she asked, shrinking into my side, her body shivering. The moment her words fell from her lips, she groaned, "I'm never gonna be able to say 'hell' again without thinking of the irony here..."

"Do not concern yourself with it. We are relocating," I told her, wrapping an arm around her waist while still covering her eyes. She weighed nothing to me as I carried her through the ether, our trip much shorter as we were not travelling far and emerged in my private gardens. I didn't stop until I toted her down the winding path that led to my private sanctuary, the stone structure bearing the symbol of me and my kingdom over the entrance, and we stepped inside. Only then did I remove my hand and reluctantly let her go.

Evangeline sagged away from me, bending over at the waist, her hands on her knees as she sucked in one long, deep breath. I watched her, nervous, wondering if she was going to faint. I've often seen humans faint when they were brought to me, and I shifted. But I was unsure of how frail she was. At first glance, given her delicate figure, I assumed she would be fragile, but her spirit was anything but. So, it was no surprise when she eventually righted herself and peered up at me, pale and shaken but holding herself together.

"So... will you tell me what that was?" she asked, her voice soft and uncertain.

I kept my eyes on her, noting every move she made, every flinch or shiver, always studying. The more I learned about her, the sooner I was sure this spell would end. "Tis, the hellmouth."

"The-the hellmouth?" Her eyelids fluttered at the word like it was something she'd never heard before, and was struggling to wrap her mind around the concept.

"The entrance to hell. The way in."

She nodded, taking in this information as her eyes stared off at seemingly nothing, her busy mind working away as always. "So those people... the ones who were falling..."

"They are the damned."

"Damned. So, they're..." she sucked in another large gulp of air as she struggled to keep up. "They were bad people?"

I could feel the corners of my mouth twitch, but I fought down the urge to crack a smile. Her words were so innocent, so naive, her large, doe-like eyes wide and lovely. I wanted to scoop her up in my arms and squeeze her like one might a hellhound pup. I quashed that urge down, holding myself back as I reached out and cupped her face, allowing myself only this as I tried to reassure her. "They were unworthy of Heaven and His love. Guilty, evil... they deserve their fate, Evangeline."

She nodded, still clearly shaken, but didn't pull away from my touch. That was, until her eyes darted to the side, and whatever sight she beheld had her shrieking and lurching away, racing around to the back of the temple where the statue of Beast was erected. I spun to face whatever had scared my human so, wishing I'd brought a blade or two, but at the sight of my waywraiths making their way over with the platters of food hidden beneath the silver domes of dishware, I relaxed, breathing a sigh of relief. I don't know what I thought she saw there... but I'd been ready to tear it to pieces if it had dared to touch her.

Now that was a strange impulse, I thought. I hadn't expected such a protective impulse in response to her. Another side-effect of human companionship?

My waywraiths scuttled about, setting up a small, round table in the space before Beast's statue, and arranged the platters nicely in the centre before they hurried away, knowing I liked my privacy. I turned to Evangeline, holding back the urge to laugh at how she tried to tuck away behind the marble coils.

"I never would have taken you for a coward," I baited her.

Sure enough, her little face suddenly reared up from behind the statue's tail, her brows tucked low over her eyes as she glared heatedly at me. "Oh, I'm sorry! It's not every day that I just happen to come across a bunch of... of... mutant crab-fish wandering around!" she snapped, straightening up and tip-toeing out from her hiding place.

"You know I wouldn't let them harm you," I said easily, pleased that I was able to predict her response to my teasing.

For some reason, my statement had her cheeks turning pink, something she did when embarrassed or... when I caught her staring at me. I don't know why this made her respond this way. I had told her she had nothing to fear during her stay. I've never felt an impulse to hurt her or see her hurt. Although I have come very close to administering some form of discipline, it wasn't the same as punishing the souls of the sinners brought to my throne room.

I decided not to address it as I pulled a chair out for her to sit on. She crept forward, casting me a quick, puzzled look before taking the seat so I could slide her forward into place. I took the chair opposite, resting easily enough as I lounged, while she sat upright and stiff, her nose crinkled. Why was she acting like some sort of unpleasant stench was fouling the space? I reached for one of the cloche coverings and pulled it up to reveal the fabulous meal I'd ordered for her.

I thought she would be impressed, or at least dive into the dishes I'd requested on her behalf, but instead, her eyes nearly bugged out, and she gagged. Confused, I set the cloche aside on the white stone floor and peered at the steaks, taking a whiff myself to make sure they smelled right. Sure enough, they were perfect. The meat cooked just right, steaming, with a pile of my favourite vegetation grilled on top. Yet, Evangeline looked like she was ready to heave.

"What ails you?" I snapped, frustrated.

"Th-that!" she exclaimed, turning her face away as she covered her mouth.

"The food? What is wrong with it?" I was seriously offended that she should turn her nose up at one of my favourite dishes. I wanted to share it with her, to see her enjoy it as much as I did. Instead, it was like it wasn't good enough for her.

Just like everything else about you in your life, right, Leviathan? You're never good enough for... I quickly shut down that poisonous train of thought in my mind and sucked in a long, deep breath between my teeth, grasping for control.

Let her explain. Let her speak so that you may understand. She promised you honesty.

"It's... it's green!" she groaned, her voice muffled by her hands.

"Yes... it is," I confirmed, still baffled.

"Meat isn't supposed to be green! It's supposed to be red! And... the smell..." She gagged again.

Ahh... perhaps this is another oddity, a difference between worlds. I knew the Prince of Gluttony, Triel, partook in human food, but I never ventured to. I thought about when I saw Gazaat attempting to feed his human the meat he'd obtained in our realm... she had refused it, too. Perhaps it was not easy to digest for them? Well, this made things a little more complicated.

I removed the cloches covering the rest of our meal, and though her response was still hesitant, she did not look as disgusted as she had with the steaks. Ruefully, I recovered the meat and summoned my servants to remove it from the table. At the reappearance of my loyal staff, she squeaked in alarm as she watched them move silently around us, cringing back ever so slightly when they brushed by her.

"You needn't be afraid. They will not harm you as they know you are mine," I told her, grabbing the empty, pale blue sea glass plate before her, and piling it with things I thought might be easier on her stomach.

"What was that?" she asked, apparently too distracted by the sight of my servants as they disappeared inside to listen.

I shook my head, sighing as I scooped up some of the delicious fruits from my own personal greenhouse and stacked them high. When I set the plate back before her, Evangeline studied everything carefully, taking small whiffs and poking at them as though fearing they may jump up and attack her. Rolling my eyes, I helped myself, watching her out of the corner of my eye, amused by her hesitancy. She must be starving, but watching her act like any of this could possibly hurt her was more entertaining than anything.

"This apple has pimples..." she muttered, picking up one of the pink *fromm's*.

"It is not an apple," I informed her, settling back in my seat as I chewed some fresh baked sweet bread that I'd covered in green *jitteroo* jelly.

"What is it, then? Do I just bite it like..." she brought it up to her mouth, and I nearly choked on my bread as I quickly righted to stop her.

"No! No, never bite into a *fromm*!" I snatched at her wrist, halting her.

"Why? What happens if I do? Are you telling me this zit-covered apple will attack me if I bite it? Are you serious? How the hell am I supposed to eat if I can't bite anything?" She was beginning to panic, and I could hear how her stomach began to rumble even from here.

"Calm yourself. And again, it is not an apple. A *fromm's* core is poisonous, but the bulbous spheres you see coating the outside are plenty safe. You twist them off like this, see?" I grabbed one of the round bits and turned, quickly tugging it free, and plopped it into her other hand.

Evangeline looked tearful and overwhelmed, and I had no doubt it was because she was so hungry. I realized then how different our worlds really were. I'd have to instruct her on every dish, it seemed. I discarded my bread and shifted my chair to be seated close to her. This was probably going to take a while...

Nervously, she held the ball to her nose, sniffing, but a *fromm* had no smell. Not until you bit in. But it pleased me to see her trust in me building as she held it before her mouth and took a tiny nibble with her teeth, testing it out. As soon as the taste hit her tongue, her eyes widened, and she smiled.

"Oh yum! Yes, that's what I'm talking about! It tastes kinda like... whipped cream. Only with a thicker texture." She said as she popped the entire thing into her mouth and chewed, sighing contentedly. I felt immense relief at the sight of her devouring the rest of the bulbs and decided on giving her some of the sweet bread I'd been enjoying. She loved that and the *jitteroo* jelly, which she claimed tasted like a mix of fruit on earth called peaches and raspberries.

For the next hour, I fed her, explaining what things were and how they were obtained in Hell. I felt incredibly smug when she seemed impressed that I grew all, if not most of it, right here in my kingdom. When my servants came around to clear the nearly empty plates, the realisation that I'd spent more time smiling, amused simply by watching her explore the tastes that were offered, finding that for once time didn't crawl, but it rushed by. I couldn't quite remember the last time I'd enjoyed something as simple as a meal.

Evangeline had tried to explain which food reminded her of things back where she came from, but some of it she admitted was utterly foreign to her, though enjoyable. I made notes about which ones she had the biggest reactions to, so I could remember to order those specifically for her. She was somewhat frail and had grown even more so after her time spent locked away in the cage. I didn't like that.

"That was amazing," she grinned up at me, the sight of her smile making my breath catch. "Thank you so much."

"You're welcome," I murmured and ducked my head over the table, hands clasped, hiding my pleasure from her.

"So... Leviathan." She tented her fingers together, elbows resting on the table-top as she leaned towards me, that mischievous look in her eye telling me I was in for a round of questioning. And I wasn't wrong. "What exactly is your role here?"

"My role..."

"Yes. I don't know much about religion to be familiar with your name and who you are."

"Who says I am anyone of importance?" As much as I wanted to boast to her, I worried that she would see me as inadequate. I was not the King, the Devil. Nor was I the ruler of a lavish, prosperous kingdom like Riker or embodied the sensuous allure of Asmodeus. I liked to think I was better than some, but I was not the first choice. As quickly as the flickering euphoria that had spurred to life in my stomach had come, it was replaced promptly with burning resentment.

Lacking, Leviathan. Always lacking. Never enough... never enough...

"Obviously, you are. You have a palace. Servants. I mean, you have a freaking throne room, for crying out loud! So, tell me, who are you exactly?"

I pressed my lips together, choosing to stare fixedly at the statue of Beast. I didn't want to see the disappointment on her face when I told her. I even considered keeping her in the dark, but... we had struck an accord, to be honest, as it would help our understanding of each other.

The sooner you understand what these feelings are for her, then the sooner you can move on with your life, Leviathan, I told myself.

"I am... the Great Devourer. The Ruler of the Chaotic Oceans," I sucked in a long breath, hating every part of this, wishing she hadn't asked. But a vow, even to me, was a vow. Honesty. "I am Dragon of the Abyss, The Gatekeeper, Grande Admiral..." I listened for some sign of recognition from her, but she gave nothing away. Perhaps she truly was uneducated about the possibilities and tales humans had managed to obtain of my world. "I am forever cursed, the tainted angel who fell from the Heavens with Lucifer. I am Leviathan, the Prince of Envy."

I braced myself for her response, waiting for her to ask about the others, to inquire about the greater princes, or the king, to learn about them. The thought of her interest pulling away from me to another was surprisingly... painful to bear. Her rejection. By all that was holy... this human had been around me for only but an earth's week, and she'd sunken her claws into me so deeply.

"Envy..." Her voice was hushed, "So... the seven sins?"

Here it comes. Her request to hear about the others. Her wish to see them, to meet with them and fall under their spell, or worse. The reverse. The thought of Lucifer taking a fancy to her spurred on that spiteful bubble that was still boiling away in me, tormenting my being. "Yes," I hissed softly.

"Why..." She sucked in a sharp breath between her teeth, her voice oddly quiet but no less curious. "Why do you call yourself the "tainted angel"?"

"Because that is what I am." I closed my eyes, regretting my promise, to be honest, more and more with each passing second. "I was not created in Heaven. Not like the other angels. I was always... *here*. From the Abyss. This is where I first drew breath and took form. It was *He* who pulled me from here, who forced me to become something I wasn't. I was always the serpent, always meant to devour, take, and spread chaos. He then tried to make me something I wasn't, and every time I displayed signs of my true being, I was looked down upon by the other angels..."

I still could not bear to look at her. How could I when I was telling her how I was never a true angel but rather the first beast He created? One he tried to tame and control to be what *He* wanted, rather than accept me for what I was? "He would not let me seek to rule over what I was designed for... until finally, He granted me the oceans, but every day that I lived amongst the angels, I was always seen as contaminated, never enough, not pure enough, not *worthy* of His love, or any love. And then, the war came to Heaven, and I chose my side."

A long silence followed this, and though I was terrified to see the look of horror on her face, the temptation, the pull, was too strong to ignore. Hesitantly, I opened my eyes and slowly turned my gaze to the little figure on my right. But Evangeline's face was anything but horrified.

Instead, her wide eyes were shining, her mouth slightly open as she watched me closely, the staggering weight of the compassion in her gaze hitting me like a blade to the gut. She reached out for one of my hands, which was splayed over the tabletop, pressed into the marble, and carefully brought it over to her lap, her fingers intertwined with mine, and squeezed it.

"I am sorry that you have lived for so long carrying such... *misery* and tortuous thoughts in your head," she said at last. I sensed that she wished to say more but was hesitant, no doubt concerned for my reaction.

"What else?" I prodded, eager to know, despite the genuine possibility that it could anger me.

"Well, did anyone actually call you that? The Tainted Angel? Or is it a name you gave yourself?"

I thought about that. When did that name begin to reverberate in my mind? When did I first hear those words? It was strange, but I couldn't remember a moment, nor a time when I could remember hearing someone utter such a thing to me. I *do, however*, remember sneering at His love for his humans, calling *them* tainted, that they were not enough and were undeserving of Him and His...

"Perhaps," she said, gently, "The name is something you conjured in your mind? Your fear of losing the acceptance and love of the others was masked behind this idea that you were unwanted? Unworthy? That it was easier to assume they did *not* want you to begin with?"

I clenched my jaw and shook my head.

No, all my existence, this was what I carried with me. That had to have sparked from somewhere. How else would I have conjured such feelings of bitterness, rivalry, and malice?

"Don't answer that now," she said, after seeing the conflict on my face. "It's okay. But thank you for telling me." Her gentleness and sincerity at this moment were more than I could ever have dared hoped for. The feeling rushing through me from her kindness was wondrous, the warmth I felt in my chest comforting rather than harrowing.

Her lips curved up a little, the smallest smile forming on her face, perking those plump, pink lips of hers just begging to be kissed.

That thought made me freeze.

Since when have I desired to kiss anyone? Ever? I was not known for promiscuity. It was never something I felt compelled to seek out. But as this kind, sweet little being at my side held my hand as I confessed the most guarded and sensitive part of myself with acceptance and no harsh judgement, I felt compelled for the first time to explore a side of life that had never captivated me.

We were still in our seats, the silence of the gardens hiding us from the prying eyes of others, and as I shifted my body towards her, she responded, meeting my gaze straight-on as always. I reached out with my free hand and cupped her sweet face, her skin soft under my touch. I leaned in close, gauging her reaction. She'd been afraid before, after witnessing my punishing power. But now, she only appeared a little puzzled, if not slightly dazed. Her pupils expanded, blacking out the beautiful browns and golds of her eyes, the pulse at her throat jumping quickly as her heart hammered away. How I wished to feel it... the life source that powered this tiny, seemingly insignificant human. I let my hand trail down the side of her neck, pausing once over the racing artery to feel it jump and skip beneath my fingers before I brought my palm down, resting it flat over the middle of her chest.

Her eyes widened in surprise, but she did not pull away as I feared she would. Gently, I let my forehead touch hers, our eyes locked, sharing each other's breath as I kept my hand over her heart, sensing the pure, beautiful soul that it kept beating, and was grateful for it.

I was *grateful*.

Grateful that this little human was alive. That she was unmarred by the evils of the world, untouched by the punishments and cruel games we play.

"Evangeline..." I whispered, loving her name on my tongue.

"Leviathan..." Her voice was as soft as mine, and as she spoke it, I closed my eyes, savouring the sound of it moving past her lips.

"Say it again?" I pleaded.

"Leviathan."

I hummed deep in my chest as I cherished this moment. For once, I felt connected with another being. The fact that she was a human mattered not. She was *my* human, and I had no intention of ever letting her go.

Unable to resist any longer, I closed the space between us, lightly pressing my mouth to hers, curious about this craving. The moment I felt her lips move beneath mine, I understood completely. At first, I was hesitant, but eventually, with her guidance, I picked up the rhythm she set for us and followed suit. She tilted her head to the side, her mouth opening as she kissed me back, the realisation that she was not pulling away only elating me more as I eagerly explored this new phenomenon.

But when my hand shifted, my curiosity got the better of me as I sought to delve into other fancies I've had in the past, she *did* pull back, though not entirely out of my reach, and she continued to hold onto my other hand, still clutched tight in her lap.

"I'm sorry," she whispered, sounding breathless, "I-I don't know... I don't know what that was. Why I..."

She appeared to be struggling with some inner turmoil, so I quickly set the record straight. "It was my impulse, my initiation. If you are feeling any sort of shame, please do not, for the fault is mine."

But Evangeline just shook her head, her eyes still shining like before, but seemed to be a little more distressed now. "It's not that. I'm not... I think I'm just... confused."

I nodded, understanding. Confusion seemed to be a shared sentiment between us. "I am rather distracted, as well. I have never done such a thing before."

"Never?" Her gaze widened with shock.

I shook my head. "It was never something I had a desire for... there was no one I wished to partake in the act with. Until now." I bowed my head over my lap. "I apologise if I have made you fearful or-"

"No, please don't," she quickly cut me off, "It's not you, it's... well, it's me. I know that saying is deceptive, but it's true."

"I have not heard it before."

"Really?" She chuckled. "Well, great! I'll use it now. It's not you, it's me. It's just been a long day, and I think I'm feeling a little lightheaded and tired."

Again, I knew nothing about how often humans required rest or sustenance. So if she claimed she wished for it now, despite the fact she has only been up for a few hours, I wouldn't question it. I rose to my feet, "Then allow me to escort you back to my rooms."

CHAPTER ELEVEN

Evangeline

What was wrong with me?

When Leviathan moved so close, his eyes were burning, the heat radiating from him seeping into me like a spell, I completely lost my mind. I felt like I was in a trance, a pull from my body to his urging us together, and when his hand rested over my heart, I was done. I had no sense like there was no conscious thought in my head that could rationalise anything at that moment. All I knew was what I wanted, and what I wanted was for him to kiss me. And he had. His lips were soft and supple, inexperienced but eager, and before long, I fell into the most intoxicating, addictive encounter of my life.

Kissing Leviathan had my head spinning, my body reacting and responding to every part of him. I drank in his seaside scent, clung to his hand, loving how smooth his skin was and the contrast to the strength I knew he had. But I wanted more. It wasn't until his hand began to creep to the side, inching toward my breast, that my mind suddenly snapped out of my rapture. I was making out with a demon... and not just any demon, but the sin of Envy himself. The first beast created by God, a Prince of Hell, not to also mention my abductor.

All I remembered thinking was, *Way to go, dumbfuck!* before I pulled away, though I could not bring myself to release my hold on his hand. Not after what he confided in me. Although my mind was reeling with everything, another part of me had its own agenda, and all it wanted was him. So I compromised. I'd stop this before it got out of hand and take some time to try to grasp all of this while still preserving his feelings. Because as terrified as I was upon learning his identity, I still felt intense empathy for him... despite everything. Everything that he was, that he's done, and what he would continue to do.

There cannot be good without evil, Evangeline, he'd told me, and he was right. In nature, there was what we classified as good and bad. But life isn't that simple. It's more complicated than that. What he was, what he did, was necessary because his sin exists in all of us. But like he'd said, our choices, on whether or not we give in, guide it to the direction of grace or impiety.

But I couldn't just let myself snog him just because some weird pull between my legs behaves like it has a mind of its own.

Okay, okay, it was more complicated than that. The feeling was more like... *longing.* A desire so strong I've never felt anything like it in my life. As corny as it sounds, it was like a magnet had been implanted in my chest, and its counterpart was in his... the lure indescribable beyond that.

The only part about all of this that was reassuring was the very fact that, as I looked up into Leviathan's bright green eyes, I could see the same lustrous yearning I was feeling. I wasn't the only one affected by the other. And when he brought me back to the bedroom, I wearily lay back up on my pillow in the cage and closed my eyes, re-living today over and over in my head until I fell asleep.

"Evangeline!"

My eyelids snapped open, my breathing quick and raspy. I stared up at the domed roof of the cage, the gold glinting in the light overhead, feeling like my heart was racing as if I'd just tried to run a marathon. I felt sickly, covered with a sheen of sweat, my lips dry, the feeling of fatigue still with me. But someone was shaking me, forcing me to stay awake. "What is it?" I yawned, rubbing my eyes. When I fought to open them again, it was to see Leviathan crouched over my figure, sitting on his knees, his hands on my shoulders, and his face etched with panic.

"You were crying out, and your skin is clammy and flushed." He lifted one hand to carefully touch my forehead and cheeks, brow furrowing as though he didn't like what he saw.

"I've just been having some night terrors for the past month and a bit," I grumbled, hating that they suddenly decided to make a reappearance after a few days of nothing. I assumed Leviathan hadn't been solely responsible for my nightmares and temperature fluctuation. I sat up, much to his objection, insisting that I lie back down and sleep some more. I wanted to laugh because all that shaking he'd done seemed to have done the trick in waking me fully. But his concern was kind of... well, sweet.

"It's okay. Once I wash up, I'll feel better." I yawned and stretched, my arms and legs cracking. As cozy as these cushions were, it wasn't the same as lying on a nice, big mattress. When I opened my eyes again, however, he was sitting upright, staring at my body with his mouth hanging slightly open. I peered down at myself, realizing that I was still in that gauzy, lilac gown from earlier, and right now, it was moulded wholly to my figure, every curve accentuated and on full display. Judging by the look on Leviathan's face, I might as well have been one of those stinky, green steaks he seemed so eager to eat earlier, all splayed out for him on a silver platter.

Let him look, a voice whispered.

Goddamn, Evie! Pull it together! I quickly rolled away out of his reach, hiding my figure from him, and wandered through the open door to the cage and into the washing room. I bent over the white granite sink, running the water, splashing it over my face, and rinsing my mouth out. I seriously needed to get a grip. Whatever this weird attraction was I had to Leviathan, the more time I spent with him, the stronger it seemed to become.

I dried my face on one of those soft, fluffy towels and turned to find him watching me from the archway. The heat from his stare was still present, and his eyes trailed away from my face, lingering over my body like he'd never really taken the time to look before. Self-consciously, I crossed my arms over my chest, now suddenly shy and awkward as I remembered our heated kiss. What was he expecting from me now that I allowed that? He'd been respectful when I indicated that I wished to stop. Would he remain that way? He *was* a representation of sin, after all. He could technically do whatever the hell he wanted.

"Are you feeling better now?" he asked at last.

I stood there for a minute, trying to figure that out. Physically? Yeah, I was feeling okay now. Mentally? Not even fucking close. "I'm alright," I said finally.

A scowl curled on his lips. "Honesty, Evangeline. Remember your promise?"

I sighed, frustrated. He was *really* clinging to that. "Physically? Yes. I feel better."

"And in what way are you not?"

Why was he pushing this? I shook my head at him and crept past, heading back into the bedroom. "It doesn't matter." Not a lie. Just an omission.

"It does matter," he countered, following me closely.

Wanting to escape him and his insistent pursuit, I wandered out to the balcony, the strange, misty drapes so soft against my skin it was like being kissed by a cloud.

I hadn't been out here yet, and the half-moon stone terrace's view was absolutely breathtaking. Breathtaking and inconceivable. We overlooked what I could only assume was the Kingdom of Envy. Despite how beautiful the inside of his palace was, the land itself was actually... horrifying.

It was a vast plateau of black rock, surrounded by strange, dark mountains that shone from the fiery light beyond. A strange mist was shrouding parts of the plain while hiding sections from view, but they were massive and extended so far that it felt like I was looking over several football fields. What gave it an even creepier edge, was the nearly thirty-foot-looking monsters that roamed in the mist. They were incredibly slender, their limbs long, scraggly, fingers about the length of my body, crooked and bark-like in appearance. They had no necks... just shoulders that hunched up around their dome-like heads and one large, lamp-like eye in the centre that cast a light beam through the fog. They wandered aimlessly, like they were searching, their steps large, lumbering, with shredded pieces of cloth hanging in rags from their backs. Overhead, there was still that same, cavern-like dome that hovered above, and soul after soul tumbled along the sides, rolling from the hellmouth down to where they would be sorted and punished for eternity. I couldn't help but feel empathy for them, despite the fact they must have been truly awful people to deserve to be cast here.

Leviathan joined me at the elaborately carved dark stone balustrade, each column carved into a serpentine shape, and stared out over the vast expanse of his land, his expression uncaring, unmoved by the sight. I suppose he's had eons to look upon this. It was nothing new nor extraordinary for him. He turned away from the view, leaning his elbows back against the stone as he leaned on the railing, his attention wholly focused on me.

"What ails you, Evangeline?" he asked, and his penetrating, sharp gaze made me feel naked. He wasn't going to let me drop this.

It was easier to talk without looking at him. The longer I stared into those green eyes, the more vulnerable I felt, and the more vulnerable I felt, the more that part of me that was so drawn to him began to come alive. So I clung to the stone rail, watching the giant, searching demons cast their light through the grey cloud, and shrugged. "Would you understand me when I said I was warring with conflicting emotions?"

To my surprise, his response was immediate, "Yes."

I glanced at him out of the corner of my eye before I quickly looked away again. "And, as I've learned so much in such a short time, can you at least imagine how confused I feel about everything?"

"Yes."

His one-worded responses were both appreciated and annoying. I was glad he agreed with me, but it would be nice if he gave me something to work with. "So, I feel like, with everything, I just need time to-to adjust... to cope." He didn't say a word at this, which was disconcerting. Did he disagree? "I understand there is no way to leave this place, not unless you allow it. So I won't waste my time trying to." I glanced at him again only to see the apparent displeasure on his face. His features looked fierce, more lethal, his eyes narrowed and jaw clenched tight. "But I need to be alone, so I can try to learn some understanding-"

"No."

My head jerked back, surprised by his sharp refusal. "No?"

"No," he said simply.

"No, to trying to understand? Or no, to being left alone?"

"To being left alone. I do not wish it."

I scoffed and shook my head at him. "Well, excuse me, *your highness.*" I couldn't hold back the snark. "But this is what *I* want."

"I don't. And I don't believe space between us will help solve any sort of misgivings or dilemmas that you are struggling with." One of his hands began to creep toward me, slowly trailing along the top of the stone, inching towards my elbow that was resting upon the surface. His eyes never left mine as he spoke, and when he locked his fingers around my arm, he leaned in close, his face mere inches from mine. "If you ignore your instincts, and try to evade what afflicts you, you are not solving anything. You are running. I never took you for someone who ran from their problems."

"It's not that simple-"

"It is." His face was still tight, his stance rigid. "It is something I have learned over the ages, and sometimes I forget. But in the end, nothing alters unless I address it directly, lest it festers and builds, further aggravating me. I do not wish this for you. So you will not avoid me and the opposing emotions you have. You will explore them and face them like the warrior you are."

I stared up at him, eyes wide, his words hitting my heart in a way I hadn't expected.

Like the warrior you are...

Even at my sickest, my parents never saw me as a fighter. They never believed I would win my battle. They gave up immediately. They handed me over to the care of others and left. When I came back and worked hard to get my strength back, my weight under control, my hair grown out, and I took classes to get my GED; they didn't see it as anything strong or struggling to gain control over my second chance at life. They took it all for granted. And yet, this demon prince, a fallen beast from Heaven, called me a warrior. *He* believed in me. He saw that fight I had inside, and yet he was practically a stranger. A stranger I felt a compelling captivation and draw toward.

And cue the confusion...

Leviathan reached up and carefully wiped his thumb beneath my eye along my cheek. I didn't even realize I was crying until he did it, and with the heat in his eyes, the unshakable faith he had in what he saw in me, I couldn't help but give in.

"Okay, Leviathan... I won't run," I whispered, my voice cracking slightly as I said his name.

The tightness in his face vanished, and his lips quirked up in a soft, beautiful smile. He leaned in, and just when I thought he would kiss me, all he did was lightly brush his lips to one cheek, then the other, before the tip of my nose, only to pull back and murmur, "Good. Now let us leave these rooms. I have never been shut away so long and I wish to leave lest I go insane."

When he brought me down to his Throne Room again, I nearly had a panic attack. It took much persuasion from him and promises that he would not eat anyone before I agreed to go in without kicking and screaming. Yeah, yeah, that soul was an asshole and deserved to suffer, but seeing someone get eaten wasn't high on my list of things to witness... ever. In fact, it was never *on* the list.

But I trusted Leviathan because he's proven to be a man of his word, and if he said he wouldn't eat anyone (what a weird promise to make, but okay), then I believed him.

However, when he drew me over to that spot at the bottom of the dais, where that damned collar was waiting, I set my feet firmly on the ground again.

"What?" he snapped, now losing patience.

"Do I really have to wear that *thing*?" I moaned, nodding dismally to where the leather collar sat, seemingly innocent, on the floor by the pillows.

"What is wrong with it?" he asked, confused.

"Well, it's sort of... degrading. I mean, it's a dog collar."

"It is not!" he said indignantly. "I have explained that I had it specially made for a purpose! I would not have put just any mark of ownership on you, nor use what you humans would put on a dog." He picked it up and stroked the design etched into the leather. "I made this with the intention of showing those who came to me here that you were mine and that touching you would mean death. This is not degradation. This is protection." He reminded me.

Okay, well, when he put it that way...

I tried to see it from his point of view, and though I still didn't like it, as *no one* owned me, even him, I suppose that with this world being so different from the human one, the rules, the beings, I had to take that into consideration. Not to mention that Leviathan actually looked a little hurt by my proclamation for this collar he had specially made for me. Though a part of me was dying inside at the idea of wearing it, I begrudgingly shuffled over, head hanging, and allowed him to magically seal it around my throat.

Leviathan ran a finger along the edge of it, trailing it over my skin, pausing at the nape of my neck like he was considering something before he pulled away. "Remain in your seat and do not intervene."

"Roger dodger." I sat with a thump on my pillow, watching as he paused his step, halfway up to his big, fancy chair.

"I beg your pardon?" He arched his brow like he had no idea what I was talking about. "I am not Roger. Who is he to you?" he snapped, sounding suddenly furious.

"Wait, what? No!" I quickly held up a hand at the intense fury twisting on his face. The last thing I wanted was for him to shift into his horrifying monster form and search for the first human named Roger. "It's just a saying that people use! It just means 'yes' or 'I understand."

He stared at me suspiciously for a moment, like he was about to interrogate me further on this, but instead, shook his head like it wouldn't be worth understanding and climbed up the rest of the way, settling on his throne.

And then, I got to witness his "work" once again.

Only this time, there were no screaming souls or naughty escapees. Just demon after demon coming in with some request or concern, two who seemed to be at odds with each other, judging by how they pointed horrifyingly, clawed appendages at each other and looks of loathing. At first, seeing all of these bizarre creatures was shocking, but after about the tenth one, I sort of got over it. Plus, I couldn't understand what they were saying anyway, as they spoke in strange languages I didn't know, but apparently, Leviathan did. Some growled and rumbled, and others spoke with some semblance of speech, but the words were so odd and the pronunciation beyond anything I was capable of, that I had no hope of really knowing what was going on.

So, I got bored.

I lounged back on the pillow, occasionally searching around for some sign of Beast. He'd be nice to snuggle into right now. But he was following his duties, apparently, and was nowhere to be seen. Hence, I lay staring up at the magnificent ceiling, humming to myself, wondering what the heck I was going to do once Leviathan decided he was through with his little experiment and let me return to earth.

We were both unaware of exactly why he took me, so I wondered if he was satiating some curiosity about people and I was just a convenient target? So whenever he got bored and sent me back, I'd then have to go on with life like this never happened, because let's be real... *no one* will believe that in the time I was missing, I was in Hell, kidnapped by a demon prince. But the idea of living a life knowing what I know now, bearing this truth alone, the memories haunting me, I felt like I'd go crazy.

I thought we were about done when a colossal figure came storming into the throne room, a demon that actually had me quivering a little where I sat. They were all scary, but this one was larger, his fury clear in the way he prowled forward, seething as his teeth gnashed together. His skin was a greyish colour, and he wore onyx armour that looked like it was made of tree bark. He was armed with long, black claws on each of his digits and a long sickle-shaped one on his large raptorial toe, and his entire body was made of muscle. When he spoke, the words were incredibly guttural, laced with growls and snapping from his overlong top incisors. His head morphed into two long, uneven horns that arched straight up into the air, and he had pure black eyes that looked like they were stuck into a glare. In his hold, a furious, red-faced human was struggling, cursing, and shouting as he was hauled forward and thrown carelessly to the floor.

"Gnaarl." Leviathan nodded at him, and I wondered if that was the guy's name or if it was a greeting in his language?

The creature growled in response, speaking in quick barks, grunts, and snarling, and bowed respectfully before gesturing to the panting man on the floor, who peered up at Leviathan with a look of pure hatred on his face. I guess this guy was either caught trying to escape, or he was a troublemaker? I sat up, now curious. Leviathan had promised me he would not eat anyone, so what would he do now? I almost didn't want to know because curiosity killed the cat, but apparently, I had a sick urge to scoop today.

Leviathan listened to the demon speak briefly, but he slowly turned his attention to the human soul on the ground. If Leviathan ever looked at me the way he sneered at the guy on the floor, I think I'd pee myself. The rage, the way he clasped the arms of his chair, his black nails seeming to carve divots into the stone, as though seeking control over his emotions, it was evident that whatever this dude did, it was a serious blunder.

"So, *human*," he spat, "you think attacking my lieutenant was an offence that would go unpunished?" His voice dropped several octaves, surprising me. I'd never heard his voice shift in such a way when in his human form. I braced myself for the possibility of him shifting. "To steal a gifted heavenly blade and attempt to use it against its owner? To defile the sword with your filth, one meant for those of divine-"

"There is nothing divine about you or any of these fucking monsters!" The man screamed, his flabby face jiggling. "Who the fuck do you think you are! I don't deserve any of this-"

"You are guilty," Leviathan raised his voice to be heard over the man's shrieking. "Guilty of harming those who were vulnerable and defenceless-"

"The torture I've gone through is *nothing* compared-"

"You took advantage of your position of power..."

"I did nothing they didn't want-"

"Children do not understand the sort of depravity you forced upon them!" Leviathan snarled, and I could see how his body began to flex... danger sign. But honestly, the more I listened to the back and forth between him and this man, the more I learned about who the soul had been when he was alive. I wanted to cheer the demon in Leviathan on and encourage him to come out and nail this guy to the wall.

"I have been suffering here!" the man shouted. "What I did doesn't warrant-"

"What you did has left your victims enduring lifelong suffering!" Leviathan rose from his chair, sending the man scuttling backward on his hands and feet. When he bumped into the lieutenant's feet, he turned and darted to the side until his back was cowering against one of the columns. "Those children will live out their lives in pain and mental scarring from what *you* did. What you wanted, what you took from them, without their understanding and consent, is why you have been damned! Instead of confessing to your coveting, disgusting lust, and defilement, you continue to think only of yourself and not the victims of your sinful actions!"

"I-I..." The man began to wildly flit his head this way and that, like he was searching for a way out. He finally noticed me, chained to the wall, sitting in my lilac gown of silk upon a cushy pillow on the floor.

"... to attack my men with a heavenly blade!" Leviathan was ranting, his rage about to tip him over the edge as his muscles strained beneath the silk shirt he wore, the sound of his pants beginning to rip at the seams. The way his wings seemed to claw from beneath his shirt, as though longing to burst free from under his skin, were all signs that he was about to shift to his demon form. "You insult not only those who are tasked with guiding you to seek penitence but dare to-"

Leviathan didn't get a chance to finish when the man took this moment to act. Before I could comprehend what was happening, the man burst from the wall in my direction, his mean-looking eyes set solely on me, his path direct and sure. I had a moment to scream before I tried to run, but the damn chain caught me, and it violently snagged me back with a jerk, bringing me down to the floor, only to be caught up by the sinner's sweaty hands.

I could hear a roar, followed by the ripping and tearing of material as the floor rumbled and shook, as a heavy, thudding bang struck the river rock floor, followed by a deep, reverberating growling that had all the hair on my body standing on end.

The man dragged me up to my feet. One arm looped around my stomach as he crushed my back to his front, holding me like a shield before himself, his other hand set in a painful grip as it twisted into my hair, jerking my head back. I opened my eyes to see Leviathan, the demon, standing at the base of his throne, watching us with glowing green eyes, smoke simmering from his nostrils, his pock-marked wings stretching out and shaking in agitation. He was immense, larger than his lieutenant, and having his glare focused my way had my entire body quivering.

"Back!" the man screamed from behind my shoulder, his spit flying onto my skin, and I cringed in disgust. "Stay back! Or I will kill your whore!" He had no weapon, but I had no doubt that this man would undoubtedly try anything in his desperation.

At the word, 'whore', Leviathan released a furious howl, the sound piercing and eerie as it pitched off-key. His lieutenant whistled over his shoulder, and immediately, a troop of grey-skinned demons, with horns, muscles, bear-like-snouts, and claws all came rushing into the room, armed with swords, spears, and weapons I'd never even seen before.

Leviathan's mouth opened, revealing the lethal fangs that had grown during his transition, a strange, green glow emanating from deep in his throat from the bowels of his stomach, a reminder that he was The Great Devourer.

"Unhand the girl, human!" Leviathan's animal-like voice rumbled from the terrifying beast before us, and the man holding me began to tremble.

Facing off with the Prince of Envy doesn't seem like such a good idea now, does it, fuckface? I thought.

"Swear to me my life!"

"Your life has already ended..."

"Promise me mercy! Promise me safe passage!" the man cried, now sounding less and less confident in his decision to use me.

Leviathan growled, his wings flexing, relaxing, and then flexing again, like a pulse. His glowing green eyes shifted to me, frozen in the man's arms, my heart thrumming so fast it didn't even feel like it was beating, just vibrating in my chest. This man was already dead, but me? I was still a living person. Still vulnerable.

The man's hand suddenly flew up to seize the back of my collar, wrenching it higher so that it snagged against my throat. I gasped, but when he pulled harder, I started coughing and wheezing against the strain on my windpipe, going up on my tiptoes in hopes of easing the pressure.

Leviathan instantly took a step forward, but the man stepped back against the wall at his quick approach, pulling even harder. I could feel the leather digging painfully into my skin, obstructing my airway, causing my eyes to well with tears. My demon prince halted his steps at once at the display, taking the warning seriously.

"I will grant you mercy," he agreed, his baritone so unlike his normal voice. It sent vibrations through my body like a booming bell, making me feel sick on top of the choking. I gasped again, squirming to try to break free. I could see Leviathan's green gaze lock on the leather before he lifted his hand and waved it. The leather gave way before anyone could react, and I fell into a coughing, spitting heap on the floor. The man yelled out in surprise, but quickly wrapped the chains around my throat, hauling me against his legs as he tightened them. "Desist!" Leviathan bellowed furiously. "I said I will grant you mercy!"

The man at my back was silent, like he didn't believe him. Meanwhile, I was kicking out my legs and flailing my arms in an attempt to hit him somewhere that would have him loosen the chains. "You give your word?" he asked, his voice a mix of hope and distrust.

"I am known for it."

A moment's pause, and then finally, he dropped the chains, and I fell forward, choking and sucking in a lungful of air. Before I could fully recover, something hooked onto the hem of my dress, dragging me a safe distance away from the sinner, before I felt a smooth, flexible, but strong blanket scoop me up from the floor. Opening my eyes, I realized one of Leviathan's wings was cradling me close. It bent around his thick frame, holding me before his face as he bowed his head low to inspect the marks that were undoubtedly forming around my neck from the attack. I could hear the hiss rise from the back of his throat as his glowing gaze slowly turned to the man grinning like a fucking fool by the wall.

"Atruro!" he barked, and all of his men stepped back at once, leaving the guilty party alone before us all. The man stared about in confusion, but he cast a smug smile about the room when he realized they weren't attacking him.

I was still wheezing at this point, and Leviathan curled me around to his back, his second wing folding around me, forming a makeshift cage of protection, as he rumbled on, addressing the man, "And so... I keep my promise."

"Good," the man spat. "Now let me out of here. I want to be taken to Heaven where-"

"You are not going to Heaven."

I peered through an opening between the two wings, just able to make out the man over Leviathan's massive, muscled shoulder. The man froze, eyes wide, perplexed by this statement. "But-but you... you said you would give me mercy? Safe passage?"

"I did not swear to a safe passage *anywhere*," Leviathan's voice deepened, each word laced with a hiss like a snake ready to strike. "All I promised you was mercy."

"Uhh..." The man stared around the room, clearly confused. "Okay? So..."

Without preamble, my demon lifted a hand, and the man rose into the air with it. His arms and legs were kicking and spasming out like he hoped to fly or some shit. I know Leviathan did not intend for me to watch this, but I wanted this man to get his comeuppance. He was scum on earth, and he was still scum here in Hell.

"Though you gave none to your victims, even though you displayed no remorse nor accepted any accountability for what you have done..." The man's eyes, nose, ears, and mouth, all began to glow with a bright, acidic green light, like a beacon was igniting within him. "Despite the fact that you are so undeserving of it... I am of my word, and so..." He twisted his hand, and the man's body froze, like it had suddenly turned to stone. "... I show you mercy."

His hand splayed open, claws stretching wide, and the body hovering in the air was absolutely obliterated. It flayed apart, ripping to shreds, sending blood, severed body parts, and organs everywhere. There wasn't even time for him to scream, let alone understand what had happened to him. He was here, and now, he was no more. Leviathan's mercy was a quick end without pain, but now, the man's soul didn't even exist. Retribution to the victims of his crimes.

"Have my waywraiths clean this up," he rumbled, speaking in English, before he corrected himself and said in a growl to his lieutenant, who bowed respectfully again, seemingly satisfied with the outcome of this confrontation. Without another word to the others, I found myself carried in the delicate hold of his wings as he walked with a heavy step out of the room and through the palace.

"I promised you I would not consume the damned," he rumbled to me as he thudded up the stairs and squeezed into the narrow halls.

"You did," I said numbly, agreeing with him.

"I hope you are not displeased with me for how I punished that soul..." Even with his growling baritone voice, I could make out the uncertainty in his tone, like he was nervous about my reaction.

"I'm not," I said simply. Though my voice was quiet and flat, I wasn't lying. I was not unhappy with how he dealt with that man. Not. At. All. "Fuck that guy."

I could hear a vibration from the depths of his chest like he was chuckling. "I concur. Fuck him."

CHAPTER TWELVE

Leviathan

Finally, in the privacy of my rooms, I felt it safe enough to release Evangeline from the protection of my wings. As much as I'd wanted him to suffer, I had sworn to be merciful, and I was. I was still shaken seeing that human filth with his hands on her, threatening something so pure and beautiful. Seeing her choke on the collar, then the chain, I don't recall ever feeling such heart-wrenching fear. Not when I'd been pulled from the Abyss and forced into the light, into a place unknown, confused, and so aware of how unique I was from the others in His kingdom. Not when I fought on the battlefield and faced the possibility of actual death at Michael's blade, nor when I fell back into darkness, my future uncertain and bleak. Seeing the life drained from Evangeline's face had been the most horrendous and utmost terrifying moment I had ever known in my existence.

Releasing her now, allowing her to leave the safety of my embrace, I moved away to sit on the edge of the bed, staring out of the swaying curtains out onto my kingdom and waiting for my body to calm enough to transition back. It was an excruciating process, one I had to brace myself for each time. It wasn't like when Lucifer changed or any of the others. What made it so difficult was that my demon form was just another way that my body had been twisted, broken, and put together again to create a new variant of my being. When I first awoke in the darkness all those eons ago, I never saw myself, so I have no recollection of what I looked like. But when He took me and forced my first change, I became something new. And when I fell, I altered again.

Now, in this warped, demonic being, I was unnatural, a combination of things that were just reminders of all the times I'd been forced to become something else.

I let my giant head fall forward into my hands, leaning my elbows heavily upon my knees, my wings quivering at my back as I sought control over my feelings, enough so I could contain them once again, to crush themselves into my back so my skin could heal over. I just couldn't stop seeing the image of her face changing colour, her eyes unfocused, gasping for air...

"Leviathan?" she whispered from somewhere at my back. Her voice was tentative, like she was nervous about being around me. I had no doubt. To her, I was a monster.

"Evangeline," I answered, unable to resist her call.

"Are you okay?"

My eyes snapped open at that, but I found I could not bring myself to turn and face her. I couldn't bear to see the terrified expression that I had no doubt was on her face, the same one I saw in the Throne Room. But her inquiry into my well-being had been unexpected.

Of course, she would ask about you. She is... good. Unsullied. Decent.

"I will be soon enough," I murmured, my chest squeezing at her words, touched by her empathy.

"May I ask you something?" Her voice sounded a little closer, like she was slowly approaching the bed from the other side.

"Always."

She hesitated, a sign of her discomfort.

"You needn't be afraid of me, Evangeline," I told her. "I would never hurt you."

From behind, the bed shifted, like she had crawled up on the mattress but stopped somewhere at my back. The warmth from her hand timidly touched one of the hooked thumbs on my wings, her fingers gently running along the fleshy membrane, over the bumps of the scarred pockmarks. "What are these from?" she asked, her voice filled with wonder.

My wings shivered under her touch, not from pain but from the thrilling, soft feel of her. No one has ever dared to touch my wings. I know many thought them weak, as they appeared to be so delicate, the membrane between the extended digits relatively thin, the scars only adding to the belief. It wasn't until today when I'd used them to scoop her up and shield her from the mess I was about to make of that soul, that *anyone* had touched them.

"They belonged to the feathers I'd had when I was an angel... or... some semblance of an angel," I told her, wondering how she would take this information. I had never been a true angel of Heaven. But she already knew this.

"What happened to them?" she asked, and I could not help but find her voice incredibly alluring by the breathy tone.

"Some of them burned away when I fell from grace." I shut my eyes, concentrating on her touch rather than allowing myself to become distracted by impure thoughts. "The others I pulled out when I settled back here." I remember it well. Lucifer, who had taken the dark pit of the Abyss and made it into his kingdom, had accepted me, grateful for my loyalty. For days, I sat amid my old lands, hiding in a cave, plucking the remaining gold plumes until there were none left. Nothing but a pile of feathers, some burnt, others still pure and shining, all coated in the blood that pooled from the pits on my wings where I'd wrenched them free.

"Why would you do that?" she asked, her voice hushed.

"Because they were never a true part of me," I explained. "The gold plumage I was decorated with in Heaven was not a natural part of my being. They were bound to me when I was taken from my home..." I released a long, shuddering breath, wiping my clawed hands over my face, and lifted my head to stare beyond the curtains at the land I knew was truly mine. "When I returned, it felt wrong to embody them. Once they were gone, they didn't heal right because they were never a genuine element of my composition. They'd damaged me when they were forced in, so when they were gone, they left their marks behind. Only when I calmed from the war, when I gained control over myself and sought to become more than what I was, did I turn into the final humanoid version of myself that you are now familiar with."

For a long time, neither of us spoke. I simply listened to her breathing, the sound uneven, as though she was having difficulty. I was about to turn to check on her, concerned about the injury inflicted by the chain, when her hands began to stroke the scars. I stilled beneath her touch, my heart clenching when she leaned in, her soft lips pressing a kiss to each wing. I shut my eyes and sucked in a sharp breath, pressing my hands to my mouth.

I felt like I was surely dying. The feelings in my chest were combusting, then quickly expanding, only to leave an ache inside. My mind was a storm of conflicting emotions I was unfamiliar with, but one thought I knew for sure, was how much I wanted her. I wanted Evangeline Kelly like I wanted respect from every other fucking thing in this world. Like I wanted Riker's wealth and drive. Lucifer's power and control. In fact, I wanted her *more*. I wanted her more than I wanted to see others bow to me, more than all the times I'd wanted something I could never have, more than I wanted to destroy that which made others so worthy.

I just wanted *her*.

And as I thought it, my body began to shift. My muscles retracted, shrinking in size, my bones painfully splintering and narrowing, my fangs withdrawing into my gums with such sharp, stinging agony. I couldn't stop myself from moaning in misery as everything shifted back. The worst was my wings, which folded in, curling in, breaking themselves joint by joint as they cut into the muscle to rest, leaving two bloody trails down my back, the skin slowly etching together again.

By the time it was over, I had sat there on the blankets, head buried in my hands, naked, shivering, eyes squeezed shut as I tried to hide just how weak I truly was from the only thing I'd come to care about.

But knowing my little human, she wasn't going to accept my shutting her out. I felt the bed shift as she crawled to my side and forcefully pulled at my shoulders. I found her attempts to turn me to face her adorable, but I wouldn't do it. I remained where I was, hiding, unable to bear her to see me so weak.

"Leviathan, look at me," she commanded, as if she could order me to do anything. When I refused to move, her little hands cupped either side of my face, resting in the hollows of my cheekbones, and tried again to make me obey. "Look at me, please!"

Slowly, I complied, finding that I could not deny her much of anything, especially when she sounded so dismayed. Gradually, I lifted my head, letting my hands drop, as I allowed her to turn my face to hers. Her shining eyes were spilling tears, her expression contorted as though she was in pain. My heart leapt in my throat, thinking she actually was seriously injured, and one of my hands flew up to grasp the wrist to one of hers, but she refused to allow me to look away.

"There is *nothing* wrong with you," she said, her voice filled with confidence.

I pressed my lips tightly together, wincing a little at her words. When I tried to shake my head, disbelieving, she sternly shook her head, holding my gaze as the hurt on her face shifted to determination.

"What happened to you wasn't right. It wasn't. And I'm so, *so* sorry that you had to go through that." Her brown eyes burned with passion as she spoke. "Just please know that whatever happened to you back then, it doesn't matter now. Fuck it all. Take that hurt, the misunderstandings, the turmoil and crush it." She gave me a fierce little shake. I sucked in a sharp breath, the backs of my eyes stinging uncomfortably at her words. That was new. It's not surprising, as I've felt many new things since I brought Evangeline to Hell with me. Again, she leaned in close and said firmly, "Fuck the others. Look at you. And all of this," She glanced around the room and nodded out the archway to the balcony, "this is yours. It's beautiful and a representation of you, and that's damned special. I don't think you realize just how blessed you truly are…" When I winced again at her words, she quickly shook her head in disapproval of my response. "No, no, don't do that. It's true. You are fucking *blessed*, Leviathan. You have so much you don't even know. And I'm not talking about just this palace, your land, and your titles. I'm talking about all that you've been through, that you've survived. None of that other shit matters now. You've made it this far. You. Do you understand that? You called me a warrior earlier, remember? Well, so are you."

I sucked in a long, drawn-out breath between my teeth, and nodded, giving her wrist an affectionate little squeeze as I realized that I would never regret taking this human from earth.

"And you know what?" she went on, her brows rose a little on her forehead, and that mischievous little twinkle in her eye sparked to life. I waited for her punchline because now that her speech was over, Evangeline's trademark was some sort of absurd comment or observation that would have me rolling my eyes or shaking my head in disbelief. "Chicks dig scars." She said at last with a wink, glancing at my shoulder to where my wings had disappeared to.

I blinked, staring at her for a moment, before throwing my head back and laughing. I laughed so hard that I actually fell backwards on the mattress, bringing her with me. I wrapped my arms around her, pulling her in tight to my chest, my stomach hurting slightly from my mirth. I didn't care that I was soiling my luxurious bedding with my bloodied back. All that mattered was her.

When she giggled in my arms, I couldn't hold back any longer. When I looked down to where her head was resting on my chest, her smile was radiant and breathtaking. Tilting her chin up to me with two of my fingers, cautious of my sharp, black nails (another disfigurement none of the others had because I was such an oddity with my beginnings), I lost myself in her gaze. I'd never before found humans pleasing to look at. I often considered them plain, less divine versions of Him and His angels. Until now...

Because when it came to her, I couldn't help but think that she was *anything* but plain.

Evangeline was beautiful, not just her physical attributes, but her soul. The soul staring out at me from behind those brown eyes, the very essence of her, was pure transcendence.

I closed the small distance between us, letting my instincts guide me, and pressed my lips to hers. When she didn't pull away, I let my hand slide from her chin around to the back of her head, where I gently cupped it, revelling in the softness of her wavy hair. My other arm, which was still wrapped around her back, glided down to her waist, looping around the curve so I could heft her up towards me. I needed her close. I needed to feel her flush against my body. But even when she lay crushed to my side, it wasn't enough.

My lips sought out the curve of her throat, where I sucked on the skin... *delicious...* ran my tongue up the lovely arc to her ear. She shivered at my touch but clung to me, her body trembling as mine was. She was intoxicating. I felt drunk off her taste, the scent of her that reminded me of sandy beaches and Lily of the Valley. The swells of her breasts moulded against the hard muscles of my chest, the feeling soft, erotic, stirring a hunger deep within that had me craving more from her.

More... *more!*

"Leviathan?" she whispered, her voice quavering, and the uncertain way she said my name made my heart clench, the thought of her being frightened of me in any way felt like a spear to my chest.

"Shhh, darling," I whispered in her ear, "I will not hurt you... just... let your mind go. Move with me. Be with me now, in this moment."

She hesitated, that very thought of her saying no had the demon inside of me screaming in a fury. I went rigid as I waited, on the brink of losing any sort of self-control I had and just giving in to the most primal impulse all beings possessed. I thought I was about to shatter apart when finally, I felt her nod against my chest, her body still shaking like a leaf, as mine was, but it was all I needed to tip me over the edge and ultimately give in to this craving. I continued to follow my instincts, my body acting on its own accord as I rolled her to her back and began to gyrate my hips over hers. The tiny sigh she breathed, followed by a moan, was like music to my ears, and I deepened the movement of my pelvis, rubbing more urgently against her as my manhood hardened painfully. But this feeling was quite unlike any I've felt before. And the fact that I was experiencing it for the first time with her, was beyond anything I could ever have conjured in my mind.

I opened my eyes, now holding her face in my hands, losing myself at the sight of her flushed cheeks, her fluttering eyelids, the way she let out a soft cry each time I swivelled my hips against her. She was absolutely stunning...

Again, I wanted *more.*

I let one of my hands explore, moving down over the silk that was hiding her body from me. It needed to go. Without ceremony, I grasped the neckline of her gown and ripped it, revealing that glorious figure that lay beneath me. Evangeline moaned as my hands sought out her breasts, the small, soft mounds tiny in my hands, another reminder of how delicate she was. I bowed my head over one and took the budded nipple into my mouth, sucking hard, needing to be closer. Though she writhed beneath me, the act proved to be satisfying and pleasurable for us both.

"I need you," she whispered over my head, her nails running through the long strands of my hair, and I swear, those words had me unequivocally falling to pieces for her. Her soft flesh against mine was gratifying, feeling the wetness between her legs as I rubbed my cock amidst her folds was riveting. But it still was not enough.

"I need you, too." I released her nipple with a loud pop and took her mouth again, only this time, I felt the flick of her tongue against my lips. When she did it again, seeming to tease me, I opened my mouth for her and groaned deep from within my belly when her little tongue massaged against mine. Eagerly, I returned the caress, finding this new method of kissing even more enjoyable than what we had done before. I had never imagined that kissing would be so thrilling. But as I pictured the endless array of women and demons that my brothers went through, I could not imagine it to be as pleasurable as what I was experiencing now, with Evangeline in my arms. No... I had no desire to try this with another. The very thought turned my stomach and had me stilling over her, my body suddenly rigid and tense as my eyes squeezed shut, trying to block the offensive picture from my mind.

"Leviathan, what-"

"All is well, darling. I just... I need..." *More.*

I felt one of her small hands slide down the front of my body, over my pecs, and the ridges of the muscle of my stomach. When it tentatively wrapped around the hard length of my cock, my eyes shot open, and I sucked in a sharp breath between my teeth. She began to stroke me, slowly pumping my length, and I clenched my jaw from the feel of her clutching me was so much more than I imagined it would be. She squeezed a little tighter, moving a little faster, and I couldn't help but push into her hand, resting my forehead against hers as I watched her watch me.

"Leviathan," she sighed, now using her thumb to smear the precum leaking from the tip. When she began to nudge it against her entrance, I knew I could no longer hold back.

"Evangeline." I wrapped my arms around her back, embracing her close, and gave a hard thrust, burying myself to the hilt within her warm, wet walls, revelling when she squeezed tightly around me. Her legs wrapped around the small of my waist, locking her heels behind my back as though to hold me to her, and I buried my face into her throat, a deep, satisfying rumble-like rolling thunder vibrating from my chest, a sound I hadn't made in what felt like a lifetime. An old sound. One I thought I'd lost when I was plucked from the darkness.

I rumbled again, the sound reverberating from my body to hers, and she wrapped her arms around my neck, pulling herself closer while gasping into my hair. My little human liked it when I did that. But the feel of her around my cock, the tight way she held me, how perfect she felt... I sucked in a breath of air to steady myself as I remained buried, not wanting to leave her just yet.

Nuzzling her throat, I smiled against her skin before pressing the softest of kisses there and whispered, "You are my reason to keep going, my warrior..."

I felt her lips on my hair. "Leviathan... please..." she begged, writhing beneath me.

And I let my instincts guide me.

I began to slowly pump my hips between her legs, revelling in the sublime feeling of her around my cock, and I knew *nothing* could ever compare to this. The heat from her, the beautiful blush that covered her flesh, how her breasts jiggled with each sharp thrust I gave, how she squirmed and clung to me each time my barbaric, bestial growl released a long vibration, the sound filling the room over the smacking of our bodies repeatedly joining together. When I tilted her hips, rolling mine into her at a deeper angle, she bit her lip and tilted her head back. The sight of her stretched out beneath me was utterly entrancing.

I began to move faster.

One of my hands roamed over her body, cupping her breasts, smoothing over her belly, curling and grasping at the soft swell of her hips. I greedily took in the sight of her, knowing for certain that I could never give her up.

Turning slightly to the side, now rearing up on my knees, I began to fuck her with more urgency, and the change in position had her absolutely wailing beneath me.

"Oh... holy... shit!" she cried out, her hands covering her mouth to silence her scream, and I felt such gratification knowing that it was I who was the reason behind her pleasure.

"Will you come with me, Evangeline?" I hissed to her, my hips pumping fervently as I ruthlessly fucked her. "Will you come?"

"Yes, please!" Her legs squeezed around my middle, her hands now gripping the sheets and blankets as though she needed something to hang on to, lest she falls away.

I slid deeper, the feeling so fucking good, the sight of her back arching as she met each thrust of mine; intoxicating. Our moans and grunts echoed around the room, and I seized her hips, roughly pulling her in to meet me each time our bodies came together. I felt her begin to squeeze around me, her hot, silky channel hugging my cock, pulling it in deeper. The smell of the sea was all around us, and unable to resist, I paused our movements as I bent over her to give her another deep kiss, my tongue languidly stroking over her own.

When I sat up and began again, picking up the pace, she licked her lips, smiling from where she lay looking like a goddess, and moaned, "Fuck yeah..."

"You like it when I fuck you like this, female?" I gritted between my teeth. I felt a little slap over my pecs and grinned, knowing she would rise to that bait. "My little human enjoys it when her demon takes her, owns her, ravishes her..."

"Mmmm," she moaned seductively, and I instantly felt weak in the knees at the sound.

"I want to take you everywhere... to fuck you on my throne, in the halls, the gardens... I want all of Hell to hear me fucking my female..." I thrusted harder, faster, the feeling of her constricting around me signalling that she was close. I lost all sense as I pounded into her with no rhythm, just giving in to the absolute craving and instinct I'd smothered my whole existence. She screamed, her inner walls spasming as she came, and I quickly followed, an explosion from my dick that wracked my body. The pleasure tingled as I came in her, a satisfaction washing over me, making it feel like I'd just come home.

We were both a sweating, panting mess. But I didn't give a shit. I slowly thrusted several more times into her, my movements gentle and careful, but I had no desire to leave just yet. I shifted my body to cover hers, holding myself up on my forearms, as I pressed kiss after kiss to her face, her throat, every part of her I could reach.

There was no doubt in my mind... Evangeline Kelly was divine.

CHAPTER THIRTEEN

Evangeline

Leviathan wouldn't let me leave his bed that night. He kept me close, both of us lying on our sides, staring into each other's eyes. His fingers traced over my body, learning every line and curve. When I shivered, he covered us in one of his silk sheets and raised his hand, closing off the curtains and dimming the light, leaving us immersed in that dim, magical sort of glow from the jellyfish overhead.

I'd always taken sex for what it was... an activity between two people that *hopefully* gave pleasure to both in the end. I'd thought I'd known what an orgasm was, but that was before tonight. Not to mention how different it felt, just being joined with Leviathan, to have him hold me and kiss me like it was vital for us to become one. It felt more... profound, meaningful. When he looked at me, I believed that he found me the most beautiful thing in the world, and coming from an eternal being such as him, I can't deny that I found it incredibly flattering and made me a little bashful. Only when I tried to burrow into the blankets to hide, he wouldn't stand for it.

Silently, he just crawled under with me, holding the sheet away from my face, so he could trace his finger over my jaw, down one side, up the other, and back again.

"Is this how it feels to be human?" he asked me just when I thought I was about to fall asleep.

"What part?"

"This... this complicated mix of emotions stirring in my mind," he murmured, his voice strained. "I don't believe I have ever felt such a diverse surge all at once."

I shrugged one shoulder and reached out to run my fingers along the planes of muscle on his body. "Honestly? I've never felt such a connection to someone before. But as a species, we *are* very driven by our emotions." I glanced up at him to catch his thoughtful expression. "Do you not?"

"I rarely, if ever, feel more than one at a time. It's usually a slow transition between one and another." His voice was quiet, thoughtful, as he spoke. "I don't believe anything I've felt has ever made me feel as... peaceful as I do now."

I wanted to cry for him, while at the same time, I was glowing because I knew that some part of the reason behind his current disposition was because of me. To know that I could bring him some sense of tranquillity was gratifying, and I couldn't help but lean in to press a soft kiss on his mouth. When I went to lie back, however, his hand gently cupped around the back of my neck, holding me in place, as he deepened the kiss, that delicious rumble from deep within his belly sending a shiver throughout my body that had me tingling.

"Will you tell me something?" he whispered, his lips brushing against mine.

"Always."

His eyes slowly opened, and I found myself lost in the mix of green shades, some unnatural, others muted and soft, almost human. They were breathtaking. "When I first beheld you... you were dead." It wasn't a question.

I hadn't been expecting that, but I knew exactly what he meant. My suspicions had been confirmed. He *had* been the shadow lurking close by when I thought I'd died. "I was..." I whispered, now about a hundred questions of my own began to pile up in my head.

"What happened to you?" he asked, his brows tensing over his eyes, his frown deepening at the memory like it upset him.

Surprisingly, this was never something I shied away from talking about, not intentionally. But it just wasn't something that really came up in conversation with others, and I wasn't one to just randomly throw out there, "Oh yeah, there was this one time when I died, but then I came back." That made for an awkward change in conversation. And because no one asked, I just never mentioned it. To finally have someone be curious enough to know, to want to talk about what I'd gone through, I felt like a weight was sliding off my shoulders.

"When I was younger, I was diagnosed with a disease called Non-Hodgkin Lymphoma." From the blank stare in his eyes, I tried to explain further, "Cancer."

"Cancer," he murmured. "I have heard of this, though I do not understand exactly..."

"So, it starts in our white blood cells or other lymph tissue, and it attacks the immune system. There are a variety of versions of lymphoma, so doctors have to narrow down exactly what type you have so they can treat people correctly and hopefully, successfully." I bit my lip, remembering the chemo I went through, the painful process, how sick I got.

"They failed you," he determined, his grip on the back of my neck tightening slightly, but it didn't hurt.

"They didn't fail me. Sometimes, bad things just... happen," I explained. "Except the strange thing about my death was that my reason for coming back didn't make any sense." As I said this, I caught how the corners of his eyes tensed. "It was seen as a miracle. I woke up and day by day, I got a little better, until finally, I was healthy again."

For some time, we said nothing. We both just remained where we were, hiding beneath the sheet, huddled close, until finally, I couldn't hold back any longer. "When you say you saw me, would you explain that?"

Leviathan sighed, as though he was not pleased by my question, but he pressed a kiss to my forehead, pulling me in against his chest so he could embrace me while he spoke, "I spotted you on your way to Heaven, Evangeline..."

I didn't know why, but him confirming that I wasn't a damned soul made me feel such immense relief that I sagged a little into his hold. "I'm sorry," I whispered.

"Why are you apologizing?" he asked, his tone completely taken aback by my response.

"I suppose because... if I had to choose where to spend eternity, I wouldn't pick Hell for myself."

He was quiet as he considered this, the entire time his sharp, black nails were combing through my hair, cautious of the sharp ends. "I cannot begrudge you that, darling, for His Paradise is where a soul like yours truly belongs. Not down here with me..." His voice trailed off sadly, and he threw a leg over both of mine, cocooning me in. "I regret to tell you that I am a selfish being, and I have no desire to give you up. The moment I saw you in death, something about your soul enraptured me so completely, I had already started to change before I even understood it was happening." I felt his lips press into the crown of my head. "The wicked creature that I am, I coveted you when I had no right to, and now, I fear I will never be able to let you go, Evangeline."

I felt my throat tighten at his words, tears stinging the backs of my eyes, as I wrapped my arms around him as best I could, gripping him so tightly as I sought comfort from the very demon who upended my life. And curse it all, as much as I wanted Leviathan, the pull to him making me feel like the need for him was the same as needing the very air to breathe. However, another part of me knew that if I had the chance to return to Earth and live my life, I would take it.

But that wasn't the case here. We were together, and ever since my brush with death, I tried to be in the moment. So, for now, this was enough.

Leviathan's lips brushed over my bare shoulder, both his hands were hidden beneath the silk of my dress as he held onto my back, crushing me to him. I was riding him while he sat on his throne, our moans and panting echoing about the room, but we were the only ones in here. I'd learned in the past week that he was kind of a tentative exhibitionist. While he did enjoy our passionate lovemaking in public places, he preferred it behind closed doors, still out of the view of others but more so we could still be heard. Yesterday, it was in the temple in his gardens, right beneath the statue of Beast. Today? His Throne Room.

I kept one arm wrapped around the back of his neck, my head tilted to that beautiful ceiling, that sensation in my lower belly building, taking me higher and higher. I felt his teeth on my throat, and I moaned in ecstasy. Being with Leviathan this way is the very definition of addiction. I squeezed around him, loving the tenor-like, rumbling that he emitted from deep within his gut, animalistic, masculine, primal...

Old... mystical... otherworldly...

When he lifted his head, his green gaze held mine, our lips brushing over one another's as I grinded down on his lap and he thrusted up into me. Our movements picked up the pace as we got closer together, and when his hand slid up to grip a handful of my hair at the back of my head, I grinned like a vixen, loving it when he was controlling this way. His teeth nipped at my bottom lip and whispered, "Come with me."

Oh fuck, yes!

I began to move faster, my heart pounding so hard I could barely catch my breath, tears stinging my eyes as I bordered the line of completely falling over the edge.

"Together," he reminded me, sucking in a sharp breath that hissed between his teeth, his sharp features taking on a carnal sort of savageness that only amplified his beauty. I nodded, keeping pace, feeling him within me, my inner walls clenching around him as I could feel myself getting closer and closer to that point.

"Oh, fuck... Leviathan!" I cried, "I can't hold back any-" but I didn't get a chance to say it before I exploded around him. He groaned heavily as he came with me, both of us clinging to each other as we reached our peaks, shaking, sweating, watching each other with such undeniable reverence that I finally felt those tears fall from my eyes. One slowly slid down the curve of my cheek, and he watched it with a sort of euphoric fascination as he came down from his climax, his gaze hyper-focused on the tiny droplet. Just as it was about to fall, he leaned in and licked it up with his tongue as though he couldn't help himself. His eyes closed for a moment, like he was savouring it before he buried his face into the side of my throat.

"It's all so beautiful..." he breathed against my skin, the hand in my hair relaxing as he stroked the locks instead. I could feel the tip of his nose as it ran up the length of my neck, beneath my jawline, below my ear, and down again. "More than I ever thought possible." And he kissed the hollow of my collarbone.

Dizzy, light-headed, I sagged against him, his words only adding to the drunken sort of gaze I found myself in every time we came together. When his arms wrapped around me, hugging me close, I did the same, encircling his neck and pressing my face into his shoulder. Every time we finished, he always whispered some ridiculously romantic, sweet thing in my ear that only tugged at my heart, adding to the clashing thoughts in my mind.

I wanted Leviathan.

I also wanted Earth.

I wanted Leviathan.

I also wanted life.

But I wanted Leviathan. I had him.

But... you've always wanted to live.

I crushed those thoughts, burying them in the back of my mind. Not now. I didn't want to go through this now. Not while we held each other, our bodies still connected, still deeply joined in the most intimate ways one could be with another being. However, one thought had been lingering at the back of my head all week, and I found I couldn't wait another day to ask.

"Leviathan?" I whispered, still wrapped around him. He sagged back into his throne, his thumbs stroking at the skin on my back beneath my gown. He was languid, every part of his body loose and relaxed like jello.

"Hm?" he mumbled, still lost in the aftereffects of sex. And here I was about to make things get real serious, real fast.

"Can... can you... procreate?" I cringed as I said it. I hated asking it, but I needed to know. I wasn't on birth control, as I'd been determined to just live with only natural supplements, just from years of having to take medication to fight the cancer in my body. I wanted children someday, and I had no idea if the chemo had destroyed that possibility or not, but I wasn't going to take anything else that could potentially hinder that. I had always used condoms until now. But with Leviathan, I'd completely lost my senses and thrown caution to the wind like an idiot and carelessly behaved like a bitch in heat. Although every time after the fact, I wondered if it was possible I could get pregnant with a demon baby. The thought of being pregnant was already terrifying enough, just because I wasn't ready at this point in my life, but to be preggo with a demon baby? That was another level of terror.

Leviathan was quiet for a minute, and though his silence had me incredibly nervous and wary, I waited, knowing with him that timing was everything. He was silent because he was thoughtful, thinking, considering. But the longer it went on, the more worried I became. What horrible news was he about to break to me?

Wordlessly, he gently lifted me up, withdrawing his now soft cock from my channel, and set me on his thigh, my legs stretched over his other leg, sitting sideways on his lap. He tucked himself away and dutifully straightened the pale periwinkle blue dress I was wearing, making sure my breasts, which had spilled out when he'd pulled the material off one shoulder, were hidden again. Ever the gentleman. With his arms looped around my middle, he clasped them together and rested them on the swell of my hip, his expression torn.

"Demon-human procreation is possible, and there are such beings here in hell. Cambion demons, they're called. A hybrid."

I raised my brows as I rested my cheek on his chest, gazing up at him, unable to ignore how captivated I was by him. He didn't sound nervous or put off by my question, which put my worries at ease, so I listened in fascination as he explained another aspect of this world that I'd never imagined possible. "So, there are other humans here?"

He nodded. "There are. Ones that were taken, found on the brink between life and death, or a soul who enraptured one of the many species that dwell here. My Second in Command, Gnaarl, whom you met last week in this very room, has one of his own. Though, as far as I know, they have not conceived."

The idea of a half-human, half-demon creature even being possible was fascinating. Yet my question was about him. And his answer had avoided that. Knowing that Leviathan always chose honesty with me, I sensed that this was not intentional, but more like he was trying to explain something more profound to me.

"Another Prince of Sin has conceived with a human woman. They have two children together."

This news had my brows shooting up on my forehead. Another sin had taken a human woman? Was there something in the air in Hell?

"So... you can father children," I confirmed, now panicking a little at how careless I'd been. Yes, I desperately wanted to have kids someday, but not now. Not here.

Leviathan's gaze, however, suddenly shifted. The straightforward, instructional sort of air he took on every time he explained something to me died away and was replaced by a quiet, almost mournful mood. His eyes fell from mine, staring down at our laps, his lips pressing tightly together, and his hold around my waist flexed for a moment before he whispered, "Do you wish for children, Evangeline?"

"I mean..." I suddenly felt horrible, realizing that he must think I did not want to have kids with him. The pain on his face made my guilt rip my heart apart. "Of course, I do. Someday. Just not now. I still have so much I want to accomplish first. But yes, absolutely. I do dream of having kids."

I thought this would reassure him, or at least console him somehow, but it only seemed to make it worse. He nodded subtly, his expression still the same, that dark, heavy mood settling even more profoundly on his shoulders as he slumped a little. "I cannot father children, Evangeline." When he finally lifted his head, his gaze was undeniably heart-breaking, the shine in his eyes only searing my guilt further. "I was not made like the others... other demons, the other sins who were once true angels. I was a creature, bent and remade again and again. I was not made to create. I was made to destroy. Ruler of the Chaotic Oceans..." he reminded me, the being he'd originally been designed to be. "If there was one thing I was always aware of, it was that when I was taken from the Abyss, I was also taken from what could have been a chance for that... the other half of my being, the only one I could have joined with, was thus removed from existence in the process. I have many things to be spiteful for, Evangeline. Being robbed of my ability to create another in my image is one of them."

I stared up at him, absolutely appalled and heartbroken for him, not knowing what to say. All I could do was cling to him and listen as he poured his heart out.

"I have not spoken of it to anyone. I never allowed myself to think of it, because the trauma from such memories instigates more pain, rage, resentment, a thirst for vengeance that will never be mine... it is fruitless. When I was taken, I lost my other. And then I was made into a twisted variation of purity, and with it, my means to sire." His arms trembled around me, but just when I thought I was losing him to his traumatic ordeals, he turned to look at me and rested his forehead on mine. "I do not remember much from my time when I was... truly me. So I cannot recall my other. But this, Evangeline, between us, this feels familiar. It feels right. But regretfully, I have been changed so much that I cannot give you something you desire. And for that, I am sorry."

If I was crying before, now I was a puddle. I couldn't stop the flow of tears as I cupped his face, pressing kiss after kiss to every part of him I could reach. "There is nothing to apologize for..." I told him vehemently. "There is nothing." I pulled him in and kissed him ardently, wishing that I could apply a balm over his wounds that keep reopening. Despite the hardship, the calamity of his origins, this part of him he's shared with me and no other, he breathes me in, humming deep in his chest as he loses himself in my hold and touch, like this is enough for him. So I hold him tenderly, as if he were a child, and whisper again and again, "There is nothing. There is nothing..."

I'm lightheaded and tired, exhausted from days and days of nearly non-stop fucking. But my need for Leviathan is insatiable, and his need for me is even more ravenous. It's like he can't get enough, and the desire I feel for him only adds to it all. We fuck in the bathing room, in the middle of his massive closet after he decorated me with an assortment of jewels he'd acquired, out on the balcony with the misty lands as our backdrop, and once in my old cage, which sat on its own, having gone unused since that first night we came together.

He crushed me against the bars, which I clung to, my legs wrapped around his waist as I took him in, and he fucked me hard, standing with his legs spread as he held me up. The thought of being screwed silly in that gold cage was thrilling enough, but doing it was something else altogether. Leviathan's naughty side was coming out full-force.

When I was busy riding him again on his throne only yesterday, there came a knocking on the double doors. He growled fiercely in his throat, but at the urgent-sounding snarling from the other side, he spun me around on his lap, facing the room, and resettled my dress, so it hid the fact that he was still buried inside of me from view. Then, placing a hand on my stomach, he crushed me to his front and waved the doors open. While my face burned red, he and the one I came to know as Gnaarl, had a long discussion about... well, I don't know, as they were speaking in demon dialect. The entire time, he remained hard as a rock inside of me, and from time to time, I could feel him shift in my tight, wet channel, sending a tingling shiver rushing over my skin. He pressed against my lower belly, heightening the sensation while maintaining a professional-looking demeanour on the outside before his lieutenant.

My forehead was beading with sweat as I nervously, and shamefully sat there, trying to look innocent and not like Leviathan and I were still very much connected. I've never been so brazen in my life. But the moment Gnaarl left, shutting the doors behind himself, Leviathan immediately gripped my waist and began furiously thrusting up into me like a crazed beast, earning a loud, gasping moan from me in return.

"That was fun," he murmured in my ear, licking its shell as he continued to fuck me in a frenzy. "I think I would like to conduct all my business this way, fucking you beneath your finery." One of his fingers teased at the silk I wore before he pressed against my lower belly again, encouraging that build within me until...

The spring snapped and I came undone, my cries echoing again and again around the room as I fell apart, trembling and nearly sliding off his lap, had he not held me against himself. He followed soon after, his teeth nipping at my shoulder, his hands moving over the silk covering my breasts as he kneaded them, pinching and teasing.

But now, I was done.

I've been in Hell for nearly a month now, and after two weeks of continuous fucking, I woke up this morning at Leviathan's side, beyond exhausted, light-headed, and my night sweats had returned. When Leviathan rolled over and began smooching at my neck, I shivered, not in anticipation, but because the blanket moving away from my body exposed me to the cold air of the room.

"I can't now..." I murmured.

At the hoarse tone in my voice, he immediately picked up on the fact that something was wrong. Instantly, he sat up and leaned over me, his gaze hard and inquisitive as he took in the sight of me. He felt the damp sheet beneath my body and furrowed his brow in confusion. "What is this?" he asked, touching my forehead, no doubt feeling how clammy I was. "What is wrong?"

"I'm just tired... a little light-headed..."

"It is because you have not been eating as much," he declared decidedly, and immediately covered me with the blankets. He rose, all naked and glorious, and I had to inwardly smack myself to snap out of it.

Not now, Evie...

"I will order you whatever you wish. Is there something I can bring you that you favour?" He knelt at my bedside, his hands clasping both of mine as he stared earnestly into my face like he was suddenly concerned. "You look pale."

"I'm just feeling a little sick, I guess. I'm not hungry," I told him, but he was already shaking his head.

"No, no, you don't. Don't think I haven't been paying attention. Your appetite these past few weeks has been dwindling." He bowed his head over our hands and kissed my knuckles. "The fault is mine. I have not been giving you the care you need."

I smiled and let my fingers play with the ends of his hair. "Oh please, this is nothing. I'm just feeling a little off. This is nothing new. Sometimes people just get sick, and they rest. Then after a few days, they get better again." As embarrassed as I was to have sweated through his luxurious sheets, it was clear that he didn't give a shit about that as he remained at my bedside, his expression still torn and guilt-ridden. "Sweating is good. A fever is a sign of the body fighting back against whatever is causing the problem. In another day or two, I'll be back to my usual, snarky self."

He narrowed his eyes as I attempted to joke and shook his head. "This isn't funny, Evangeline."

I shrugged. "I disagree."

He sighed heavily. "Of course you do." Rising to his feet, he stalked off to his massive walk-in closet and returned in only a pair of black, tied pants, the leather hugging the lean muscle of his legs, his chest bare and hair messily strewn about his head. As I stared, his expression changed from one of worry to scrutiny and confusion.

"Huh? What?"

"I asked again if there was anything you favoured for a meal and you just lay there staring at me like you'd suffered some sort of a stroke." That statement, and the fact that he appeared to be thoroughly alarmed, had me losing my head completely and I burst into a fit of giggles. "What do you find so humorous, darling?"

"Just... just the fact that I-I literally zoned out..." I gasped in my fit, "... I zoned out just by checking you out." I cackled, falling back onto the bed, now feeling a bit better.

"This isn't a time for your fastidiousness, Evangeline!" he snapped, heading toward me, his face etched with disapproval. "I am concerned for your welfare, and you don't seem the least bit troubled."

I sat up, waving his hands away as I rose to my feet and stretched. "Honestly, I'm feeling better. I think I just need to bathe and then get some food in me, okay? Really, I've been off for a while now. It's probably just some flu bug you have wandering around Hell that I've caught."

A lie, Evie... why are you lying to him? You know what this could be...

Leviathan's eyes were locked onto my face, and I swear, it felt like he was overanalysing me, trying to determine if I was being honest or not. I had no doubt that he could detect human deceit, but I wasn't trying to be malicious. I just didn't want to face the possibility that I could be sick again.

As I grinned up at him, resting my chin against his sternum as I batted my lashes, trying to look as innocent as possible, he finally gave in and rolled his eyes, though he wrapped his arms around my back. "Infuriating female."

I didn't bother correcting him, as I knew he liked to use the term when I was challenging him. It was sort of becoming a pet name. I decided that while I didn't like being called, *human*, or *female*, I didn't mind it when *he* did it. "Oh, I absolutely am. I'm the worst. Aren't you glad of all the girls you could have thrown over your shoulder and hijacked you picked me?"

Leviathan snorted and shook his head, like he really didn't know what he was going to do with me.

"That's the spirit!" I poked his ribs, enjoying the sight of him jumping from the contact, like he had been tickled. "Now... I don't suppose you have blueberry pancakes and whipped cream kicking around this place, do you?"

CHAPTER FOURTEEN

Leviathan

Seeing Evangeline so pale and clammy that morning had only reminded me of her mortal nature. Since she awoke sweating and shivering, I'd been careful to pay closer attention to her health and habits. I decided that she *was* rather skinny. Too skinny. Much more slender than when I'd taken her. I ordered for only the tastiest foods from my staff to be delivered, gathering together her favourites in hopes to entice her. Nevertheless, much to my chagrin, though she thanked me endlessly for being so considerate, she only nibbled at the meals.

Though she got out of bed and tried moving around, when I brought her into my Throne Room for business, she fell asleep in my lap, as I chose to now keep her directly at my side after that incident with that guilty soul. Her head fell back against my chest, and I peered down to find her completely out, her mouth opened slightly, her eyes shut, and her lashes fanned out beneath her lids. Carefully, I positioned her into a more comfortable position on my lap and summoned Gnaarl. I was done fucking around.

He came at once, and though he appeared momentarily taken aback at the sight of the girl in my arms on my throne, he didn't question it. In fact, he seemed oddly smug and relieved. I could only assume his fear that I would take his Kys from him had been temporarily disregarded since I now found myself completely enraptured with my own little human. But as he approached and bowed, I could see how his black eyes narrowed even more upon a second glance at her, and I knew he noticed her sickly pallor.

"My lord?" he said, keeping his voice hushed so she could continue sleeping. "You summoned me?"

"Gnaarl, my female has been ill as of late." He glanced at her again before meeting my stare, as though he knew I would dislike someone ogling her. And he was right. I did dislike it.

My men had learned quickly not to let their eyes stray to the small figure in my lap when they met with me, lest I snarl in warning. That old rumble had since come back to me, thundering around the room like a guttural, rolling, before pealing up into a higher, sharp, quick groan, like a door swinging on a creaking hinge. That was new, but when one of the demons who worked in the eighth plane punishing those guilty of sins led by his envy came to me with a request, his eyes stared a little too long at Evangeline's delicate figure. That newly discovered rumble began to churn in my gut now. When he ignored the warning, it escalated to that higher pitch, the sound resounding through him in a way that had him cringing and staggering before he collected himself and looked away.

"What sort of illness?" Gnaarl asked, his usual rigid features twisting as he puzzled over this.

"Loss of appetite, weakness, fatigue, night sweats." I peered down at her and stroked her cheek, hating how cool her skin was. I removed the elegant, fur-lined cloak I'd been wearing and wrapped it around her, hoping to preserve her warmth.

"How is her mood? When my Kys had a bout of depression, I brought her things she liked from Earth. Books, seashells from a beach she had mentioned, and obtained a strange black and brown beast she called a dog." He made a face as though the creature he'd brought down for his human was more of a nuisance than anything. "Perhaps, yours is in need of things familiar to her?"

I thought about what I knew of Evangeline and felt crestfallen when I realized that there was not much I could say. Everything I knew of her was from her time spent with me here. I thought hard about what I could remember of the shabby little room she'd once lived in. It was a struggle, for everything in the small, cramped space was worn, old, nothing I would look twice at. I needed to explore more.

"Thank you, Gnaarl. I shall consider this."

He bowed respectfully, careful to keep his eyes averted from my female, and retreated from my room. Carefully, I carried my Evangeline up to our private rooms, carefully tucking her into bed so she wouldn't catch a chill. Running a hand down her face, I whispered, "I will fix you, my warrior. Keep fighting. I shall return."

It was even worse than I remembered.

As I drifted from one world to another, stepping through the swirling black smoking portal from the ether, I found myself in her old dwelling. It appears as though she's had visitors. Her things had been rifled through, the door had a padlock in place, and out the small, dirty window; night had fallen upon the city. I stared around the small, dark space, finding my way with ease. The absence of light had never troubled me.

Whoever had been here, they'd left a filthy trail in their wake... muddy foot-prints, tiny traces of white powder scattered here and there on doorknobs, the window ledge, the light... I didn't understand any of it. I could smell the age of the building, but it wasn't pleasant like some structures I've dared to visit. No, this smelled... like rot. The entire building was in decay. Picturing my Evangeline here angered me and only reaffirmed any question of my taking her. She deserved more than this. I could give her what she wanted. Her life would be better spent with me.

But as I told myself this, the more I condoned the increasing sense of shame I felt for plucking her out of her life and throwing her into mine, a small part of me spoke up in the back of my mind, the voice ever so faint. Still, the words no less hitting me hard as they reminded me, *You cannot give her a child, Leviathan...*

More shame. More of those suffocating and building guilt that had been start-ing to churn in my gut. I quickly quashed it down, reminding the other side of me I was here for a reason, to help Evangeline, to prove that I could care for her the way she needed. Her illness was hopefully just a passing bout of homesickness, but soon, I would set it to rights, and she would settle comfortably with me in my home. Soon, everything would work out the way I wished... instead of my forcing her to stay, she would want to, and we would be happy together.

You know you can't just...

"Stop it!" I hissed under my breath. Not now. I was on a mission, and I didn't have time for this plaguing guilt. So I moved on, searching through her things as best I could, hoping to learn more about the little creature that quickly had me wrapped around her tiny finger. I prowled around her space like a shadow, investigating what little my human had in her life.

There were things like a bag full of clothing that had been pulled out from beneath her bed, all of her belongings shuffled through by some other trespasser. Though her old clothes were at least clean, they were worn down, made of strange, simple fabrics, some rough and scratchy, which I did not like. She was better off in the silk gowns I had made for her. I discarded those and moved on to the small, rickety desk beneath the little window and continued to pry. Numerous books of text had caught my eye at first, but after scanning through the pages, I nearly fell asleep on my feet from boredom. Whatever she'd been reading these for, it couldn't possibly have been for anything other than educational.

That was when I discovered the mess of strange supplies scattered over the other half of the tabletop. There were several silver tins, stacks of different coloured and patterned paper, jars of beads, stickers, coloured sticks, and items that reminded me of blades and scalpels. What in the hellmouth was all of this for?

I picked up one of the tins, which she had covered in the shining paper, beads, and stickers, curious as to the purpose. When I opened it, several items fell out, a few which I recognized. Candles, several tumbled stones, a bird's feather, a bit of cloth, a shell, and several small glass jars stuffed with various natural florae. What was my little human doing with such things? Was this all some part of a practical joke? I wouldn't be surprised. More often than not, I was amused by her humour, but other times, I found myself entirely at a loss as to what she was thinking. This was clearly one of those times. So I moved on.

But all I found was nothing more than a few boxes of strange, dried food that looked incredibly unappetizing, a simple, flimsy table, a chair, and a washing stable, which was too small for me to fit into. Disheartened, I sank down on the edge of the bed, feeling helpless. At first, I was frustrated, for I learned nothing about my little companion. But the longer I sat there, the more I realized that, despite the simplicity of her old home, she had still been happy with so little.

As I glanced around the space more and more, it all became so clear. I'd missed it before, as I'd been too busy sneering at her few, shabby belongings; I'd completely overlooked something about Evangeline Kelly.

I'd called her a warrior for fighting back from her childhood ailment. But looking around myself now, I realized she was also a survivor. She didn't need to be surrounded by splendour and lavish belongings. It was not something she strived for. She had found happiness by just... living.

I grabbed a handful of her blankets in my hands and clutched them tightly in my grasp as I stared around myself, in the little room my female had lived in for God knows how long, happy and working hard to make something of her second chance at life. I felt an unfamiliar clench in my chest, a strange sense of inadequacy pooling in the pit of my stomach. How much has been awakened in me since I met this girl?

She was just a human. Insignificant. One of those whom He betrayed my love for. She belonged to a species that I had spent the last age punishing, torturing, seeking to destroy, every soul gained in hell, every single one that I took, consumed, or flayed was one less for him. I used them to hurt *Him*.

And yet...

Evangeline Kelly had become so much more than that.

I buried my face into her blankets as my tumultuous thoughts whirled in my head, tormenting me. Nothing was sitting well, and this onslaught of unfamiliar emotions was becoming unbearable.

When I finally lifted my head, my eyes shining with unshed tears as the pain in my head and heart spiralled, something caught my eye. From where I sat, I was staring directly at her table and chair, the flimsy, offensive piece of furniture nothing I would look at twice. But that was until I noticed that there were colourful drawings decorating the piece in the low light. I rose to my feet and moved closer, crouching slightly to see better. I touched one of the green vines that had been decorated along the table leg, moving up to the surface, covered in a beautiful array of flowers. My Evangeline was an artist.

A thought occurred at this understanding, and for the first time in days, I felt hope. Perhaps this could be a possible resolution to her ailment? Her homesickness? I needed to give her a piece of home somehow. I could do it this way.

I would try it. Because it was becoming clear to me that, despite the influx of overwhelming feelings and complicated inner disputes I was having with myself, I knew I'd fallen completely for this frail, little being. As I lifted my hand, summoning that smoking portal that would lead me between worlds, I knew that whatever spell she'd cast upon me, I'd fallen completely under, and what was more... I had no intention of removing its hold.

CHAPTER FIFTEEN

Evangeline

Something nudged my side, and all I could think of was that Leviathan was none-too-subtly hinting that he was in the mood. But as my sleepiness started to wear off, I only became more aware of how shitty I felt. I cleared my throat and rubbed my eyes, waking up with that same, uncomfortable night sweaty feeling all over my body that I wanted to wash away, but what was worse was how my throat felt. I swallowed and winced, reaching up to lightly touch the area beneath my jaw, only to find it a little swollen. At once, my eyes flew open in horror, and a cold awareness rushed over me.

It was happening again...

Another nudge.

I'd completely forgotten that I wasn't alone, and when I quickly rolled back over, expecting to see Leviathan lying next to me, I found Beast, coiled up, his nose prodding my side as he begged for attention.

I sighed and fell back against my pillows, staring up at the ceiling, idly stroking his cool, scaly head as he hummed with excitement, and got lost in thought.

There was no doubt in my mind. I could tell something was wrong with my body. It reminded me of before, when I'd first gotten sick. People are more attuned with themselves than you realize, and all these weeks, I could tell something was wrong. Stupid me had been playing it off as a simple upset in my life... like being dragged to hell by a demon prince of sin. Little did I know that actually hadn't affected my physical health. That was all on me.

And now, here I was in the Kingdom of Envy, sick, and I had no clue what I was going to do. I mean, no, I wasn't one hundred percent, but deep down, I knew. I was positive that if I went to a hospital and went through the whole process again, it would be confirmed that my Non-Hodgkin Lymphoma had returned.

My hand trembled as I unconsciously continued to pet Beast, who at this point had snuggled up completely against my side and was snoring away on my stomach with actual drool trailing from his mouth through the sheets and onto my skin. It was comforting having him here, but inside, I was still terrified. What was I going to do?

Before I could dwell too long on that thought, the door to the rooms opened, giving Beast and I a start, before Leviathan's tall frame came into view, his eyes sparkling with delight, and his mouth slightly upturned into a tiny smile. "Ah, good! You are awake!" he declared, hurrying into the closet briefly before returning moments later with a jade green silk gown. "Wash up and dress! I have a surprise for you."

"A surprise for me?" I sat up, putting aside my worries as I hadn't seen Leviathan looking so excited before. Beast groaned, opening his milky eyes, and I swear, he was glaring at his master for the interruption. "Sorry, buddy. I gotta get going." I gave his snout a little kiss before sliding out from under him and hurried into the washroom to clean up. For now, I'd keep my concerns to myself.

Leviathan was so excited that he rushed me until I was stepping out in my dress, hair pinned back with two gold clips, away from my face, only to be scooped up in his arms and carted off, like my pace would slow us down.

I laughed as I wrapped my arms around his neck. "What's got you acting all eager-keener?"

"I beg your pardon?" He furrowed his brow. "What did you call me?"

"Nothing bad. It just fits your bubbly mood."

"Bubbly?" Though his pace didn't break, he noticeably looked agitated with this comparison. "I am not bubbly. I am-"

"Animated?" I offered another word, but it didn't fly, either.

"Will you desist with the name-calling? I am only looking forward to surprising you with something I've been working on all night."

"Okay, okay, I'm sorry." I gave the hollow of his cheek a little kiss, which earned me an affectionate nuzzle in response. "So, what is this surprise?"

"Just along here..." He had carried me out of our wing and down to an area near the back of the castle, not far from the Throne Room. I was pretty sure, judging by the round, stone wall on the outside of it, that it was set in one of the massive towers. When he opened the large, black wooden door, I couldn't help but stare in awe.

It was a circular room, cozy and intimate. The walls were made of that same grey stone as the bedroom, only this one was covered with bright, colourful starfish and seashells. It trailed around the room and up toward the peaked ceiling. The three narrow, arched windows that followed the path of the shells were made of broken pieces of pale blue stained glass, with fresh light beaming in. I didn't know how that was possible, as the only light available in Hell came from what I learned was the massive circling river Phlegethon that looped around the outskirts of the black mountains that shielded this plane from its heat. The floor was the same river rock but covered with several soft, white-furred rugs. However, what had me speechless was the desk made of howlite that was literally covered in strange tools, long sheets of parchment, an assortment of rock, wire, and metals, crystals, and bowls of dye.

"What is all of this?" I asked as he set me down on one of the fur rugs.

"Your new art studio!" he announced, like he'd been holding this in for far too long, as he practically shouted it.

I stared at all the unfamiliar gadgets he'd arranged so neatly on an emerald, green spread of cloth. The crystals and stones he had accumulated for the purpose of my creative whim, the piles worth a small fortune on Earth. The metals of golds and silvers, bronzes, all of it were materialsI'd never worked with and far beyond my welding capabilities. But...

I slowly turned and peered up at Leviathan, who was watching me with a careful, sort of guarded expression on his face, his eyes so full of hope and anticipation. He'd done this for me. Somehow, he had discovered that I had a creative bug in me and had gone out of his way to put together a space where I could design. Sure, the materials weren't anything I was used to working with, but that didn't matter. The gesture was so incredibly sweet and thoughtful that I couldn't even express how much it meant to me.

So I just threw my arms up, standing on tip-toe to reach, wrapping them around his neck so I could pull myself up to kiss him. I pressed my lips firmly to his, and judging by how he stumbled back half a step, I knew I'd caught him off-guard. But soon, he hummed deep in his chest and wrapped his arms around my waist, lifting me off the ground and tilted his head, his tongue running over my mouth before delving in to languidly massage mine.

I could kiss this man forever.

When I finally pulled back a bit to see his face, I could make out how pleased and surprised he was by my abrupt passion, but obviously wasn't going to complain. Especially when he leaned in to peck one last little kiss on me before he said, "Therefore... I take it that you are happy?"

"Very," I confirmed. "This is amazing." The smile that spread across his face was wider than any I'd ever seen from him. He was practically glowing; he was so proud. "This is so sweet, I can't begin..." my words trailed off as I took in the beautiful space and all the little things he'd put together for me.

"Do you feel better now?" he asked seriously, his brows lifting hopefully as he stared into my face.

Oh my God... that was why he did this. He thought this would cure me.

I felt my throat tighten as I swallowed hard, blinking fast to keep tears from welling up in my eyes. I nodded, unable to bring myself to tell him that I suspected it was more than he realized. Much more. But I didn't want to break it to him. Not now. Especially when, after he lowered me back to my feet, he lifted his hand, the air around it shimmering like the air had gone up several hundred degrees for several seconds, before lowering it as though what he'd done wasn't the most random, bizarre thing in the world.

I got my answer a moment later when two of his freaky, scuttling minions came rushing into the room carrying the biggest silver platter piled high with blueberry pancakes and a silver bowl of whipped cream, fresh fruit, and a glass vial full of amber liquid... maple syrup.

"What the hell is this?" I asked, breathlessly, as they arranged the platters and bowls upon the small section of cleared space on the desk.

"The breakfast you requested," he said, his voice incredibly smug as a third smaller demon-crab thing came running in with a tray holding a fancy-looking blue sea glass mug and a silver pot, the smell of coffee quickly filled space.

"Holy shit... I think I love you," I said without thinking and immediately shut up. My word vomit was on point today, apparently. I quickly turned away, covering my mouth with my hands, hoping beyond hope that he hadn't heard me. I should have known better. Because next thing I knew, he clasped my shoulder tight and forced me to turn to face him. I wanted the earth to swallow me up before I could look into his eyes, but he wouldn't have that. Of course not. This guy was the most stubborn I'd ever met. The moment he tilted my chin up to meet his gaze, I began my panicked, rambling babble, hoping to spare myself the embarrassment.

"What I meant by that was-was that I love that you did all of this for me," I said in a rush. His face was blank, giving nothing away, which only added to my jumbled nerves. "Getting this all put together to make me feel better? I wasn't expecting that. I mean, not that I wouldn't expect you to do something nice for me, because you have many other ways. Like the dresses and exotic foods and stuff. Not that I'm into material things. But other stuff, too. I mean, the sex is amazing-" *Holy shit, shut the fuck up now, Evie!* I could feel my face burning. I can't believe I said that out loud. "Uh, I mean, yeah, the sex *is* great, but it goes deeper than that, you know? A more intimate level. Not love. But definitely something..."

Yeah, that was it. I was done.

My weight shifted from one foot to the other, my entire body burning like I'd sat out in the sun too long. My hands clasped together, my fingers twisting as I squirmed uncomfortably before him. "Please, say something?" I begged at last, unable to stand that lingering, straight, green gaze any longer.

Leviathan released my chin, only to slide his sharp, black nails up along my jaw to gently trail small, curling patterns along my cheek. His expression was still void, blank, unreadable, and intimidating as fuck. He simply stared into my eyes for several heartbeats, his breathing deepening as though trying to catch my scent. Slowly, he bent his head, running his nose along my collarbone. Oh *hell*! I hadn't been expecting this! I froze as his hands drifted to my shoulders, carefully holding me still as he slowly crouched to his knees before me and, without pause, pressed a kiss to my chest, right over my heart.

"Evangeline," he murmured. "You are beyond charming, even when you are spouting nonsense. Now please, eat your food and enjoy yourself. I will be by to see how you are faring." He sounded so damned hopeful it tugged at my heart. He honestly thought this was going to cure me.

And I was going to break his heart...

"Thank you so much," I whispered, glad that his forehead was resting over my chest, the tears in my eyes and hopelessness that was no doubt etched upon my face hidden from his view. "This just... it's one of the sweetest, kindest things anyone has ever done for me."

At that, his gaze snapped up to mine, the fury evident in his eyes, like the thought of me living my whole life without this simple kindness and consideration enraged him. He rose to his feet and kissed me, his lips firm and unyielding over mine before pulling back to whisper vehemently, "I sincerely hope that is untrue."

I'd only been able to eat the smallest fraction of the mass amount of food Leviathan had procured for me. As delicious as it was, I felt sick trying to finish even one plate. My loss in appetite, the swelling in my throat, the recurring exhaustion... I tried. I *tried* hard to put a dent in the food, to show my appreciation, but I simply couldn't.

He'd given me privacy in this space, this cozy little room he'd arranged for me to work in. It was warm, the chair before the desk cushy and soft, and my weary body longed to sleep some more. But my determination not to waste this precious gift he'd given me, to explore the interesting selection of materials he'd brought me, pushed me through. As I played around with the metal, winding, bending it, an idea occurred, and for the first time in a long while, I felt a creative surge rush through my veins.

I'd been making my kits for a long time by this point, and I'll admit that while they brought me a nice income, I'd grown bored of making the same things over and over. Trying something new like this was like a palette refresh. Cutting a length of gold wire, I began twisting and shaping a small cage of sorts, trying to make the metal as appealing looking as possible as I looped and bent it.

When I carelessly missed a sharp point and stabbed myself with it, I gritted my teeth in frustration, muttering, "Oh, you're a dirty little bitch, aren't you?" Before I grabbed one of the files to smooth out the edges.

Initially, when I searched through the crystals he'd obtained, I began with the flashier ones, admiring their sparkle and shine. But when I discovered a raw, obsidian chunk and a small, bead-sized smoky crystal quartz, I changed my mind completely. Slipping the natural black stone into the cage, I began tightening the metal around, making sure that none of the gaping holes were big enough that it could slip out. Almost finished, I took the smoky quartz bead and twisted it in at the top of the cage, where I threaded a gold chain through to make it a necklace.

I spent the remaining time tightening everything into place, knowing that this first attempt wasn't the best; nonetheless, I was pleased with the outcome.

When Leviathan reappeared an hour or so later, poking his head into the room as though expecting to see me buried amid a project, I laughed at the discreet way he tiptoed in as I hid the gift I'd made behind my back. His green eyes took in the remaining plates of food and visibly deflated, but upon seeing the small mess I'd made on the desk, there was a spark in his eyes that was so hopeful I felt my heart break again. He shut the door behind himself and headed straight for me, stooping to his knees before my chair, his arms encircling my waist as he curiously studied the broken pieces of metal and chain I'd tampered with.

"You have been busy," he said, sounding satisfied, as if this was the progress he wanted. Except when his gaze drifted up to mine, I could see the hint of dismay flickering there. "You did not eat very much, darling."

I melted at the affectionate name and ran my free hand through his silky, wavy hair. "Don't worry about that. It was delicious, I promise. I just..." My voice trailed off as I tried to think of a way to tell him without lying, but also without worrying him. "I was too eager to get started with my crafting."

That sad, sorrowful expression shifted, and he scanned the desk again. "And what, may I ask, did my little human create?"

I rolled my eyes at the term, though he smirked at me as he said it, his tone playful. "Well, my demon prince," I said, my voice heavy with sarcasm, which he missed, of course, "I've been making a present for you."

At this, his brows shot up in surprise, now looking even more eager and curious. "Have you now?"

"I have." I grinned, loving the teasing. I knew he wanted to see what I'd made immediately but making him wait was too much fun for me. "I slaved away this entire time, trying to think of something I could make that would be worthy of the Great Leviathan, Grand Admiral of Hell, Ruler of the Chaotic Oceans, Dragon of the Abyss..."

His eyes flared at my praise, the corner of his mouth tilting up as he gazed at me from my lap. His large hands, which were gripping my hips, gave a little squeeze, and he leaned in closer, wedging his body between my knees so that I had no choice but to spread them so he could fit. Resting his chin against my stomach, he smiled up at me, reminding me of a mischievous child who was getting ready to sweet talk to get his way. "And where, may I ask," he practically purred, "Is this creation?"

"Around," I grinned, clenching the necklace tight in my fist behind my back. His vivid green stare flickered to my arm and back up to my face, that playful grin broadening.

"May I have it, then?" He pressed a long, firm kiss to my stomach, his touch warm over my cream-coloured silk dress.

"That depends."

"On?" He kept his eyes on me and trailed kisses down my stomach.

"On how nicely you ask for it."

"Mmmm," he rumbled, his arms wrapping around to cup my ass as he buried his face into my gown, his lips moving over my navel. "Evangeline..." he murmured, the reverberation vibrating against my skin so deliciously I couldn't help but sigh as I gave in to his touch. "My beautiful, perfect Evangeline, who owns my dark, crooked soul so completely in the little palm of her hand... would you please reveal what item your talented artistic mind has assembled? For any treasure made by your hands will be forever cherished by me."

I wanted to laugh and cry at the same time because of the way Leviathan said it, the way his eyes so innocently stared up into mine while he spoke; I knew every word was his truth. He was not one for false praise. He was too literal for any of that. To think that this wicked, dark being thought in such a way of someone like me was so moving, I felt a lump catch in my throat, and tears stung the backs of my eyes. But I held it together as I slowly brought forth the simple trinket, now feeling silly to present him with such a flawed, imperfect thing.

Knowing Leviathan, how he saw things, this would seem like a joke to him.

Sure enough, his head snapped back as he took in the gold chain and rough stones I'd entwined within them. His eyes followed the pendant as it swung minutely before his face, until finally, one of his large hands reached up to cup it in his palm. He stared at it silently, no doubt taking in every blemish and rough edge, and suddenly, I felt so self-conscious I wished I hadn't done it at all.

"I-I know that it's nothing fancy. It's ugly, really. I mean, I can make another one and use one of the nicer stones, I suppose." I glanced over at the emerald and sapphires, thinking I could incorporate them into something instead. "And I can make anything. It doesn't have to be a necklace. I get you're a guy, and... and... you probably wouldn't want to wear such a thing, and you don't have to-"

Leviathan, however, pulled on the pendant, freeing the chain from my hand, and stuck his head through the loop for his neck, the rough stone settling against the space between his pecs. He admired it for another minute before meeting my uncomfortable gaze and murmured, "If you dare try to take this back from me, I shall be most displeased, Evangeline. This is something you have made for me, and therefore, it is the most exquisite piece in my collection. I will never remove it."

I sucked in a sharp, shaking breath and nodded, bowing my head over his as my tears began to fall free. I couldn't stand it any longer. I could feel myself suffocating the sweeter he became, the truth I was withholding from him eating away inside of me. He tilted his head back so that our foreheads touched, his hands caressed my sides, both of us sitting in comfortable silence.

"Leviathan?" I whispered, closing my eyes, finding it unbearable to watch his reaction, "I have to tell you something..."

"Tell me," His voice was soft, gentle. It almost seemed like he was hoping for a sweet secret, shared confidence between us. It only made it difficult.

"This was all so kind, so thoughtful..."

"Mmmm," he rumbled again, sounding immensely pleased. Goddammit...

"And I appreciate it so much, but..."

"But?" I could hear the instant wariness in the word as he snapped, caution rearing to the forefront.

I reached up, my fingers touching the hollows of his cheeks, my forehead still touching his, my eyes closed as I summoned the strength to speak. "I am unwell."

"I know this, and I will fix you." I shook my head slightly, but he wouldn't hear of it. "I have access to anything you require, to anything that will make you more comfortable. Is there another fare you wish for?" He pulled back from me then, and when I finally looked at him, I could see him glance at the remaining pancakes.

"Or perhaps a more comfortable sleeping space? I will upgrade our rooms. I can have oils delivered from my brother's kingdoms. If there is something on Earth I missed, I will have my followers obtain it for you-"

"Leviathan," I cut him off, unable to bear it any longer. "It's not like that."

He stared up at me, his brows furrowed, lips slightly parted. He looked so lost, confused, like a child trying to grasp something beyond their capability of understanding. I gently cupped his face again. "Humans get sick, and sometimes, they can't get better."

His green eyes turned to stone at my words, but he remained silent, listening.

"Once before, I told you I had been unwell, that I passed away, and miraculously, recovered,"

"When we met."

"Yes."

He nodded, trying desperately to follow and understand, and it occurred to me how little he really knew of humans.

"It's back."

He stared and said nothing.

I sighed wearily. "How I've been feeling... it's like it was before, that time when I was younger. I know that I'm not a doctor, but I know my body, and I recognize this for what it is. I'm not going to get better with fancy pillows or expensive oils and luxuries, Leviathan."

"No..." he began to shake his head.

"It's just a part of being human-"

"No, I won't allow it!"

"It's something we all face. Our mortality is-"

"You cannot!" he shouted and reared suddenly to his feet, his breaths coming fast and uneven, his eyes crazed and wide. "You will not! I won't allow you to pass. I will fix it!"

I rose to my feet, swaying slightly from the head rush, and clung to the desk for support. "Do you have the power to heal, Leviathan?"

He opened his mouth but stopped short, his lacking in this ability apparently hitting him now hard.

"This is Hell, where people are brought to be punished. I doubt many of you actually have the capability of healing."

"I... I cannot just..."

"If I can't get the help I need here, then I must return to Earth-"

"No!" he cried, moving into my space, his hands clasping both of mine. "You cannot leave me, Evangeline!"

"And if you do not let me return to Earth, I will die here."

"NO!" he screamed and fell to his knees with a heavy thud. He hugged me around my waist, burying his face against my chest, only this time, there was a sort of desperation behind it. "No, if you die, I know you are meant for the heavens! Your soul would leave me-"

"Then you must allow me to return to Earth so I may get help from my own kind."

"No!" He shook his head, hissing the word. "If you go, I will only bring you back here!"

"And if I die here?"

"Then I will cling to your soul and keep you with me!"

I sighed heavily, both my hands fisting the hair at the back of his head, my heart wrenching, my tears falling into his waves as my sobs had me trembling. "Would you be so cruel as to damn my soul to Hell because of your own selfish desires? You won't even ask me what I want?"

He shook his head again and pressed his face into my body. "I would be so lost without you!" Leviathan's voice cracked, breaking on every word, and I hiccupped as I cried over him.

"Do not think that my leaving means anything more than only my wish to live..." I said to him, cradling the back of his head. "I fought like hell when I was younger because I wanted to experience life. When I got my second chance, I tried to take every advantage of living it to its fullest. I never thought I'd be ripped away from it and brought here with you. I never expected any of this-"

The wail from his lips was absolute heartbreak. He sagged against me, and I had to reaffirm my stance to keep from falling over from his bulk. He pressed his ear over my heart, and his face screwed up in pain. "Then stay!" His words were full of desperation and grief.

"And perish? Humans are only given one chance to live their life, Leviathan... I was lucky enough to be given a second chance. How can I throw that away?"

His body was shaking from his wracking sobs. Pressing his lips to my heart, he wept, "But... I *love* you."

I broke down at this, bending over him, my arms wrapping around him protectively. "Love is not selfish, Leviathan."

"I do not care!" He held me tighter. "You have brought so much to my miserable existence... you have blessed me with your soul... never in all the ages that I have lived have I felt such fulfillment, tasted such serenity and simple joy. I have never known any sort of love such as this before! I don't want to lose it! I don't want to lose you!"

I closed my eyes, shuddering over his body as I sobbed, "You told me once I could not leave Hell unless you wished it, and that's true. I can't just walk out of here, I know that. So, the decision is yours, Leviathan. Keep me here and when I inevitably die, you will keep my soul as yours, and all of this, despite everything I have told you of what *I* wish for. But know this... that is not love. It is not. You are destroying what I want for your own selfish needs. That is the very epitome of your sin... to destroy the happiness of another so that you can be satisfied."

He shivered before slowly lifting his head to look at me, and at first, the sight was horrifying, for I'd never seen Leviathan actually cry, but seeing him now, it was a reminder that he was a contorted, dark mix of three beings... for his tears ran black down his face like oil, filling the whites of his eyes, his appearance never looking more demon-like than it did at this moment. When his mouth opened, the sharp upper and lower canines of his teeth seemed to have lengthened and he released that primal, monstrous rumble, the almost mechanical sounding vibration unearthly and ancient.

"I will fix you!" His voice had dropped to a dangerous tenor, the sound ominous and so unlike him, I knew he'd further tapped into his first original being. It frightened me, but still, he was Leviathan.

Ignoring the black streak marks that bled from his eyes, the animalistic appearance of his facial features, the terrifying growl of his voice, I ran my fingers through his hair, the love I had for him still ever-present, as I whispered, "This is one battle you cannot win."

Chapter Sixteen

Leviathan

Never had I ever felt so inadequate, so incompetent, in my entire existence. I had always revelled in my powers, but now they were nothing to me. I could not heal the sick or wounded. It was never something I even coveted, until now. Although there was one being in Hell who *could*, and it was toward the Kingdom of Pride that I carried myself to, ignoring the very fact that today was not the day Lucifer would usually see his subjects to listen to their plights, but he was my last resort. I'd have him heal Evangeline, and then I could keep her forever. Over time, I was sure that she'd forgive me for keeping her in Hell at my side. Then as her words echoed again and again in my head, a sense of shame and guilt began to churn and writhe in my gut, making me feel ill.

I travelled through the ether, teleporting as close to his kingdom as I possibly could, the spot he held open on meeting days being closed. Determined, I strode up the road to his palace, a pathway made of actual souls he had damned here, uncaring of their well-being. The only one that mattered I'd left safely in my private rooms, and I was on a mission to save her.

Two of his demon guards were blocking my way, and upon my approach, I could see the apprehension in their stances as they wavered. No doubt I had caught them off-guard with my untimely visit, not to mention that my appearance had shifted into something quite unlike my familiar image, but I did not care.

"Uh, The King of Darkness, The Great Red-" one started to stammer when my gait did not slow, but I hadn't the patience for this.

With the power surging through my veins, I seized the air around his throat, squeezing it so that it constricted like a snake. Though I was ten feet away, the demon gasped and spat, clutching at the invisible force holding him, while the second one backed away. Any other being besides one of the royals of Hell would never dare such a thing, nor be capable of it, and I'm sure Lucifer would be less than impressed with my attacking his guard, my mind had gone oddly unequivocal and straightforward, only comprehending one thing at a time.

And right now? All I could think of was... *Evangeline... Evangeline... Evangeline...*

I stalked up the steps and shoved open the doors, sending them flying open with an ear-breaking, echoing bang, as I found myself staring down the long hall that led to the devil's throne, which was empty.

"Lucifer!" I roared, stalking down the gallery, flanked by the marble columns, "Lucifer! I need your assistance! I need help. Immediately!" In the past, to even say these words out loud would have sent me into a spiral of agitation and angst. I never wanted to appear so weak that I would need the aid of one of my brothers or sister. But now, I was screaming the words to the deceptive skylight above, the blue skies with rolling white clouds having never agitated me before now. I didn't feel light or like celebrating the beauty of Heaven. I wanted to drag it down to my mercy, to rid it of existence so that Evangeline's soul could remain mine forever. "Lucifer!"

"Holy fucking shit!"

I spun to see the ass himself stride in from the archway of an adjoining hall, his fiery wings stretched out, dressed in his usual mortal garb. Most likely, he'd only recently returned from Earth as he travelled amongst the mortals, spreading chaos, and encouraging sin. He shoved his blond hair off his face, his blue eyes widening in shock at the sight of me. "What in the fuck happened to you? You get stuck halfway through transition or some shit?"

I ignored his swipe, following him into the clearing before his grand chair, hot on his heels. When he turned to find me looming almost directly at his back, the flames from his wings warming my skin, he reared back in surprise by my impatience, as it was quite out of character.

"What the hell is going on?" he asked, stepping back before climbing the steps to his throne, settling in to stare down at me, appearing skeptical and curious all at once.

"Lucifer," I bowed deeply to him, placating his vanity in hopes of him becoming more amiable and sympathetic to what it was I was about to request from him. "The Great Red Dragon, Son of Perdition, Angel of Disaster, and King of Darkness and all Hell... I come to you now in most desperate need of your powers of restoration."

Lucifer's brow cocked at that. Whatever he'd been expecting, it wasn't this. Though his interest was piqued, he indulged me by waving his hand, signalling for me to continue.

Still, on bended knee, I stared intensely up at him, my blackened gaze pleading, my face still stained from the black tears I'd somehow produced. "I have a companion-"

"You've taken a whore?" The delight on his face was immediate. "My, how things have changed in such a short time! Conventional, tight-assed Leviathan finally gave in and decided to get his dick wet, eh? Who is she? A succubus, perhaps? Or one of those demon bitches with the claws around their va-"

"My *companion*," I hissed between clenched teeth, "Is of a delicate nature and whose health has been slowly deteriorating."

At this, Lucifer sagged back against his throne, his expression now even more puzzled. "And what exactly is it they are suffering from? Have they been inflicted by a curse? Sustained a wound from a divine blade? What?"

"An... an illness..." I cringed, knowing that it was inevitable that he should know I've taken a human for a companion. This is what I feared to say, for I had no idea what his reaction would be. Would he laugh? Or set out to see her with his own eyes to convince himself it was true? And what then? The devil had no love for those who wandered Earth, no pity. I had hated humans, but it was nothing compared to the way Lucifer begrudged them.

"An illness?" His eyes narrowed in suspicion. "What sort of illness is there that a being of our dimension would succumb to?"

"A mortal one."

There was a deathly silence at this that seemed to stretch on and on. Still, I remained where I was, watching his expression as it slowly took in this information, shifting from uncertainty to coldness to an eerily calm fury as his hands clenched the arms of this throne, sparks flying off the tips of his wings as he suppressed his displeasure. "A mortal one..." he repeated, his voice soft in a way that sent a tremor around the room, like the very walls themselves shivering at his ire. "You mean to tell me that you have taken a *human* for a lover?"

"I have," I said firmly, not backing down. "And she has fallen ill to a disease that is fatal to mortals. As I haven't the power to heal her myself, I have come to you in most desperate need. I beg of you as my King, my brother and friend, whom I've always shown loyalty to, to heal her."

Lucifer stared down at me from the great height of his dais, his body frozen as he appeared to be considering what I was asking. Finally, after what felt like an age, he crossed one leg over the other, resting his ankle on the knee, and sank back in his seat. The smallest, cruellest smile crept upon his handsome face, and he murmured, "No."

I stared at him, a feeling I hadn't felt in what felt like an eternity returning to me in a wave. I stood at the gates of Heaven, with Michael at my back, my neck and hands bleeding from the blade of his sword. I'd stood at Lucifer's side then. I swore loyalty to him. And then, I was thrown. I fell through the air, my body burning and breaking, altering once more, taking me even further than what I had once been. That feeling in my stomach from the fall, the surge that made me sick, that overwhelmed me, had me almost collapsing completely at that soft, *no*.

"No?" I gasped, feeling like I was struggling to fully comprehend his refusal.

"No," he replied simply, his tone terse, his face smug and callous.

And there it was.

That old friend, that part of me that has been becoming more and more alive, suddenly reared its head, and as my body trembled, my rage intensifying beyond anything I'd felt before. My demon burst free and my wings ripped through my back, my limbs lengthening and growing, muscles bulging, as my eyes started to gleam. I became even more monstrous as I bellowed in that old tenor, rumbling roar. Standing tall, I was now looking down upon my king, who, though he appeared startled by the changes in my demon body, hadn't moved from his spot. He still sat there like the smug prick he's always been, and I opened my mouth, letting the beam of acid green light shine upon him, the air wavering from the heat of the death lights that lived in my gut.

"I have shown you nothing but loyalty!" I growled, my bass-like voice thundering around the space. "I fought for you. I fell for you! I have always shown you endless respect and reverence. I have come to you to ask for one thing, one thing that would only cement my allegiance forever... and you deny me?"

"You did not fight for me, Leviathan!" Lucifer barked, still sitting as he glared upwards, his wings now sparking with even more vibrancy and animation, his own rage coming to the surface. "You fought for yourself! Everything you have shown loyalty to me for, was for your own personal gain. You have proven loyal, yes, but only because I gave you what He did not! How soon would you cast me aside when someone else comes along with the promise of more?"

"I killed for you!"

"You killed because of your own personal vendetta with Him!" At this, he rose to his feet, shouting up at my massive figure, unfazed and unthreatened, "Humans are nothing to us! You've been infected! You are weak, Leviathan. Unworthy of everything I have gifted you!" I winced as his words summoned those dark memories to the forefront of my mind. "The best thing in this scenario is to just let it die, unless you wish for me to put it out of its misery now?"

"No!" I screamed, almost ready to flee from his palace to reach her first, to hide her away where he could not channel his dark energy upon her innocent soul. "Please no…"

"Then leave!" he snapped. "Leave, and go to your pet's side and watch her die. If you truly cared for the creature, I suggest ending it now to save it from pain. That is as far as my mercy would go," he taunted as he descended the steps and headed toward one of the archways leaving the hall. He paused beneath the stone, glancing back over his shoulder at me in disgust. "Don't ever come to me for such a request again, Leviathan."

"I won't come to you again, ever, Lucifer." My body was shaking, vibrating as I seethed on the spot, refraining from attacking the devil in an attempt to rip his head from his body. But it would be fruitless, as I did not have the strength or power to kill him. But I did one better. "You are alone for a reason… because your fucking arrogance has alienated you from everyone. You will forever be alone, Lucifer. I promise you that. I will never forgive you for this…"

He curled his lip at my curse. "At least I am a king, while you, Leviathan, are nothing more than a snivelling ass-kisser, always wanting what you can't have…" he sneered.

"It matters not," I said to him, thinking of Evangeline laying in my bed, sick, dying... "It matters not."

The puzzled expression on his face was the last thing I saw before I reared back, stretched my wings, and shot up, bursting through his false skylight into the skies of Hell, the sounds of his furious screams ringing behind me as I flew out of range of his power so I could transport myself back to the only thing in that mattered to me... the human female that was slowly being taken away, and I was powerless to stop it.

I stepped out of the swirling smoke, finding myself standing out on my balcony to my private rooms. I had to stoop to fit beneath the archway, my wings snagging on the misty drapes. The room was semi-dark, the lights cast low, but there was no mistaking the delicate little figure lying upon the bed. Evangeline's hair was fanned out over the silk pillow, her eyes closed, the dress she wore smeared with the black, oil-like tears I'd shed. Her breathing was shallow, and as I quietly approached the bedside, I could make out the swollen tissue beneath her jaw, something I'd overlooked before.

Kneeling at her side, I stretched my arms over the silky blankets until I could carefully clasp one of her tiny, frail hands in both of my own. It was cool to touch, as light as a feather from my old wings, and all I could do was cling to her and sob quietly so as not to disturb her sleep.

It didn't matter anyway, for only seconds later, I could hear her soft voice coo, "Leviathan?"

I lifted my head, knowing I looked like a monster right now, my body incapable of shifting back as I endured the worst sort of torment I'd ever known. But she did not shrink back, nor avert her eyes in fear. She only smiled sleepily at me, the shadows around her eyes more prominent. I kissed the back of her hand, cautious of my fangs, revelling in the softness of her skin. Her fingers, however, maneuvered past my hold, reaching towards my throat. I peered down to see her lightly touch the pendant she'd made for me, the chain of the necklace digging into the skin at my neck, but it held fast, nonetheless. I'd meant what I said... I would never take it off. Ever.

Her hand dropped with a soft thud to the mattress, her head sinking to the side into the pillow, as though she was beyond exhausted. For a brief moment, I thought she'd passed, and I stared in horror, frozen, thinking the worst before her chest rose to take another breath.

"Unfurrow that brow, mister," she whispered, her tone still as playful as ever. How she could tell my face was screwed up in pain while in my demon form, I could only think it was because she knew me... she knew me better than anyone. My little human never missed a thing. She could see right through me, and still smile at what she saw. "Do you know how much I love you?"

Hearing those words from her lips had me sucking in a ragged, shuddering breath, but I needed to know. "How much, my darling?"

"The very fact that, despite all the reasons why I shouldn't, when I look at you, I'm always dazzled. Your soul is beautiful, and it breaks my heart knowing you refuse to see yourself for what you are... you are so deserving, Leviathan. Please stop punishing yourself."

"I never-"

"You do... everything you do is to shut others away because you are your own worst critic. I fell in love with you because I embrace everything about you, even what you would consider your 'flaws.'" She shook her head limply from side to side. "They are not flaws. They are beautiful parts that make you who you are. But *you* need to embrace them, too."

I kept my head bowed as her words hit me hard in my heart. I felt... *awakened* by her speech, while at the same time, that other part of me was screaming and writhing in pain, refusing to believe it.

"Evangeline," my voice trembled as I said her name, "Please..."

"The power is yours, Leviathan," she said, her voice filled with suffering, sadness.

"How could I let you go, when you are the only thing I could ever want forever?" When I lifted my head to gaze upon her lovely face, it was met with a sorrowful stare, her eyes shining.

She squeezed my hand, her hold fragile and weak, and I gently returned it, always remembering how much stronger I was than her. Though, at this moment, I've never felt so powerless in my life.

You are weak, Leviathan. Unworthy of everything I have gifted you... His words had stabbed me deeply, but they did not compare to this moment.

"Goodbye doesn't mean forever," she whispered. "It just means, while we're apart, that until next time... I will wish for your protection, healing, and forgiveness."

"Forgiveness?"

"You are not tainted, Leviathan. In your own mind, you have believed what was not true. You have never been punished. You were never cast aside. You..." She squeezed my clawed hand again, "... have *always* been loved. You just couldn't see..."

"I only want yours," I pleaded with her. "I'm afraid of being without you. Your love is all I need."

"But I need more," she wheezed, "I need life."

I bowed my head over our clasped hands, heaving from my sobs. I could hear her sniffling as she joined me in my cries, but the weight of her words was true. I knew it. I knew that if I truly loved her and wanted what was best for her, it was to allow her to leave Hell, get the help she needed from her own people, and let her live her life. Even if that meant she lived one without me, and inevitably when she passed, if her soul was virtuous, it would pass through the gates of Heaven where it belonged for eternity. Because that was what she deserved.

"Evangeline?" I choked out her name, the pain in my heart weakening me beyond all measure. "You have awoken so much in me, and I will never forget it."

One of my massive, clawed hands carefully thumbed the necklace she'd made for me only that day, hours ago, when I was the most happy and hopeful, thinking I'd cured her, that I'd get to keep her forever. And now? What I was about to do would be the most painful, the most challenging endeavour I've ever faced.

"You, my darling, you are my reason for being," I said as I beheld her, endless tears falling from her shining eyes, her lip quivering as she listened to every word I spoke. "You are what reveals the very best in all things, and I consider myself truly blessed to have been gifted this time with you. And as much as I wish to keep you with me, I wish for you to return to earth to live out what is left of your life, as you so desire..." Leaning over her tiny frame, I pressed a tender kiss to her lips the very moment I lifted my hand to summon a portal. Along with my vow, I summoned a part of my power I'd never tapped into before, sending a cloud to her mind and memories. She kissed me back, her sweetness seeping into me one last time until her body vanished like the sea beneath my hands, falling away from the shore, leaving me on my own as the smoke carried her back to where she needed to be.

She was gone.

And I was alone.

Furiously, I wiped the tears from my eyes, the emptiness in my heart ripping me apart. Sitting here at my empty bedside, all the reminders of her already haunting me the longer I stayed there, until the point in which it became unbearable. I could not linger another moment. So, I travelled to the only place I could think of, ready for the long wait... purgatory.

I sat at the edge of the River Styx, watching the souls drift idly by. I had no idea how long it had been since I settled here on the bank, sitting on the grey sand, studying the faces of the deceased as they moved on. I would wait here, so I could see her one last time before she entered Heaven and left me forever...

I could very well go to Earth and watch her, but the temptation to take her back would be unbearable, too much to resist. I would break my promise.

So here I sat, having long since fallen back into the humanoid version of myself, though there were several small changes...

Besides my sharper canines and black nails, my eyes had taken to continually weeping that strange black liquid, falling from my jaw to the grey sand beneath me. I was ready to sit here until the end of her life, that was until a familiar figure appeared on the bank opposite... Michael. I noticed him in the corner of my eye, but I did not bother to look his way nor acknowledge him. I had no desire to listen to his berating lectures or scoldings for taking a human from the mortal realm. No doubt he and Him were all aware of what I'd done by now. But I was grieving. I didn't need to hear him belittle me or mock me in my despair.

However, as time passed, he never left. He remained on the other side, some-times stepping into Charon's place, The Last Stop, for a meal or a drink before moving back to stand opposite me.

It wasn't until he stood upon the stone bridge, the last section of the neutral zone between Heaven and Hell, his blue eyes watched me earnestly, as though keen for my attention. I sighed wearily, unable to remember the last time I slept or ate. How long had I been sitting here? Days, weeks? Months? I knew not. But I suppose now, at least, I was ready to move a little, even if it was to hear Michael's bloody lecture. Might as well get it out of the way now so I could go back to my spot on the riverbank, watching and waiting.

I stumbled to my feet, my muscles and limbs stiff from sitting endlessly in one place. I felt like my body was numb, my mind lost, as I wandered like one of those souls with unfinished business who drifted along the shores. I climbed the steps, crunching the dried, black moss beneath my feet, as I then found myself at Michael's side, leaning over the railing, staring at the endless sea of the dead.

"Leviathan," Michael's voice was gentle, soft, like he was afraid of my reaction.

I couldn't even summon the strength to respond. I simply stood there, leaning all my weight against the stone balustrade, waiting for him to get on with his criticism so I could continue to wait for her.

"She is going to be alright," he said at last.

His words turned whatever sort of blood I had flowing inside of me frozen like ice. But I was too afraid to ask him to clarify.

"Evangeline," he went on, "She will be okay. I promise you that."

Hearing this news that He would spare her and allow her health to recover, had my knees weakening as I heaved a long, shaky breath of relief. I found myself smiling at this, the joy of learning that she would once again become healthy and strong too much for me to handle. I fell to the stone ground, uncaring that those patrons within The Last Stop could see the Great Leviathan half-laughing, half-sobbing like a crazed lunatic on the bridge of peace. I was so grateful at that moment that I actually reached over the line for Michael, waiting for him, until finally, I felt him take my hand and hold it, as I wept and convulsed with laughter as my conflicting emotions crashed together. "Thank you," I gasped, finding breath, "thank you... thank you..."

I sensed him sitting on the stone beside me, still holding my hand in comfort as I fought for control.

"You put her needs before what you wanted, Leviathan," Michael said when I'd somewhat calmed. "The selflessness that you bestowed upon her has redeemed your soul."

"What soul?" I scoffed, holding my head in one hand as I gently removed his hold from the other.

"You have always had a soul..." Michael disagreed. "*He* has always loved you. I have always loved you. You just wouldn't let us."

I shook my head, his words hurting my heart more than he could know.

"I know it is hard for you to accept, and I hope that in time, you will. But please know, Leviathan... you were always loved."

I felt my lungs compress at his words, and I could not bear to look at him. I hid my gaze behind my hand, trembling where I sat.

Michael squeezed my shoulder. "She will live her life, brother, and you need to continue to live yours. Do not spend eternity in despair for how this has ended, but rejoice that it happened, and cherish those memories."

He released me, his steps carrying him away.

Nevertheless, I remained where I was, sitting outside the cafe as demons and angels drifted by, ignoring all of them as I focused myself, thinking about what Michael said over and over.

I wiped the black ink from my face, realizing what a mess I was. He was right. I needed to pull it together. What was important was that Evangeline was getting that second chance at life that she always wanted, and I would treasure my memories with her and what she awakened in me.

I rose to my feet, watching the souls drift beneath the bridge, seeing them differently now. Humans, like her, lived their one chance at life before meeting their mortal end. Had they loved? Had they suffered? Did they deserve punishment for the sins they committed?

There cannot be good without evil...

Some would not come to me to receive their reckoning. Some would travel to the Golden Gates of Heaven and receive His love for eternity. I would return to Hell and do my part, for despite that I am a representation of what is considered wicked, it is a part of nature, a balance. I was necessary. I was needed.

I cast one last look at the River Styx, wondering when the day would come that Evangeline would drift one last time amongst the souls before inevitably going to Heaven. Would I be lucky enough to witness it? To gaze upon her one last time and remember the human girl who, for just a fraction of time, had made a more significant impact on my being than any other. Who awoke something within me that changed my perspective forever...

Not now... but maybe someday.

EPILOGUE

Evangeline

I was elsewhere... drifting, the sensation of moving in a cloud of mist, a memory from long ago, one I'd forgotten. But this feeling of moving along in the cool dark, waiting, waiting to know how I will be judged, I find I am ready to meet my end. For some reason, I recalled the sensation of being hunted, stalked by an evil presence... that couldn't be, could it? Was this a dream I'd had? It must have been, because now I'm drifting to the light, to warmth, to love...

I emerged on the shores before the Golden Gates, an old woman, having died comfortably in my sleep, unafraid. I'd lived my life to the fullest. I'd been happy. Alone, but happy. I travelled the world, ran a successful jewelry line, lived in a beautiful cottage by the sea, and enjoyed my last chance at life. And now, I was welcomed into Heaven, to rest for eternity basking in His love.

But something was missing.

What was it?

When I was diagnosed for the second time with Non-Hodgkin's Lymphoma, it was like I went to bed one night and awoke in the hospital, surrounded by doctors. My whereabouts apparently were a mystery for weeks and weeks, but I had no memory of it. My parents came by to see me, frantic with worry, claiming they'd had the police searching for me, all wanting to know where I'd been, yet still...

There was nothing—just a cloudy fog.

I couldn't think of any reason behind my amnesia, nor how I managed to disappear for so long and survive without any hint of where I'd been. I could only tell the police my side of the story so many times. I'd gone to bed, and the next thing I knew, I was waking up in a hospital.

After beating my lymphoma, a second time, I'd made the most of what I called my last chance at life. I focused on my business, on living my life on my own terms, and not by my parents or anyone else's. I hadn't found love, but that was okay. Though initially, I'd desired children, it became less and less of a priority as time went on. And then, the wish for a child was gone completely. And that was okay. Plans changed, and mine certainly did. Not everyone had to have the same dreams.

Although I'd been happy with my life, in the evenings as I sat on the porch of my cottage which overlooked the sea, breathing in the salty air as I sipped on a hot mug of tea, I thought about what was missing... a strange hole in my heart that, no matter how busy I kept myself, no matter how much I travelled or delved into my creative impulses, never seemed to go away. Something was always missing, a part of me that I figured I would discover in time. But I never had.

Now, however, as I stood on the bank of Heaven, everything that I'd lost came rushing back to me. The memories that *he* had removed from my mind, freeing me so I could make the best of my life, flooded my senses. Every kiss, every touch, every whispered word... his voice, his lips, his *eyes*...

Leviathan.

My eyes stung with tears as he came back to me, the memory of him rushing through my body like an electric current, a longing in my chest that swelled, knowing that I'd lived a full life without him, crushed me. He'd kept his word. He'd stayed away. But what I didn't realize until now was how much I actually needed him.

Heaven beckoned, the gates opening wide to reveal the bright, golden light, almost blinding me. I lifted my wrinkled, weathered hand, shielding my gaze. All I had to do was take a few steps, and I'd be welcomed into His Grace forever.

But...

I peered back over my shoulder, the trail leading to heaven a mist of souls, the light from this place drowning out the path that led elsewhere... to him.

I stood there, my chest heaving, the pains I'd gotten in my knees and hands in my later years now gone, my body feeling younger despite my outward appearance. Moving forward was the obvious choice, to pick peace and serenity forever, but it wasn't *mine*.

"If you please," I whispered, somehow knowing He could hear me. "I wish to return to *him*."

There was nothing. The gates did not close, no deep voice from the rolling white clouds beyond boomed its displeasure at my turning down the welcome into Paradise. No. Instead...

An angel, the golden aura around him blinding his features from my view, stepped out from the light, his wings stretched wide, the feeling of safety and protection radiating from his divine being. I felt his hand upon my head, and a warmth spread through my body, like warm molasses trickling down my form until...

Lifting a hand, all my wrinkles and sunspots had vanished, replaced with the tanned, smooth complexion from my youth.

"Granted," the voice whispered before giving my forehead a chaste kiss, a goodbye. The air around me shimmered, like the air coming off a road on a hot day, blurring my sight as it shifted and transformed, swirling all around me as it darkened and changed. Disoriented, dizzy, I fell to the ground, squeezing my eyes shut as I reeled, trying to calm the vertigo. When I opened my eyes, however, my wish had been granted. I was curled up on the floor in the middle of the entry hall of Leviathan's kingdom, the stairwell at my back, the stone floor unchanged beneath me. Shakily, I rose to my feet, my heart pounding, unable to think of anything other than seeing him again.

I turned to those doors that had been long forgotten from memory until only the last few minutes. Without thinking, I raced to them and shoved them wide, fully expecting to see him seated upon his glorious throne, but all I was met with when I burst into the room was emptiness. Slowly, I stepped in, letting the door close behind me with a click, my bare feet silent on the river rock stone floor. The throne was the same, but there was no Leviathan. No sign of the pillow nor chain having ever existed.

"Leviathan?" My voice was quiet, but it still managed to echo in the space, like a ghostly whisper.

It was met by silence for a moment until a flapping at my back had me spinning round to see that familiar, misted drapery fanning apart, revealing the archway that led out onto the balcony. Beyond the hazy, smoky curtains, a dark figure stood on its own, staring off over the foggy lands as tall, dark beings drifted through the cloud, the spotlights that were their eyes searching for those wandering, running...

I carefully pulled one of the drapes aside, drinking in the sight of him standing there, his back to me. Of course, he was dressed in finery, his caramel-coloured hair the exact same... long, wavy, beautiful. The pale hands resting on the stone railing still feature those sharp, blackened nails. His head was drooping like he was lost in thought, and a horrible thought occurred then... *what if he doesn't want me anymore?*

"Leviathan?" I whispered his name once more. This time, it was heard.

His head snapped up, still staring out, away from me. His body went incredibly still, like he'd turned to stone, hesitating for several agonizing seconds before he turned.

The man Leviathan was there, but so was the beast. His handsome, pale face was the same, those high cheekbones, the androgenous look about him, but with several changes. The tips of his canines were ever so pointed over his bottom lip, more than the other teeth in his mouth, like a part of his demon side just could not fully retract. But what broke my heart was the sight of his eyes, the green still there, but the whites were blacked out, just as they were the last time I'd seen him... with dark streaks lining his face, as though he'd been crying forever...

His lips parted with a sharp intake of breath at the sight of me standing there, and at once, one of his hands flew to something at his chest, clutching it tightly.

"This is a dream, surely?" he breathed.

I shook my head, my heart bursting with love at the sight of this man, and as tears pooled in my own eyes, I took in the sight of him, that beautiful myriad of monster, man, and demon, I knew I'd made the right decision. "I choose you, Leviathan," I whispered to him, my voice wavering as I spoke. "I choose to spend eternity with you."

He continued to stare at me in disbelief, his face a mix of despair and disbelief, still clutching at whatever he had at his neck.

I took a step closer, reaching for him with one hand, letting him decide if he wanted this, too, and whispered, "You are *worthy*, Leviathan."

Those words, those simple yet powerful words, had him crumbling. His hand fell away from the object at his chest, the rough obsidian stone still cocooned safely in the gold wired cage I'd made so many years ago, still adorning his neck like he'd never taken it off. Wordlessly, he stepped forward, sliding his hand into mine, and the moment he did, the blackened tears stopped flowing. In fact, they cleared completely from his face, leaving his eyes that lovely bright green I remembered, the whites returning at last.

"My warrior," he grinned, both beautiful and heartbreaking as he stared into my face like he was witnessing a miracle. The fangs in his mouth had retracted, and all I could see was his dazzling smile. "If I can have just this moment with you, I will be thus satisfied for all time."

I beamed, almost laughing as the memory of his old-fashioned speech came back to me. Reaching up to play with the ends of his locks, I breathed, "For love is enough."

We didn't need to say more. We had all the ages to talk, to grow together. All we wanted now was to bask in each other's presence, knowing that this was all we would ever need... our love for each other.

Leviathan gently tilted my chin up, his eyes holding mine before his lips pressed to my own. We lost ourselves in our kiss, this moment one we'd both waited a lifetime for.

Around us, the air swirled, and the sweet hum of Beast trilling happily as he wrapped around our two figures had me smiling against Leviathan's mouth. This was our beginning, and whatever the end to all of this was, to Heaven, Hell, life, we would face it together. For as He says, *above all, love each other deeply because love covers over a multitude of sins.*

The End

FOLLOW

Follow Dylan Page to keep up with all the fun and upcoming releases! Stalk her at...

Made in the USA
Middletown, DE
09 August 2023

36436970R00168